The diary of a
mad bride

The diary of a
mad bride

LAURA WOLF

MARGARET TAYLOR
ROOM 22

ORION

First published in Great Britain in 2001 by Orion
An imprint of Orion Books Ltd
Orion House, 5 Upper Saint Martin's Lane, London WC2H 9EA

Fourth impression 2004

A CIP catalogue record for this book is available
from the British Library

ISBN 0 75284 612 4

Typeset by Deltatype Ltd, Birkenhead, Merseyside
Printed in Great Britain by
Clays Ltd, St Ives plc

www.orionbooks.co.uk

FOR KARL
Who helped the writer to wake up

(And without whom I never
would have been a bride)

ACKNOWLEDGMENTS

IN PRAISE OF WOMEN . . .
All of whom helped to guide, shape and support this book.
My editor Kirsty Fowkes, my literary agent Tracy Fisher,
Beth de Guzman, Cori J. Wellins, and Lauren Sheftell

IN PRAISE OF FRIENDS . . .
Who took the time to read my early drafts and to offer
invaluable advice. Garret Freymann-Weyr, Mikie Heilbrun,
Albert Knapp, Elizabeth Marx, Giuliana Santini and Matthew
Snyder

IN PRAISE OF FAMILY . . .
Who have always given unwavering support to my creative
efforts, and who bear absolutely no resemblance to the
fictional families that I've created

And lastly to my father who, in a moment of stunning clarity,
suggested I write a book.

PREFACE

26 June

My best friend Mandy is getting married and no one is suffering more than my secretary Kate.

> KATE
> I'm an administrative assistant.
> Not a security guard.

> ME
> And I appreciate everything you do for me. Didn't I get you that gift certificate from Saks last Christmas?

> KATE
> Macy's.[1]

> ME
> Whatever you say. But I can't talk to Mandy right now. Just take a message.

> KATE
> I already did that. Six times.

---

[1] Don't be fooled. The Macy's in Manhattan is really nice. It's their *flagship* store. She was just angling for sympathy.

ME
What'd she say?

KATE
'Urgent – call me.'

ME
It's a bluff. Tell her I'm in a meeting.

KATE
That's what I said the first time she called.

ME
I'm in the ladies' room.

KATE
Used it twice. Once more and we'll be saying urinary tract infection.

ME
Hey, that's a—

KATE
Forget it. I have my pride.

ME
All right. Put her through. But if I'm not off the phone in three minutes call my other line.

KATE

You know, this wasn't in my job
description.[2]

Kate struts out of my office. I wish I could go with her.
Instead I pick up the phone.

ME

Hi, Mandy. What's going on?

MANDY

Just the usual bridal nightmares.

ME

What nightmares? You found the guy.
He found you. In just three months it'll
be eternal bliss—

MANDY

Three months and two days.

ME

Like I said ... Now, relax and enjoy
yourself.

MANDY

Oh, you couldn't possibly understand,
Amy. You've never been married.

---

[2] Technically an argument could be made against this comment. One of
the nice things about working for a big corporation like Hind
Publications is the way the employment contracts use broad, undefined
terms such as 'general support', thus leading the way for grand abuses
of power like the one you're seeing here.

ME
Then why'd you call me?

MANDY
What?

ME
Never mind. Just tell your spinster friend what's ailing you.

MANDY
You're mocking me. Don't mock me.

ME
I'm not mocking you.[3]

Suddenly there's loud sniffling at the other end of the phone.

ME
Don't cry, Mandy. Everything's going to be okay.[4]

MANDY
I'm just so tired. Today the florist called to say that her original quote on Holland tulips was under by 15.78 per cent.

---

[3] I was totally mocking her.

[4] That's right. Throw me a huge party, buy me an expensive dress, make me the center of attention and to top it all off shower me with gifts of my choosing and I'll cry too.

4

ME

Wow! 15.78 per cent? How'd you even figure out how much that was?

The sniffles become sobs. Did I say the wrong thing? My other phone begins to ring. Kate's just earned a pay raise.

ME

Oops, there's my other line. I've gotta go. Just remember this is about you and Jon getting married. That's all that matters.

MANDY

But the tulips are an integral part of our floral concept.

ME

We'll talk soon!

I hang up. I know I should feel guilty but all I feel is relief. Moments later Kate returns to my office with a scowl.

KATE

We both know she's calling back in an hour.

Kate – so young. So wise.

ME

You're probably right. Now tell me why

getting married turns normal people into
total freaks?

KATE
Don't ask me, Ms Thomas. I'm not
married.

ME
That's why I like you, Kate.[5]

It's true and you know it. People who are about to be
married magically transform into raging narcissists. Able
to hear reports of burning day-care centers and worry only
that the scent of charred diapers might waft into their
wedding reception. They're like those robot dolls we had
as kids. The ones that transformed from a human to a car
to a prehistoric animal. Well, put a veil and a string of
pearls on one of those T-Rexs and you've got yourself a
bride-to-be whose personal evolution is powerful enough
to sweep every living man, woman, and child into its
turmoil. And that's not malicious. Just fact.

Trust me. I know.

Mandy's asked me to be a bridesmaid at her wedding
this September. On a certain level it's flattering. She's been
one of my closest friends since sophomore year in college.
Stunning, determined – and extremely high maintenance –
she's the only person I've ever known who arranged her
clothes by season. It's an odd mix of awe and incredulity
that seals our friendship.

But now the terms of that friendship dictate that I

---

[5] That and the fact that I love being called 'Ms Thomas', even if it is
by a twenty-one-year-old who has a Backstreet Boys screen-saver on her
computer.

appear at her nuptial *soirée* in a yellow satin dress with an Empire waistline. Mandy has convinced herself that the 'buttercup' color and the Empire line are a subtle yet elegant interpretation of Camelot-era gowns.[6]

Yeah, right.

First off, the fabric may be called 'buttercup' but it's really 'pucker-mouth lemon' – like cheap mustard at picnics and ballparks. Or New York City taxi cabs. And only young girls with eating disorders look elegant in Empire line dresses. The rest of us look pregnant and dumpy. So you can forget Camelot.

But I'll wear it and smile. Because Mandy loves it and I love her.

Besides, I'm secure enough to appear in public as a livery vehicle. I'm an attractive twenty-nine-year-old brunette. I've even been told that I look like Julia Roberts. The size ten version. But shorter. With smaller boobs. So for one day I can endure the shame and humiliation of joining seven other women in pucker-mouth lemon dresses as we cruise down Mandy's wedding aisle to the tune of three hundred bucks a pop.

Oh, did I forget to mention *that* part?

And the spewing wallet doesn't stop there. There's still the engagement gift, the shower gift, the wedding gift – it all adds up.[7] Then there are the eight groomsmen who

---

[6] That's Camelot as in King Arthur, *not* Jackie O.

[7] People always say you don't have to bring a gift to the engagement party. They're lying. They never forget who brought what and who showed up empty-handed. The first person who told me engagement gifts weren't expected is still waiting by the mailbox for my present to arrive. That was four years ago. She stopped speaking to me after two. But I don't care. I'm not sending it on principle: liars really tick me off.

have to buy suits or top hats or full body armor (I've been too afraid to ask). Not to mention the two hundred and fifty guests she's invited to share in this intimate event, which she's been painstakingly planning for twelve long and laborious months . . .

I sound callous. I hate that because I'm not. In fact I try to be as patient and understanding as possible. I try to remember, as Mandy constantly reminds me, that I've never been through this. I really *don't* know what it feels like to endure the tumultuous storms that mysteriously accompany weddings. I try to remember that all those insane brides used to be my thoughtful, intelligent, truly enjoyable friends. Women I loved being with. The whole 'do unto others as you would have them do unto you' doo-doo.

But it's difficult. It's like they've been stricken with some Mad Bride Disease. And it's not their fault – it's the diet powder they've turned to in a desperate attempt to shed those ten extra pounds that they've failed to lose for the last thirty years.

Yet not for a second do I begrudge them their happiness – or their hysteria. I'm thrilled they've found soul-mates, partners, whipping boys, playthings . . . Heck, life's hard. A spouse is an invaluable bonus. No one prepares us for the lonely weekends watching mediocre TV, wishing we had something better to do. Sure I've got a great boyfriend and terrific friends. But boyfriends come and go and friends make other plans. A spouse is always on-call. You can stay at home and do nothing because you're doing it *together*.

But enough is enough. These days every time the phone rings it's another person calling to say she's getting married. They're bursting with excitement, spewing from the mouth, as their joy overfloweth for hours and hours and hours … Wedding dates, bridal dresses, flowers, registries, *hors d'oeuvres* and gifts. Next they'll be calling about babies and twins and in-vitro fertilization. Hours of birthing details. Placentas, epidurals and tearing. Do they *have* to talk about the tearing? Then it'll be Little League and Cub Scouts and car pools and extramarital affairs and couples' therapy and divorce court … Soon I'll have to get a second phone just to order Chinese food!

Breathe. I must remember to breathe.

The thing that I really don't understand is the whole *desperation* to marry. I wasn't one of those little girls who sat around and fantasized about my wedding dress. I didn't know how I'd wear my hair or what type of flowers I'd hold. And I certainly didn't have visions of myself floating down the aisle as hundreds of guests quietly wept into handkerchiefs while whispering in hushed tones about my exquisite beauty. My remarkable poise. My stellar choice of veil.

In fact I pretty much assumed I'd never get married. I mean, why bother? I'm not religious. My family doesn't really care. And I have a sister who made it clear from infancy that she intended to lead the most traditional suburban existence possible thereby assuring my family of at least one joyful nuptials.

I still remember the first week of college when a girl in my literature class told me in all seriousness that college was our last chance to find a husband. According to her, it was the last time we'd be in an environment with an abundance of men of the appropriate age, educational background and financial stratum. I was horrified. Here was an intelligent, good-looking, very young woman declaring that her main goal in college was to meet a mate. The degree she was getting in macrobiology? Merely a footnote. College was simply an episode of *The Dating Game* honed to its sharpest point.

By junior year she was engaged to a guy with chronic dandruff and a history of kleptomania. She liked his sense of humor and thought his love of tennis would make him a good dad. She stopped talking to her friends and socialized exclusively with his. They were married two years later. I'm no devil-worshiping Satanist, but I just don't get it. Wasn't the whole point about birth control to liberate us from these shackles of dependency? Isn't that why we had the 1970s? Wasn't that why halter tops were invented?

And it's not like I'm 'out of touch'. As the associate features editor of *Round-Up* magazine it's my job to know what people in New York are thinking and doing. And not just the Donald Trumps and models of the moment. But real people who worry about public school violence and look forward to eating hot dogs at the next street fair. In fact, I'm so 'in touch' that I've been appointed editor of next year's 'Faces In The City' issue. So I know weddings are important and meaningful events. I just don't understand why they diminish my girlfriends' capacity for rational thought, increase their ability to cry ten-fold, and entirely vanquish their fashion IQ. I mean, for God's sake, *I'll look like a taxi cab with dyed-to-match shoes.*

I think my sister Nicole innately understands my genetic inability to deal with marriage. Nicole, my vaguely younger sister, got married five years ago to her college sweetheart Chet. A sincerely great guy. So storybook-touching it almost made me puke. But she was smart enough to plan the whole thing while I was backpacking through Europe. I returned just in time to slip into a pale pink spaghetti-strap dress and march down the aisle along with four of Nicole's nearest and dearest girlfriends.

The photos from that day are beautiful. People are joyful and excited and then there's me. My eyeliner smeared into raccoon eyes and my pale pink dress so close to my skin tone that it looks like flesh.

Yeah, that's me. I'm the haggard naked chick on the left. Nicole knew what I've suspected for a very long time. Weddings just aren't my bag.

10 July

We're in Frutto di Sole, a little Italian restaurant in the West Village that we've been coming to since the day we graduated college. Small and cozy, it's filled with checked tablecloths, cheap wine and woven baskets of flour-dusted bread. Its owner, Rocco Marconi, a stocky old man with a Neapolitan accent,[8] calls our favorite table – the one in the back near the fireplace – the 'Sirens' table. He claims it's because my girlfriends and I are so pretty. But I know it's because we're louder than most emergency vehicles. Which makes sense because Frutto di Sole is where we toast promotions and curse unfaithful boyfriends. Where we celebrate birthdays and mourn birthdays. Depending on the year.

---

[8] Despite the fact that he's from Bayside, Queens.

But tonight Mandy, Jon, Stephen and I have come just to relax and spend time together. Something that's been difficult to do since Mandy and Jon got engaged. Except it's already 8.30 p.m. and Stephen's late.

> MANDY
> So we've decided that you and Stephen
> should get married.

Here it comes. The international conspiracy of married people just itching to have you join their cult.

> ME
> Like I've told you before, Stephen and I
> are happy with the way things are.
> Besides, I'm in no rush to get married.
> Maybe I'll *never* get married.

You should see them shudder when I use that one.

> JON
> Single women always say that.

Did I mention that Jon's a real ass? And that Mandy could have done a lot better if she hadn't freaked out when she saw thirty approaching?

> ME
> Well, some of us mean it.

> MANDY
> Of course you do. It's just that you and

Stephen have been going out for almost
a year now. You guys are great together.
He adores you and he's gainfully
employed. Why wouldn't you get
married?

ME
The cashier at my dry-cleaner is gainfully
employed. Why don't I marry him?

MANDY
Because Stephen's in *software
development*. It's the plastics of the
twenty-first century.

ME
You sound like your mother.

MANDY
Yes. And my mother's a very smart
woman. You'd be wise to follow her
example.

Mandy's mother – like her mother before her – is a
stickler for detail, a tyrant for tradition, and a devotee of
Emily Post's etiquette guide. Oh, yeah, and she married
the senior legal counsel for a huge conglomerate. Thankfully Mandy has broadened the example to include a
career – in real estate.

ME
Well, you're right about one thing.

Stephen and I are happy. Things are
perfect. So why screw it up by getting
married?

JON
It sounds like you're in denial. No
offense.

ME
Don't be ridiculous. Why would your
telling me I'm in denial offend me, Jon?
On the contrary, it strengthens my belief
that married people push single people to
wed because they're uncomfortable with
their *own* decision to devote themselves
exclusively to one person for the rest of
their lives.

That's right, Jon. Smell the coffee. No more Winona
Ryder fantasies for you, you little perv.

MANDY
Well, it wouldn't hurt you to at least
consider marriage. Let's face it, you're
not twenty-five anymore.

ME
So?

MANDY
So if you don't want kids that come

14

through a mail-order catalog you'll need
to settle down soon.[9]

JON
Plus, looks don't last forever.

Jeez, I hate this guy.

Sure I think about getting married. How could I not
with all this badgering? But it doesn't feel right yet. It's not
my time. It may never be my time. And that's okay. I'm a
well-educated, intelligent woman who loves her career and
has plenty of friends. And yes, I have a terrific boyfriend.
I'm really happy. So why do I need to get married?

The answer is, I don't. And I certainly don't need to be
married in order to have kids. Anyone who's ever played
'Doctor' knows that. Besides, I can always offer sanctuary
to Jon and Mandy's devil-offspring who will undoubtedly
grow to loathe and despise their father the minute they
gain the ability to understand the English language.

ME
Oh, Jon. You always know exactly what
to say.

12 July

Stephen and I first met at a birthday party for our mutual
friend James. In his birthday cheer it occurred to James
that Stephen – recently split from his onerous ex-girlfriend

---

[9] Why do people keep telling me to 'settle down'? I *am* settled. I'm
associate features editor of *Round-Up* magazine. I have cable television.
I get junk-mail in my own name!

Diane – and I, single for so long that I'd blocked it from my memory, might hit it off. We did.

I knew nothing about computer programming and he'd never read *Round-Up*. But we both liked Dick Francis novels, Chinese food, and having sex. I don't exactly remember how that came up but it did. So we did. Three nights later in his apartment. And for the record, it was *really* good.

But that night at James's party I had no idea that the sex would be so good. All I knew was that this handsome, thirty-one-year-old guy, with light brown hair, hazel eyes, and a smile that tilted to the left, was single and didn't seem like a stalker. Furthermore he was intelligent (his knowledge of politics extended beyond soundbites), he was charming (he told me I had the prettiest blue eyes he'd ever seen) and he was endearingly awkward (after mistakenly calling me 'Ann' he apologized profusely, then blushed for the next twenty minutes).

But what I remember most from our first meeting was his willingness to laugh.

Soulful and embracing, that laugh enveloped me. And I was gone. Lost in the euphoric haze that precedes first kisses and tells your heart to beat faster.

Four months later, after dating steadily, I happened to be searching Stephen's wallet for change for a twenty. Instead I found a picture of myself. Lovingly protected in a clear plastic slip and tucked neatly behind his driver's license – there I was, asleep in a hammock during a trip we'd taken to Fire Island. The words 'Amy takes a nap' had been lightly inscribed on the reverse side with a pencil.

Right then, I fell in love.

15 July

Stephen and I played hooky today. Instead of going to work we went to the beach.

It's one of Stephen's most attractive qualities – spontaneity.

Unlike the rest of us, when he gets an idea in his head he actually pursues it with gusto. So while my inner voice is telling me that I have to go to work and be a dutiful employee, Stephen's inner voice is saying, 'Mmmm . . . beach weather.' And it's not like he's irresponsible. In fact, it's his hyper-sense of responsibility that keeps him at the office for twelve-hour days. But today he saw an opportunity and seized it. So who was I to be a party pooper? Besides, I may be a control freak but even I recognize the value of occasionally cutting loose.

Or at least I did the minute my toes were wiggling through the sand and the ocean breeze was fluttering across my bare skin. And when my mind wandered back to work and deadlines and calls I had to make, Stephen gently calmed me with a kiss.

Mandy's mother is wrong. A ring couldn't possibly make this any better.

17 July

On a superficial level summer is pure fun. Concerts in the park, tons of daylight and iced tea. But the truth is that Memorial Day to Labor Day is like one big walk down the aisle.

It's difficult not to feel a little disenfranchised.

Invitations fill your mailbox. Wedding dates thwart vacation plans. And television commercials use tearful fathers[10] walking their 'little girls' toward the altar in an effort to massage our heartstrings and awaken our fears so that multinational companies can sell us everything from expensive champagne to wedding insurance.

The business of marriage is being rammed down our throats and my gag-reflex is working overtime.

For a person who's not engaged I find myself thinking about marriage a lot. Which can't be healthy. It's like thinking about an insulin shot when you're not a diabetic. It'd be a fabulous boost but would ultimately kill you.

Not that marriage itself is bad. But the Cult of the Married is lethal. It annoys me, angers me and, more often then I care to admit, it makes me feel like utter crap. As if being single says more about me than the fact that I don't have a husband.

Humiliating: when people want you to marry so they can stop 'worrying' about you. So they won't feel obligated to call you on the weekend or live in fear that when you're old and alone you'll expect them to entertain you.

The minute I expect Jon to entertain me is the minute I welcome anyone with a side arm to blow a bullet through my brain.

Frustrating: when the love bug bites married people so hard that it causes amnesia. Suddenly all their memories prior to marriage are erased and they're unable to fathom another lifestyle.

This *is* Mandy. Trust me, back when we were nineteen

---

[10] Why do we still assume fathers are paying for these events?

18

Mandy was *not* looking to get married. Sure there were girls who were. But not Mandy. She wanted to lay anything that moved and wore a football jersey. Choosy she wasn't. And marriage was certainly not on the agenda. But here she is years later, reincarnated as her mother, preaching to the single on the evils of going it alone.[11]

And The Ultimate Nail in the Coffin of Decency: the fact that men are rarely badgered on the topic of marriage.

Sure the times they are a-changin' and the occasional homophobic parent will prod their son toward marriage. But parity on this subject? No way. When I'm with Stephen no one utters a word about our getting married. And if they do, they let it rest with our initial response that we're not interested. None of the needling and shaming. And among men, forget about it. It's rare that any man will turn to another man and say, 'Hey, Joe, shit or get off the pot.' *No* man wants the responsibility of pushing his friend to the altar.

It's like aggressively advocating vasectomy to your best buds – there are certain regions of life you just don't mess with.

18 July

After a particularly taxing day at work Stephen came over to my apartment where we went to bed early and played Connect the Dots.

With a can of whipped cream.

Anything which is vaguely round on your partner's

---

[11] 'Alone' being defined as any state other than legally married. As if Stephen is simply a sexy mirage.

body qualifies as a dot. You'd be surprised how many portions of the male anatomy are round.

30 July

Stephen's been distracted and edgy these past two weeks and it's starting to get on my nerves. Last night he became apoplectic because I made plans to see Anita on Saturday night when he and I had already agreed to see a movie. So I'll reschedule with Anita, right? Wrong. It was like I'd told him I was planning on canceling his cable just before the play-offs: 'How could you do that? What were you thinking?'

'I was thinking it'd be nice to see Anita. But it's fine. I'll just see her some other time.'

'I certainly hope so because we have *plans*. We've *planned* to go to the movies.'

'Relax. You're totally overreacting.'

This is where he became defensive. 'I'm not overreacting. I'm reacting in a manner that is perfectly acceptable, considering the fact that we made plans days in advance, which you completely forgot about. Now, tell me you honestly can't understand what the problem is here.'

'Okay. I honestly can't understand what the problem is here.'

It wasn't the response Stephen was hoping for. But he was pissing me off. And I really didn't appreciate him acting like I was the one with a problem. One thing I'm sure of – *I* don't have a problem.

As much as I hate to admit it I think the end is near. Either he's trying to precipitate a break-up or he's getting really possessive. Either way it's a clear signal to bail. Which is depressing as hell. It's not like I was planning on marrying the guy but I was positive we'd last well into my thirties. He just seemed so right for me. He's intelligent, he's handsome, and he likes four of my five favorite things: laughing, eating, reading, and sex. So what if he's not big on shopping?

And I was actually beginning to tolerate his fanatic love of sports![12]

How could this not work out? Why are some people destined for good fortune in relationships while the rest of us play giddy-up on the merry-go-round of losers and creeps?

Maybe I should just break up with him tomorrow night and see Anita on Saturday. After all, I haven't seen her since she started her new job at *Teen Flair* magazine. Maybe she knows someone I could go out with. Maybe there's a cute sixteen-year-old in her 'Acne Before the Prom' focus group. Or maybe I should find a really old guy who's been divorced a couple of times. Someone who wants to subsidize our purely meaningless fun . . .

Ick.

What am I talking about? I can't dump Stephen. I mean I could, but I don't want to. I love him. I was about to suggest we move in together. This is just my defense mechanism kicking in. But it's always better to be the dumper than the dumpee. Right? And what if he's about to give me the boot? Shouldn't I spare myself the humiliation?

---

[12] Okay, fine. Maybe I wasn't learning to tolerate his love of sports. But I was definitely learning to ignore it.

Absolutely!
Except I can't imagine living without him.

1 August

I'm getting married!!!!!!!!

1 August – 11 p.m.

Stephen's been a pain in the ass because he was so nervous about *asking me to marry him*! Some jerk at his office told him this horrible story about proposing to a woman. Instead of saying 'yes' the woman turned him down, told him off, then married his brother. No wonder Stephen was a mess. He *hates* his brother. But so do I! And now we're getting married!

There I was at the movie-theater concessions counter with Stephen, about to see the new Jackie Chan film, wishing that I was going to see the new Sandra Bullock movie instead, still deliberating whether or not I should break up with Stephen before he dumps me when – boom! Before I can ask for a medium Diet Coke and a bag of Gummy Bears Stephen drops to one knee and asks me to marry him. In front of everyone. I couldn't believe it. The next thing I know the women on line are screaming for me to say 'yes' and some guy at the back is yelling at us to hurry it up so he can get his nachos and Sprite before the previews start and all I can think is –

How much I love Stephen.

How this feels more right than anything else in the world.

How I wish I could stop crying long enough to say, 'Yes!'

And who the hell orders *nachos* at the movie theater?

2 August – 3 a.m.

I can't sleep. Every time I close my eyes the words 'I'm getting married!' roar through my head. It's definitely surreal. But does it count if I haven't told anyone yet? Is it like when a tree falls in the woods and no one hears it? Or is that 'no one can hear you scream in space'? I don't know. I can't think straight. My mind just keeps spinning and spinning like a ballerina pumped full of amphetamines.

Holy shit! *'Yes.'*

Just one word and my whole future has changed. I can't handle this. *I am going to explode.*

2 August – 4 a.m.

I had to wake Stephen up.

> ME
> Do you realize that this is the
> only moment in our entire lives
> when only you and I know that

we're engaged? We should
cherish this moment.

Stephen's eyes vaguely crack open.

STEPHEN
You're right, Honey. I do
cherish it.

His hand reaches out limply to stroke my arm.

STEPHEN
But could we talk about it
tomorrow? I've got an 8 a.m.
conference call and I really
need to sleep.

Puckering his lips he manages a kissy sound before passing
out.

Do I get annoyed that he won't cherish this moment
with me, or do I rejoice that even at 4 a.m. he's considerate
enough to call me 'Honey' before blowing me off to go
back to sleep? I go with loving and responsible. After all,
he does have an 8 a.m. meeting and he could have gone
back to his apartment to sleep but he wanted to spend our
engagement night together.

I'm marrying a man who's romantic *and* gainfully
employed. What a rush! Goodbye, losers!

– Jonas the painter: an 'abstract-impressionist'?
– Anthony the inventor: who's going to wear Velcro
  swimwear?

24

– Rick the conga-drum player: constantly sweet-talked me into doing his laundry. What was I thinking?

It all seems like ages ago. As if my decision to marry has suddenly put decades of distance between my life before Stephen and now. Our commitment to each other has solidified our union and built this impregnable wall around us. This is for ever.

2 August

Work was a complete waste today. I couldn't stop smiling and I had the concentration span of an attention deficit disorder poster child. I was certain that someone would figure it out. I mean, for Christ's sake, I was glowing! All during the department meeting – glow, smile, glow, smile, glow, smile . . .

But no one noticed. Which is strange because I work at New York's least-read magazine. No one ever smiles. Or glows.

Further complicating matters was the fact that I couldn't tell anyone about my engagement. I decided on my way to work that my mother should be the first person to know. After all, she gave me life, right? It's a matter of respect. So here I was with the greatest news since control-top pantyhose and I'd sworn myself to silence.

Silence isn't my style. Just ask my secretary Kate who pops Advil throughout the day and routinely complains of carpal tunnel syndrome when I dictate letters.

I decided to take the commuter train upstate this weekend and tell my mother in person. Face to face so we can embrace in this most intimate of mother-daughter moments. The minute I got to my office I called to tell her I'd be arriving on Friday night.

Unfortunately the woman who gave me life is too busy to see me for the next two weeks. School starts in less than a month and she's got to prepare a new curriculum for her fourth-grade class. So I'll wait. I may have to staple my mouth shut but I'll wait so those lice-infested, snot-encrusted nine-year-olds can have a shot at a decent education. But it's worth it. After all, how many times does a girl get to tell her mother she's getting married?

3 August

This silence thing is killing me. Stephen thinks I'm crazy. I think I'm driving him crazy. He's the only one I can talk to about the engagement so I've called him forty-six times since yesterday morning. That's approximately once every half-hour. I've gotten no work done and he's forwarded his phone to voicemail.

So in an effort to contain myself I channeled my exuberance toward a worthy cause: shoe-shopping.

I pass the Kenneth Cole shoe store every day and this was the first time I noticed the display of bridal shoes in the window. After work I tried on a pair of simple, classic, reasonably priced white satin slingbacks. I actually considered buying them before it occurred to me:

I'VE ONLY BEEN ENGAGED FOR SEVENTY-TWO HOURS AND ALREADY I'M BUYING FOOTWEAR?

Talk about over-zealous. It's like preparing the spit before you've shot the pig. How Mandy of me! So I hurried out of the store and bought a low-fat blueberry muffin instead.

5 August

I don't understand why people have such trouble organizing weddings. All you need is a good list.

Luckily, I'm the list queen.

I've always made lists. That's why I'm so good at my job. I'm organized and in control. I'm on top of the situation, always. As a fast-rising magazine editor I've overseen articles on housing scandals, crack babies and boat shows. Not to mention a six-part series on yo-yo dieting. I think I can handle a wedding.

It drives me nuts to think that people like Mandy actually spend thousands of dollars to hire a wedding planner. Sure she wants everything done 'just right' but how about putting that money into something practical? Like a retirement account. Or a new vacuum-cleaner. Those are investments. But thousands of dollars on a wedding planner? Another couple thousand on flowers? Not to mention the million-dollar dress you only wear once. Forget it. I refuse to wake up in debt the day after my wedding.

> LIST OF THINGS TO DO FOR WEDDING
> 1. Choose wedding date
> 2. Tell boss wedding date
> 3. Vacation time for honeymoon

4. Decide on honeymoon
5. Get minister/church
6. Choose reception venue
7. Make guest list
8. Choose maid-of-honor
9. Choose best man
10. Register for gifts
11. Arrange for engagement party
12. Buy engagement ring
13. Buy wedding rings
14. Buy wedding dress
15. Choose maid-of-honor dress
16. Order wedding cake
17. Hire caterer
18. Hire band for reception
19. Order flowers for ceremony
20. Buy shoes

6 August

It started as a lark. Since I can't actually talk about my wedding I figured I should at least use my time wisely and get all the planning out of the way. You know, zip through that Things To Do list, then get back to the important things in life like my stories ideas for the October issue of *Round-Up*. So looking for guidance I stopped at the newsstand to buy a bridal magazine.

Except it wasn't that simple.

I work in the magazine industry and even I never realized how many bridal magazines there are. And they cost a fortune. Ten dollars a pop? That's what some guys get for sperm donations. And sperm's got a longer shelf-life. These magazines are useless after I'm married. Even if I give them to a girlfriend, she's got to get married within the next year or the dresses will be out of fashion, the prices will have changed, and the vendors will have moved.

And they're 90 per cent ads.

But which one to buy? I probably should've waited to ask Mandy but I still have nine *long* and *torturous* days of silence left and I see no reason to be idle. So I purchased ten. I'm too busy *living* to waste a second agonizing over how to choose a bridal magazine.

7 August

After studying the bridal magazines and weeding through all the advertisements, it seems I left a few things off my list. Although only freaks and Mandys would seriously consider numbers 30, 31, 36, 38, and 39.

LIST OF THINGS TO DO FOR WEDDING
(AMENDED)
1. Choose wedding date
2. Tell boss wedding date
3. Vacation time for honeymoon
4. Decide on honeymoon
5. Get minister/church
6. Choose reception venue
7. Make guest list
8. Choose maid-of-honor

9. Choose best man
10. Register for gifts
11. Arrange for engagement party
12. Buy engagement ring
13. Buy wedding rings
14. Buy wedding dress
15. Choose maid-of-honor dress
16. Order wedding cake
17. Hire caterer
18. Hire band for reception
19. Order flowers for ceremony
20. Buy shoes
21. Plan rehearsal dinner
22. Invites to rehearsal dinner
23. Hire musicians for ceremony
24. Decide on dress code
25. Get marriage license
26. Hire videographer
27. Hire photographer
28. Order table flowers
29. Order bouquets
30. Order boutonnières for men
31. Order nosegays for women
32. Order invitations
33. Decide on wine selection
34. Postage for invitations
35. Choose hairstyle and makeup
36. Buy gifts for attendants
37. Buy thank-you notes
38. Announce wedding in newspaper
39. Buy headpiece

9 August

I showed my list to Stephen. After looking it over he felt confident that I'd remembered everything. And, just as I suspected, he agrees that we should not, under any circumstances, allow our parents to get involved with the planning. Stephen's folks live only a few towns away from my parents upstate so it's not like it'd be impossible for them to commute to the city and help. But where my parents can be overbearing, especially my mother, the Stewarts are just plain insane. That's Stephen's word, not mine.

Mr Stewart owns an electrical-repair company and Mrs Stewart's an interior decorator with a passion for dogs – in particular her little chihuahua named Chuffy whom she carries everywhere in her handbag. The Stewarts separated ten months ago after thirty-five years of marriage. Mr Stewart now lives in a bachelor pad across town and is dating a woman with whom Stephen and his brother Tom went to high school. Perhaps 'insane' doesn't really begin to capture the family spirit. In any event we'll take their money with sincere gratitude, then handle all the details ourselves.

Actually it looks like I'll be handling most of the details. Stephen's entire company is relying on him to complete production of a new software program by June so they can release it in September. He hasn't got a moment of free time. So he's agreed to let me handle all the wedding details – except the band, which he wants to choose. The only thing he asks is that the meal be 'real'. He hates finger food.

Not a problem. I've got plenty of time, my trusty list, and an easy-going fiancé whom I adore.

How hard can this be?

10 August

Little Women was on TV tonight. Overwhelmed with love, Professor Bhaer proposes to Jo in the pouring rain.

No movie theater, no concession stand, no artificial butter-flavored popcorn. Just romance.

11 August

It's my first mini-crisis. The Maid-of-Honor Dilemma. Mandy, Anita, or my sister Nicole? It seems so small and insignificant a decision but the more I think about this the bigger the problem gets. A mis-step so early in the wedding process could seriously cripple my chances for smooth and harmonious sailing, not to mention lay the foundation for years of bitterness and latent hostility.

I guess Nicole's the easiest to edge out since she didn't ask me to be her maid-of-honor and, honestly, we may be sisters but we're not that close. I mean, let's be real. She's Mr Coffee and I'm a double espresso. Blood may be thicker than water but, unlike me, she'd know exactly what cleansing product to use to get it out of your carpet.

But Mandy or Anita? My *yin* or my *yang*? I'm not Mandy's maid-of-honor, and Anita will never have a maid-of-honor since hell will freeze over before she ties the knot, so I can't use the pay-back principle. On a practical level Mandy is better able to handle the responsibilities. After all, she is the repository of all wedding knowledge. And I doubt Anita even knows about bridal showers let alone that it's the maid-of-honor's responsibility to throw one. But certainly a party spearheaded by Anita would be significantly more fun than the Stepford Wives' luncheon Mandy's likely to pull together.

It's the difference between Sabrina, the teenage witch, and Buffy, the vampire slayer. Neither is truly 'right' for the job but somebody's got to do it.

13 August

I went over to Stephen's apartment last night to work on the wedding.

We decided on an evening ceremony with 'festive attire', which means sharp and elegant. Although Stephen and his best man will definitely wear tuxedos. After all, Stephen *is* the groom.

But it wasn't the planning that alarmed me that evening. It was his apartment. I've been there a hundred times since we started dating. We've had meals there, entertained friends there, had sex in his bedroom, his bathroom, and on his kitchen floor. But this visit was different. This was the first time I ever really *looked* at his apartment. The apartment of the man with whom I am going to share my life and my living space. Sure it's well lit and fairly clean but when did it get so *tacky*?

Is he going to keep that horrible plaid couch after we're married? Not to mention the light blue toilet seat, the collection of plastic cups from his favorite sporting events, the neon bar sign that reads 'HOT ICE', and don't get me started on the entertainment center with the remote-controlled doors.

Sure these things were cute and fun when we were dating but now that we're going to be sharing an apartment they're positively TERRIFYING. I can't live with a neon bar sign.

Never before have I thought about the concept of joint property. His stuff is my stuff and my stuff is his. By virtue of our marriage I practically own that entertainment center. What an awesome sense of culpability that brings. And whoever thought I'd be the proud owner of a vintage 1990 *Playboy* magazine featuring Pamela Anderson as Playmate of the Year? On a brighter note I also own the foot massager, the big screen TV, and the framed Ansel Adams prints.

But the couch!

14 August

I have gone two weeks, two *torturous* weeks without telling anyone about my engagement because I felt it was important to tell my mother first, in person, at our monthly family meal. After all, she *is* the one who gave me life. Did she not birth me? Did she not scream in agonizing labor for thirty-six hours so that I could come into existence?

I actually kept quiet about the most outrageous thing that's happened to me since my orgasmic one-night stand with the guy who played Tom Cruise's younger brother in that pirate movie. That's right. I slept with what's-his-name. But this was bigger. Better. The best news I've ever had and I saved it for my dear sweet mother.

Who couldn't have been less enthusiastic if she'd been doped up on cough syrup.

Sure she smiled. She hugged me. She told me how happy she was and how great she thinks Stephen is. But then she turned around and finished scrubbing the grout on the kitchen counter. No champagne. No euphoria-induced prancing throughout the house. Just grout. Grout so clean you could perform invasive surgery on it.

Dad gave me a hug. A big generous hug followed by a litany of questions ranging from how it felt to be engaged to whether Stephen's family was planning on splitting the expenses.

And while Chet and Nicole congratulated me there was none of the weeping hysteria I was expecting from classics like *Beaches* and *Steel Magnolias*.

> NICOLE
> That's terrific. I'm really happy for the
> two of you.

> ME
> That's it?

That's our *femme à femme* bonding? Thirteen years I share a bedroom with you and that's all you've got to give?

> NICOLE
> What do you mean, 'That's it?'

ME

I mean, here I am sharing some pretty incredible news. No, correct that. The *most* incredible news I've ever told you—

NICOLE

I don't know. Sleeping with the guy from the pirate movie was pretty cool.

ME

Cool, yes. Incredible? No!

CHET

What guy?

NICOLE

The one who played Tom Cruise's younger bro—

ME

Can we focus here? I'm getting married and all you can say is 'I'm happy for you'?

NICOLE

Well, I am happy for you, Amy. Stephen's a really nice guy and I know you love each other. I guess I'm just a little surprised.

ME
By what?

NICOLE
By the fact that you're actually getting
married. I've never thought of you as the
marrying kind.

There it is. Here we go. The gloves are off.

ME
What's that supposed to mean? What's
the marrying kind? And why am I not
it?

NICOLE
I just can't imagine you settling down
with one person.

CHET
Did you and Stephen consider living
together first?

ME
Yeah, but we decided to get *married*
instead.

Thank God Stephen was sick with the flu and didn't
witness this delightful family tableau.

NICOLE
I didn't mean it as an insult. I just meant

that some people seem better suited to
marriage than others. Maybe that's just a
part of your personality that I'm not
aware of.

ME
How could you not be aware of that?
Even Mandy's mealy-mouthed fiancé Jon
knows that I'm the marrying kind. He
thinks it's a great idea!

CHET
Jon, the guy you said had the IQ of dog
shit on a stick?

ME
Yeah, Chet. That's the one. And by the
way, thanks for listening.

I can't believe this! Chet is a social-studies teacher at the
neighborhood junior high. Nicole is a paralegal for a local
law firm. They are the *embodiment* of traditional living. So
why were they advising me to live with Stephen instead of
marrying him? My head began to spin and for the first
time in my life I literally could not speak.

Why wasn't my family happy for me? Was I expecting
too much? Or did they know something I didn't? Had I
jumped too quickly? Was I making a mistake?

My palms were suddenly cold and clammy and as I
walked to the living room I realized that my feet had gone
numb. Thank god Gram was sitting on the sofa.

GRAM

I heard the exciting news. How
wonderful!

Gram moved in with my parents after my grandfather
died two years ago. It seemed the natural thing for her to
do. Once a large, regal woman who had won a slew of
tennis trophies, she had gracefully shrunk to become a
silver-haired septuagenarian who insists that she's five feet
five although we all know she's five two. My only
surviving grandparent, she has always been my favorite.

GRAM

Your Stephen's an absolute doll.

ME

Thanks, Gram. That means a lot to me.

GRAM

He's so dark and handsome. Just like
Clark Gable.

ME

No, Gram. That was Jeremy. Stephen's
shorter. Lighter hair. You know, more of
a runner's build.

GRAM

The Dan Quayle lookalike?

ME
Dan Quayle?

GRAM
A little around the face but it doesn't matter. Come here. Let me give you a big Grandma hug.

And just then, as she stood from her armchair to give me a hug, she tripped over the television cable and fell to the ground. It was pretty horrifying. She didn't scream too much but it was clear from her expression that she was in excruciating pain. The whole family had to carry her back to the sofa. And while nothing was broken she must have smacked her head on the ground because she kept complaining of a ringing in her ears. We spent the rest of the evening bringing her tea and adjusting her pillows.

All because she wanted to give me a congratulatory hug. Now *that*'s the spirit.

15 August – 12.30 a.m.

I just couldn't contain myself. The moment I got back from upstate I had to call everyone. Sure it was 11.45 p.m. but good news is good news no matter when you get it. And wouldn't my dearest friends want to hear my good news regardless of what time it was?

– Hey, Mandy.

– It's a quarter to twelve.

– Yeah, at night. Listen, I'm sorry to wake you but I've got great news to tell you . . . No, actually it can't wait. If it could wait, I wouldn't be calling you at midnight now, would I? . . . I'm *not* getting testy, just listen to me. Stephen and I are getting married. Isn't that wonderful? . . . No, we haven't set a date yet . . . Of course I remember that your wedding is on September twentieth. You call me every friggin' day about it . . . Do you really think that I would schedule my wedding on the same day as yours? . . . What's that? What's Jon saying? Oh, just put him on the phone . . . Yeah, that's right, Jon. You found me out. All the single girls just say they like being single. Boy, are you clever. So listen, tell Mandy to call me tomorrow. And, Jon, it's been a real pleasure sharing this intimate moment with you.

15 August

Mandy called me back at 7 a.m. She apologized for being so sleepy last night, then got all crazy with excitement – but not before verifying that my getting married would not in anyway conflict with my duties as her bridesmaid or interfere with her wedding. Clearly she's experiencing difficulty focusing beyond her own existence.

Freak.

We spent the next hour giggling like idiots . . . Until Mandy asked if I was going to keep my name.

Of course I'm going to keep my name. I've been Amy Sarah Thomas my whole life. To suddenly change my name to Amy Sarah Stewart seems as logical as changing it to Amy Groucho Marx. Besides, I'm not Mrs Stewart. Mrs Stewart is some recently divorced eccentric from upstate

New York who carries a dog named Chuffy in her purse. I'm Ms Thomas, a fast-rising magazine editor.

16 August

I've spent the entire weekend calling people about the engagement. It's been educational. Just when you thought it was safe to divide the population into those who shave and those who wax, there appears a whole new criterion – those who can successfully feign enthusiasm, and those who can't.

I just assumed that everyone would be delighted. After all, doesn't it signify my happiness and shouldn't that please my friends? Apparently not. People I figured would be mildly pleased were overwhelmed with joy and emotion, and those who I was certain would be elated weren't.

And I will never in my entire life forget who those people were. Yes, that *is* a threat. And a promise.

> ANITA
> Married? But why? You've always been
> so anti-marriage.

> ME
> I'm not anti-marriage.

> ANITA
> Sure you are. You're the poster child for
> non-legally binding unions. You abhor
> blood tests. Shirk at the thought of

wearing white. And you Crazy Glued
your toilet seat down.

ME
Is this some deeply coded way of
congratulating me?

ANITA
Oh, screw congratulations. Of course I'm
happy for you. Stephen's a major piece
of ass *and* he's got a sense of humor.
Just as long as you're certain this is what
you want.

Why would she ask such a thing?

17 August

Last night was Stephen's turn to make the pilgrimage
upstate and tell his family about our engagement. Considering his parents' acrimonious divorce he thought it would
be best if he went alone. Reading between the lines – which
in this case an illiterate could do – this means that his
parents are still duking it out over their financial settlement
so the topic of marriage might not be met with the usual
enthusiasm.

Judging by the migraine that Stephen's had since his
return, I think he was right. Apparently Mrs Stewart was
so thrilled by the news that she fed Chuffy a fresh can of
Beef Feast before dissolving into a deep depression. Her
comment, 'My son's getting married. I'm getting old', set

the tone for the evening. After putting his mother and Chuffy to bed, Stephen went across town to see his dad.

Mr Stewart celebrated the news with a group hug: Stephen, himself, and Misty – Mr Stewart's new girlfriend and Stephen's ten-grade lab partner. Being wedged between his father's armpit and Misty's left breast was just about all the happiness Stephen could take. But Misty insisted on a champagne toast. And, though it's a gesture most clear-thinking adults would recognize as thoughtful and kind, Stephen was disgusted. He viewed it as Misty's self-serving attempt to ingratiate herself to the family and specifically blames the champagne for his migraine.

And as the threesome drank champagne, Mr Stewart made a toast, 'To a happy marriage and, if necessary, a painless divorce!'

The minute he saw my jaw drop, Stephen knew he shouldn't have repeated it. I was livid. What kind of creep puts a divorce provision in the middle of a marriage toast? But Stephen quickly reminded me that if I wanted to be pissed at his dad I'd have to take a number and get in line … behind him, his mom, his brother, and his sister. Apparently I have yet to earn my right to bitterness.

I met the Stewarts for the first time ten months ago. Mrs Stewart had invited us to dinner so she and the rest of the family could meet me. Everyone was there, including Stephen's older brother Tom and his little sister Kimberly.

It was a disaster. The entire family was completely nuts. Straight out of the Menendez family Christmas album. Mr Stewart complained bitterly about the food, which Mrs Stewart had made. Mrs Stewart did her best to ignore him by spoon-feeding Chuffy at the table. Tom repeatedly told us how much smarter, better-looking, and sexually active he is than his co-workers at the Xerox Corporation.[13] And Kimberly, who had recently graduated college and was about to start work at a local public-relations firm, was presented with a brand new Honda Accord. A new car! When I graduated college my parents handed me a diploma and a debt-repayment schedule.

Kimberly was moved to tears. She had wanted a Camry.

The Stewarts announced their divorce two days later. I remember feeling relieved.

18 August

Mandy called me this evening in hysterics. She'd just come back from her parents' country club where she's getting married. It turns out that the club won't allow their fancy chairs to be moved outside for the ceremony. They're available for the indoor reception but they insist on using folding chairs (*quelle horreur!*) out on the lawn. I tried to convince Mandy that it didn't matter. That no one was going to notice the chairs because she was going to be such a beautiful bride and there would be all those stunning Holland tulips to focus on and of course eight bridesmaids in 'special' *buttercup* dresses. But it was no use. No matter what I said Mandy continued to insist that folding chairs would make her ceremony look like an AA meeting in a church basement.

As a bride-to-be I tried desperately to look inside my soul and locate some empathy for Mandy and her disastrous plight.

---

[13] Note to self: consult doctor about the genetic probability of Stephen and I reproducing anything remotely resembling Tom.

But I couldn't.

19 August

Who proposes on a movie-theater candy line?

Am I evil for being dissatisfied with my marriage proposal?

20 August

I finally reached my great-aunt Lucy. She's eighty-five, lives in Wisconsin and refuses to get Call Waiting. Technically she's my mom's second cousin once removed but ever since I spent summer vacation with her when I was ten I've called her my great-aunt. She's the only relative I have who enjoys rollercoasters and at sixty-six she drove two hours to the Grand America amusement park so we could ride the 'Devil's Pitchfork'. After using her advanced age to jump the queue we rode it nine times and she won my undying affection.

Recently she's been confined to bed with a bevy of medical problems ranging from high blood pressure to poor circulation. I had hoped that news of my engagement might help to lift her spirits. And it did. She hooted, hollered and no doubt terrified her neighbors with shrieks of delight. After demanding a front-row seat at the ceremony, a nimble dance partner, and the inside track on my bouquet toss, she vowed to attend.

And when she said that she hoped Stephen was worthy

of me, I started to cry. It was the kindest thing anyone had ever said to me.

Now I really can't wait to get married.

21 August

I don't want this wedding to be just about me and Stephen. I want it to be about everyone – our parents, our siblings, our friends. After all, I'm the last child in my family to marry and Stephen is the first. This isn't about two people. It's about two families.

22 August

I told Kate about my engagement today. She met my news with a particularly frosty reception. When pressed she admitted to her selfish feelings of anxiety. She didn't actually use the word 'selfish' but that's what it amounts to. Instead of congratulating me, or even mustering a fake smile, she cringed. I'm her boss, for Christ's sake. You'd think she'd at least be smart enough to suck up.

Instead she's choosing to focus on the negative impact my wedding could potentially have on her job. What my wedding will mean to *her*. I assured her that it would not impact on her job in the least. At most a few extra phone messages. And you can be damn sure I won't inconvenience her with an invitation to the event.

Thankfully my boss, Mr Spaulding, was a little more supportive. A little. At first he seemed more surprised than anything else. That's probably because we never discuss our private lives at work. All I know about Mr Spaulding is what I can tell from his appearance: a man in his mid-sixties with a receding hairline who wears nice blue suits with gaudy ties because he thinks they make him seem hipper than he is. He used to wear a wedding ring and keep a picture of an attractive middle-aged woman on his desk. Then one day the picture and the ring disappeared. A few weeks later someone tacked on the cafeteria bulletin board a photograph of him with an extremely young woman from the society section of a suburban newspaper. I was sure he'd freak when he saw it. But no. He just smiled and re-tacked it straighter. Okay, so I also know he's a big pathetic cliché. If our office building had a garage he'd be cruising around in a cherry-red Corvette with a license plate that read 'Loaded'.

But Mr Spaulding was decent about my engagement. After cautioning me not to use company time to plan my wedding, or to allow my wedding to interfere with my job – the monthly review and assignment of feature articles – or with my new appointment as editor of our annual 'Faces In The City' issue, he gave me a hearty handshake and reminded me to request my honeymoon time as soon as possible. Of course I will. That's No. 3 on my list of Things To Do.

Do men get this much 'counseling' when they announce their wedding at work?

23 August

I had dinner with Suzy Parks tonight. It'd been months since we last spoke so she hadn't heard about the engagement.

I met Suzy eight years ago at South Publishing when she was a junior-level editor in the YA division. She hired me after a summer internship to be her assistant. That was back when I was still naïve enough to find book publishing attractive and glamorous. I quickly realized that only masochists and people with trust funds can survive in book publishing. Suzy is the first and has the second so needless to say she's done well for herself. She's moved up through the ranks and last year at age forty-two was appointed senior vice-president of East Coast Publishing. We get together for dinner every few months to catch up and for her to admit to a secret fantasy of my returning to work as her assistant.

While Suzy respects my career choices it seems that I'm the best message taker she's ever had.

But I don't mind. It's flattering, in an odd sort of way. After all, I consider Suzy to be my professional role model. Besides, she *always* picks up the check.

After an hour of chitchatting about our jobs, books we've read, movies we've seen, and dream vacations we'd take if she had the time and I had the money, I told her I was getting married.

Suzy fell silent and before I knew it her eyes were welling with tears. Now we're talking! This is the type of reaction I expected from all my friends.

As her tears rolled down her cheeks and her nose began to run she tried desperately to catch her breath and say something. But she couldn't. She was overwhelmed with emotion, and I was amazed at the depth of her love and affection for me.

Then I started to get emotional. So much has happened over these last eight years. I remember back when Suzy used to dream of being a senior editor. And I used to dream of dating someone for longer than six weeks and here I am getting married!

I suddenly felt an overwhelming sense of kindness toward Suzy. I even considered answering her phones for a couple of days.

Suzy continued to cry. Her napkin was soaked. I gave her mine and when the tears showed no sign of stopping I signaled the waiter for more. He took one look at the river of mucus flowing from Suzy's nose and raced to the stockroom. It occurred to me that Suzy must care more about me than I realized. That after all these years she'd come to look on me as a little sister rather than a friend.

But now I was starting to get worried. Okay, not so much worried as embarrassed. Suzy had progressed from tears to sobs to all-out hyperventilation, and people were beginning to stare. I didn't know what to do. I'd never seen anyone act like this, especially in public. She struggled to speak but her inability to breathe stood in her way. It was mortifying. I WAS MORTIFIED.

I began to pat Suzy's hand, the one not covered in mucus, and to assure her that there was no need to speak or to cry. That I was flattered by her reaction but that I didn't want her to hurt herself. Maybe we should talk about something else—

Did you know there's only a three-gene difference between humans and chimps?

Then, through her sobs and drool, Suzy managed to utter, 'I can't believe you're getting married. Everyone's getting married except me. I'm going to be the last single person on the face of the planet. I will die alone!' She continued to sob. People tossed *me* accusing stares. I didn't know what to do. The *maître d'* asked us to leave. We hadn't even finished our entrées. It occurred to me that what I'd mistaken for Suzy's love, good wishes, and affection had in fact been a complete nervous breakdown.

Then she made me split the bill.

Now I really was mortified.

24 August

Stephen called his grandparents in New Jersey to tell them about our engagement. They were thrilled. He says they can't wait to meet me. Apparently after being married since World War II only to witness their daughter's marriage fall apart after thirty-five years and have her now ex-husband date a woman young enough to be his child, they view our marriage as a beacon of hope in a storm of a disintegrating generation. I am honored to oblige.

25 August

A beautiful arrangement of lilies was sitting on my desk when I arrived at work. I assumed they were from Stephen. A small token of his endless love. I saw a blow job in his immediate future.

> Congratulations and felicitations on your recent engagement.
>
> Barry

Barry is the office butt-kisser and resident troublemaker. If you're late for work or leave early or happen to miss a deadline, Barry is the one to let everyone know about it. He's nosy, obsequious, and calculating. Unfortunately, in addition to sharing a secretary, the ever-lovely Kate, we're both associate features editors, which means that someday, when Mr Spaulding leaves, retires or is secretly murdered in his sleep by Barry, one of us will have his job. And the other one won't. Barry almost had an aneurysm when I got the 'Faces In The City' issue.

But today I'd barely been in my office five seconds when Barry burst through the door – grand, effusive, and smacking of disingenuousness.

> BARRY
> Oh, good, you got the flowers. I ordered
> them the minute I heard the fabulous
> news. Congratulations. It's just
> stupendous.

> ME
> Why the sudden interest in my private
> life?

> BARRY
> Don't be silly. We're a family here. You
> and I are like siblings.

Cain and Abel, anyone?

> BARRY
> So have you set a date yet?

ME
No.

BARRY
Well, hurry up and get on to that. You
wouldn't want that man of yours to
chicken out.

ME
Don't worry.

BARRY
Who's worried? I'm thrilled! Now tell me
how Dream Boy popped the question.

There's no way I'm telling Barry about my concession-
line proposal.

ME
Did you remember to wish Mr Spaulding
happy birthday?

BARRY
His birthday isn't until June fifteenth.
He's a Gemini.

ME
That's odd. He loved the birthday card I
gave him this morning.

And before you could say, 'Brown-noser,' he was out the
door.

26 August

I've decided to forgive Anita's less than enthusiastic
endorsement of my wedding plans and ask her to be my
maid-of-honor. She'll keep me laughing, honest, well-
dressed, and entertained – even if she maligns the concept
of marriage in between shots of Jagermeiser. Short of
asking her to bear my child it's the greatest compliment I
can give her. And, honestly, she's been my best friend since
she hustled me into the ladies' room during a press
conference to inform me that I'd tucked my skirt into my
pantyhose. So she deserves it. I just hope Mandy isn't too
upset when she finds out.

Who am I kidding? Mandy's so self-absorbed these days
she barely notices Jon.

27 August

ANITA
I know this is supposed to be an honor
and I'm flattered that you thought of me.
But I just can't get into it.

ME
What do you mean you can't get into it?
Does that mean you're saying, 'No'?

ANITA
Exactly.

ME

You can't say, 'No.' No one ever says,
'No,' to that question. Besides, you're my
best friend. It's the greatest compliment I
can give you.

ANITA

Come on, Amy. You know how I feel
about marriage. From where I stand the
only thing worse than being someone's
maid-of-honor would be bearing their
child.

28 August

I knew Mandy would appreciate the maid-of-honor
position. With her high regard for marriage and the 'show
of shows', which is a wedding, she would acquit herself
admirably in the role. She will provide me with the perfect
balance of support, guidance, assistance – and, when
necessary, fealty.

Crass as that sounds, I've begun to sense that fealty will
have its moments in this ritual. As will loose tea, pink
balloons and prissy little finger sandwiches at my Stepford
Wives' bridal shower.

ME

Listen, Mandy. You've been one of my
best friends since college and I can't
think of a better way to express my

appreciation than to ask you to be my
maid-of-honor.

I practiced this speech several times before delivering it.
I've cherished Mandy ever since she held back my hair
while I vomited profusely from my first encounter with
grain alcohol. So it was important to me that she knew my
offer was sincere and heartfelt. Because it was.

But most of all I wanted to ensure that she'd say, 'Yes,'
because the thought of two people refusing to be my maid-
of-honor was just too damn depressing.

MANDY
So you finally got around to asking me. I
guess this means Anita said no.

ME
Who told you?

MANDY
You did. Just now.

ME
Shit!

MANDY
What were you thinking asking Anita to
be your maid-of-honor? That's like
inviting Kate Moss to the Betty Crocker
Bake-off.

ME
Well . . .

MANDY
Anyway, I'd be delighted to be your maid-of-honor.

ME
Oh, thank goodness! It really means a lot.

MANDY
It should. You clearly need all the help you can get. Although I can't possibly do anything until after my own wedding.

ME
Of course. But what do you mean I need help? I've got everything under control.

MANDY
Do you have a wedding date?

ME
No.

MANDY
A wedding dress?

ME
No.

MANDY
A wedding song?[14]

ME
No. But I've read all the bridal
magazines and I've compiled a detailed
list of things to do.

MANDY
No offense, but those magazines are
worthless. With the possible exception of
the one by Martha Stewart. Hey, she's
not related to Stephen, is she?

ME
Not that I know of.

MANDY
Too bad. Anyway, the fact remains that
any bride worth her floral budget knows
that the single most essential tool when
planning a wedding is the *Beautiful Bride*
book.

So Mandy had been holding out on me. Sure, she *could*
have mentioned the *Beautiful Bride* book weeks ago when
I first announced my engagement. But no. She had to see
me squirm until I finally got around to asking her to be my
maid-of-honor. Talk about passive-aggressive.

---

[14] *Song?*

Luckily I really do have things under control. The date and the dress can be chosen in under fifteen minutes. As for the song – has anyone ever heard a little ditty entitled 'Here Comes The Bride'? Please. As much as I want to benefit from Mandy's experience, I refuse to succumb to her neuroses.

29 August

Not surprisingly, *Beautiful Bride*'s glossy cover boasts a picture of an attractive blonde dressed like a bride. I've decided to name her Prudence.

Prudence has creamy white skin free of wrinkles, pores, and pimples. Her hair is molded into a massive bun that should protect her from falling debris in the event that she passes a construction site. But if she *is* wounded at a construction site the tiara-like ornament mounted on top of her massive bun will undoubtedly transmit an emergency distress signal along any of the AM frequencies.

And don't for a minute think Prudence broke the bank on the tiara and skimped on the gown. Her elaborate taffeta dress could easily make bed skirts for all of Kensington Palace.

But what alarms me about Prudence is her smile. It's big and long, as if the corners of her mouth have been stretched back and taped to her earlobes, and her teeth, polished to a high-intensity white, bulge in an effort to break free.

It's the smile of someone struggling to convince herself she's happy.

30 August

I introduced Stephen as my fiancé for the first time today. Very strange. It was like telling someone he's my brother. Or my gynecologist. It had to be a lie. How could he be my fiancé? That would mean I'm getting married. And how ridiculous is that?

So I dissolved into laughter.

31 August

I have seen the future. It's not pretty.

Mandy's bridal shower was today. Her sister Kendall threw it in the Cranbrook Hotel. The Cranbrook is famous for its women-only policy. When it realized that the policy had failed to ensure chastity within its hallowed halls it adopted a tacit, constitutionally illegal, albeit impossible to prove policy of no homosexuals. What a warm and embracing environment in which to celebrate love.

I only knew a handful of the shower guests from college. The rest were women whom Mandy had met over the years who share her love of shelter magazines, summers in the Hamptons and QVC. Bubbly young women whose nail polish matched their lipstick and whose legs were always crossed.

For what seemed like an eternity we oohed and aahed over gifts, giggled innocently at lingerie barely racy enough to get a clock-radio started, and used the discarded ribbons to decorate a paper plate for Mandy to wear as a hat. As an expression of my affection and to assuage my guilt over not asking her to be my maid-of-honor first (especially since I was busted on it) I maxed out my credit card and bought Mandy an extraordinarily expensive tea set. I knew she'd love it. Martha Stewart did.

During this time I kept discussion of my own engagement to a minimum and actively avoided the topic of marriage proposals. The last thing I wanted was the outpouring of pity that my concession-stand proposal was certain to elicit from this crowd.

The highlight of the event was seeing Mandy eat. She's been starving herself since May. If it's not steamed, poached or in a Weight Watchers wrapper she's not going for it. But today she celebrated by eating a slice of cake so thin you could shine a light through it. Afterward, to alleviate her potential consternation, one of the guests offered her an Ex-Lax. Clearly love has no bounds.

As I drank my peach-flavored iced tea I began to worry. I don't want a bridal shower like this. A cookie-cutter affair that follows all the 'rules' and bores me to tears. I'm not like those Bubbly Young Women. I'm creative. I'm rational. I don't cross my legs when I sit on the toilet! My bridal shower should be exciting. A gambling junket to Atlantic City. All-night club-hopping. Naked karaoke. Anything but a lobotomized gathering featuring laxatives and cake. Where's the fun in that?

Ugh.

1 September

Beautiful Bride is closer to a computer circuitry book than a primer for weddings. It's filled with pointers, tips, rules, charts, diagrams, and a ton of very fine print.

I've only been engaged for a month and already I'm three months behind 'schedule'. Who knew I had a schedule? I don't even have a wedding date yet.

Additionally it appears that I've left a number of very important items off my list.

Official THINGS TO DO List

1. Choose wedding date
2. Tell boss wedding date
3. Vacation time for honeymoon
4. Decide on honeymoon
5. Get minister/church
6. Choose reception venue
7. Make guest list
8. Choose maid-of-honor
9. Choose best man
10. Register for gifts
11. Arrange for engagement party
12. Buy engagement ring
13. Buy wedding rings
14. Buy wedding dress
15. Choose maid-of-honor dress
16. Order wedding cake
17. Hire caterer
18. Hire band for reception
19. Order flowers for ceremony
20. Buy shoes
21. Plan rehearsal dinner
22. Invites to rehearsal dinner
23. Hire musicians for ceremony
24. Decide on dress code

25. Get marriage license
26. Hire videographer
27. Hire photographer
28. Order table flowers
29. Order bouquets
30. Order boutonnières for men
31. Order nosegays for women
32. Order invitations
33. Decide on wine selection
34. Postage for invitations
35. Choose hairstyle and makeup
36. Buy gifts for attendants
37. Buy thank-you notes
38. Announce wedding in newspaper
39. Buy headpiece
40. Buy travelers' checks for honeymoon
41. Apply for visas
42. Get shots and vaccinations
43. Order tent if necessary
44. Order chairs/tables if necessary
45. Make budget
46. Divide expenses
47. Make table-seating charts
48. Choose bridesmaid dress
49. Decide on menu
50. Decide on *hors d'oeuvres*
51. Decide on dinner service style
52. Decide on staff–guest ratio
53. Decide seated or buffet
54. Reserve vegetarian meals
55. Reserve band/photographer meals
56. Make photo list

57. Choose hotel for wedding night
58. Hire limo for church–reception transport
59. Buy guest book for reception
60. Find hotel for out-of-towners
61. Decide on liquor selection
62. Hire bartenders
63. Verify wheelchair accessibility
64. Choose processional music
65. Choose recessional music
66. Choose cocktail music
67. Choose reception music
68. Choose ceremony readings
69. Prepare birdseed instead of rice
70. Schedule manicure/pedicure/wax

2 September

My parents keep their wedding album neatly filed between a biography of Eleanor Roosevelt and a Sidney Sheldon paperback, which my babysitter left behind in 1976.

As kids, Nicole and I would flip through the album and laugh at how funny everyone was dressed. Our dad in a *beige* tuxedo. And Gram, impossible to miss, in her floor-length gown covered with giant gold sequins. But now when I think about that wedding album it's my parents' youth that strikes me most. They were barely in their twenties. My father had just been hired as a manager at the local supermarket and my mother was studying for her teaching certificate. They had no idea what life had in store for them. Yet their joy is impossible to deny.

This is what I see in my relationship with Stephen – a love that's strong enough to brave an unknown future, joyfully.

4 September

I met Mandy for lunch today. It's less than three weeks until her wedding so I expected the usual hysteria about place cards and *hors d'oeuvres* and wine selections. But there was none. Far from hysterical she was truly depressed. Apparently her mother and her aunt had a fight about her aunt not giving Mandy and Jon an engagement gift and now her aunt won't come to the wedding. It seems her aunt withholds gifts as a way of expressing her dissatisfaction. When pressed she told Mandy's mother that she was dissatisfied with the graduation gift Mandy's family had given her own daughter three years earlier. It was too cheap and thoughtless. When Mandy's grand-mother heard this she got so mad at the aunt that she decided to disinherit her. This made Mandy's cousins so angry that now they won't come to the wedding either. It all sounded ridiculously petty.

But it did make me appreciate my family. Bud and Terry Thomas may be stingy with their enthusiasm but at least they're not dysfunctional. Which is good because Stephen and I have chosen 2 June as our wedding date and nothing is more unpleasant than dysfunction under a hot summer sun.

5 September

Wedding planners. What a joke. I've already made an impressive dent in my 'Things To Do' list.

Official THINGS TO DO List
1. ~~Choose wedding date~~
2. ~~Tell boss wedding date~~
3. ~~Vacation time for honeymoon~~
4. Decide on honeymoon
5. Get minister/church
6. Choose reception venue
7. Make guest list
8. ~~Choose maid of honor~~
9. Choose best man
10. Register for gifts
11. Arrange for engagement party
12. Buy engagement ring
13. Buy wedding rings
14. Buy wedding dress
15. Choose maid-of-honor dress
16. Order wedding cake
17. Hire caterer
18. Hire band for reception
19. Order flowers for ceremony
20. Buy shoes
21. Plan rehearsal dinner
22. Invites to rehearsal dinner
23. Hire musicians for ceremony
24. ~~Decide on dress code~~
25. Get marriage license
26. Hire videographer
27. Hire photographer

28. Order table flowers
29. Order bouquets
30. Order boutonnières for men
31. Order nosegays for women
32. Order invitations
33. Decide on wine selection
34. Postage for invitations
35. Choose hairstyle and makeup
36. Buy gifts for attendants
37. Buy thank-you notes
38. Announce wedding in newspaper
39. Buy headpiece
40. Buy travelers' checks for honeymoon
41. Apply for visas
42. Get shots and vaccinations
43. Order tent if necessary
44. Order chairs/tables if necessary
45. Make budget
46. Divide expenses
47. Make table-seating charts
48. Choose bridesmaid dress
49. Decide on menu
50. Decide on *hors d'oeuvres*
51. Decide on dinner service style
52. Decide on staff-guest ratio
53. Decide seated or buffet
54. Reserve vegetarian meals
55. Reserve band/photographer meals
56. Make photo list
57. Choose hotel for wedding night
58. Hire limo for church–reception transport

59. Buy guest book for reception
60. Find hotel for out-of-towners
61. Decide on liquor selection
62. Hire bartenders
63. Verify wheelchair accessibility
64. Choose processional music
65. Choose recessional music
66. Choose cocktail music
67. Choose reception music
68. Choose ceremony readings
69. Prepare birdseed instead of rice
70. Schedule manicure/pedicure/wax

6 September

According to *BB* I'm alarmingly late in reserving a venue for my wedding reception. Flirting with disaster. Treading that thin line between a life of happiness and a dream unfulfilled.

And it's starting to worry Prudence. I can tell by her refusal to blink.

It seems people typically reserve their venues a year in advance. I only have nine months. But I refuse to worry. If a human being can sprout in nine months from some spare biological matter, then I can plan a wedding. Besides, this is New York City, not some little suburb with one church and a town hall. There are literally thousands of hotels, 'event' spaces, and gardens for us to choose from. We could do a turn-of-the-century mansion, a hotel ballroom, a loft, a theater, a botanical garden, a private club or a waterfront restaurant. And, Lord knows, this city of sin isn't lacking in places of worship. Even Gomorrah had churches.

Besides, how bad can it be? After all, I'm going to be a June Bride.

Holy shit.

8 September

While compiling my guest list for the wedding[15] I realized that it's been a while since I've seen several of my friends.

This is strange because I'm very social. I'm the one you call if you want to go out. I'm always up for a movie, a gallery show, or a meal. I love debating local politics and discussing career goals. Then it occurred to me that all these 'lost' friends are married. I've only seen them a couple of times since their weddings. One by one my married friends have disappeared. How did this happen?

Where did they go?

I'm vowing here and now that THIS WILL NOT HAPPEN TO ME. I will not fall off the face of the Earth after 2 June. I will not cease to exist.

I wonder if my married friends made the same vow?

9 September – 2 a.m.

I can't sleep. It's just occurred to me that marriage is emblematic for lodging.

---

[15] According to *BB* you can't start looking for a reception venue until you know how many people you're inviting.

The Jewish wedding canopy is symbolic of the roof on the couple's new home. The Catholic church is the *house* of the Lord. And then there's the 'institution' of marriage, like the Institution of American Dentistry, which you 'enter into' like a home, a supermarket, or a car wash. But do you ever come out? Will I fade into my friends' memories as that brunette with the great smile?

And what if the lodging is sub-standard like a hut? Or a log cabin? Or a studio apartment with roaches and no hot water? Who do I complain to?

10 September

I went to Frutto di Sole with the girls tonight. Anita, Jenny, Kathy and Paula. We just laughed and bitched and ate really great bad food. I felt like I was back in college. Except Mandy wasn't there to complain about my use of profanity. She was too busy putting the fear of God into her wedding caterer.

Several times during the evening I thought to ask my girlfriends about wedding venues, dress suggestions and creative party details ... but I decided against it. I'm not going to be one of those brides who won't shut up about her wedding. As much as I love her, I'm no Mandy.

Furthermore, I'm going to make a point of doing this at least twice a month when I'm married. Going out with the girls. Kicking back and talking, maybe rollerblading in the park ... I just hope Stephen won't feel threatened. Forgotten. Left out. Neglected. Abandoned. Hurt. Ignored.

For Christ's sake! This is why I don't own a pet!

13 September

Barry held the door open for me on the way into the conference room.

Something is very wrong.

14 September

I went over to Stephen's apartment for dinner. We needed to buckle down and come up with a rough estimate on our guest list. And though I purposely sat on and tried to bond with his plaid couch, visions of Goodwill just danced in my head.

Since I always want sushi and he always wants Mexican we generally compromise and order out for Chinese. But tonight Stephen surprised me with a homemade dinner. Seafood paella served by candlelight. And on our table was an ice sculpture the size of a milk carton that Stephen himself had made.

The man can cook but he can't sculpt. He claimed it was a rose and though I praised his artistry I couldn't help but think how much it looked like a human brain. Shrinking and dripping before our very eyes on to a saucer. All through dinner – drip, drip, drip. And when I suggested that we move it away from the candles Stephen insisted on keeping it where it was. Drip, drip, drip, went the human brain.

Then, just as we were finishing dessert, and the human brain had shrunk to the size of a small tumor, I noticed something sparkling within it. Minutes later Stephen's hand-carved rose revealed a dazzling jewel. He plucked it out and, slipping it on to my finger asked how I liked my engagement ring.

It was the most romantic, creative, thoughtful gesture. And the ring was sparkling and stunning and NOT A DIAMOND.

It's a glorious emerald set in a gold band. Lovely and elegant but NOT A DIAMOND.

> ME
> Oh. Wow. It's an emerald. I don't know
> what to say.

> STEPHEN
> I'm so relieved you like it. I thought you
> might prefer a diamond but my
> grandmother convinced me to give this to
> you. It belonged to her mother and she's
> been keeping it all these years waiting for
> one of us to get married. I even had it
> sized to fit your finger.

> ME
> Oh, yeah, it fits great.

What could I say? It was his great-grandmother's ring. To refuse would be insulting four generations of his family. So what if his wedding proposal was cut-rate? The ring is stunning and he cooked me dinner and he hand-carved a human brain from a block of ice but it's NOT A DIAMOND.

I know this shouldn't bother me. After all, I'm the one who keeps insisting that we avoid the shackles of tradition, blah, blah, blah, but when else in my entire life am I going to get a diamond ring? Never. This was my one chance and I blew it.

15 September

> EVERYONE IN THE ENTIRE WORLD
> Your engagement ring is lovely.

> ME
> Thank you. It's a family heirloom.

> EVERYONE IN THE ENTIRE WORLD
> Ah, I was wondering why you didn't get
> a diamond.

Yeah, me too, asshole.

19 September

Mandy's a walking time-bomb. Say the wrong thing, touch her the wrong way, suggest she eat something more substantial than low-sodium consommé and she'll snap your neck like a diseased twig.

But she smiled continuously from the wedding rehearsal to her rehearsal dinner at the oh-so-elegant Chez Jacques. And when Marcel, our snotty waiter, mistakenly referred

73

to her as Madame instead of Mademoiselle I swear I thought she'd take her butter knife to his heart. But her smile never once faltered. Like Prudence – but armed with cutlery.

And thank God for that cutlery because the food was terrific. All sorts of delicacies you rarely get to eat because you're too old to order the children's portion but old enough to owe rent. *Escargot*, *foie gras*, baked Brie and pâté. Stephen and I ate everything that would fit into our mouths.

But not Mandy. No sluggishness, hangover or water retention for this bride-to-be.

The highlight of the evening came when Mandy's dad made a toast. He praised her for growing up to be such a poised young woman. And while this made me suspect that he'd been out of town during her anguished search for place-card holders to co-ordinate with her burgundy-organza overlays, it did make me teary. I mean, here was this sixty-something corporate lawyer, who's spent the last forty years downsizing companies, facilitating hostile takeovers, and pink-slipping entire towns, choking up while publicly professing his love for his child. Sure, he'd deny his own mother medical treatment if her insurance didn't cover the procedure but his love for his daughter was just so touching. In fact, the whole evening was loving and heartwarming and would have been perfect had Jon not been there. I mean, come on. Even *his* family doesn't seem to like him.

I can only imagine what tomorrow will bring.

As for our rehearsal dinner, I have to admit that I think it's old-fashioned to expect the groom's family to pay for it.[16] It's like a throwback to the days when women viewed their engagement rings as an insurance policy against their virtue. If they got dumped before the wedding then their diamond's trade-in value would compensate for their sullied purity.

Well, these days, purity is more about soap than sex so I see no need to be prehistoric about our wedding costs. On the other hand, the Stewarts are a bit on the traditional side – except for Mr Stewart's generationally challenged girlfriend – and I wouldn't be surprised if they offered to pay for the whole thing. I just hope it's not too outlandish. As a decorator Mrs Stewart spends every day preoccupied with appearance and taste and style. She may insist on turning it into a real 'affair' at Le Cirque or Tavern on the Green.

I'd be happy with a celebratory gathering down in Chinatown. After all, nothing says I love you like a plate of sesame noodles.

20 September

Talk about overkill. Mandy's wedding was more like a coronation than a blessed event. From the two hundred and fifty guests to the doves and the horse-drawn carriage, EXCESS had its day. *Dynasty* meets Liberace, Marie-Antoinette and Cher.

And no, that's not the wind whistling. It's the jubilant

---

[16] Although I'm certain the prospect of pawning their son off on another family was enough motivation for Jon's folks to shell out the cash.

cheers of a wedding planner putting an extension on to her house. Who knew Mandy's parents had so much disposable income?

Our pucker-mouth lemon dresses were UNDERSTATED in this setting. And Jon, what an idiot! He wore a morning coat at *night*. Do top hat and tails mean anything to anyone? If you're going to overdo it, at least do it right. Like Mandy. If you're going to act like a princess then dress like one. Which she did. Right down to her ten-foot train that everyone stepped on. But she looked radiant.

The more weddings I see the more I thank God that I've got common sense. More is not necessarily better. Sometimes more is just annoying. The floral centerpieces, those damn out-of-season Holland tulips at 15.78 per cent over their original quote, were so big that we couldn't see across our table.

And the entrées. Would you like fish or meat? The grilled salmon or the beef medallions? How obvious. Where's the thought? The creativity?

And I know Stephen feels the same way. We simultaneously reached for each other's hand when the horse-drawn carriage appeared.

ME
Be afraid. Be very afraid.

STEPHEN
Trust me. I am.

And as one of the horses began to neigh uncontrollably, Stephen looked into my eyes, desperate.

STEPHEN
Please tell me you don't want livestock at our wedding. Because honestly, I don't think I could take the pressure.

Stephen can relax. The only animal at our wedding will be that jackass brother of his. In fact, Mandy's wedding really drove home how much I value Stephen and his down-to-earth sensibilities. It even helped me make peace with my engagement ring. So it's no marquis-cut diamond. Big whoop. It's stunning and it's unique.

22 September

A recent poll of my friends, presented as a potential story idea for the magazine, revealed what I suspected: my marriage proposal stank.

Margo: husband delivered a personalized fortune cookie to her at a Chinese restaurant. Done before? Sure. But it demonstrates good planning skills.

Mandy: Jon presented her with a two-carat diamond ring while they were watching the Boston regatta from his parents' waterfront penthouse. Proves the old adage: birds of a feather . . .

Lisa: hand in marriage asked for at Café des Artistes. No particular creativity but illustrates ability to choose romantic locale.

Meghan: got engaged while ice skating at the Rockefeller Center. Displays romance, youthful charm, and a solid knowledge of cheesy eighties movies such as *Ice Castles*.

Jessica: husband proposed during a picnic lunch in an apple orchard. It doesn't get more Hallmark.

And then there's my *secret shame* . . .

Amy: the Multiplex Concession-Stand Proposal.

Sure, Stephen got down on his knee and, yes, we skipped the movie and celebrated with a nice dinner, but is this really the tale you want to tell for generations to come? Me, Stephen and the unmistakable stench of stale popcorn? And it wasn't spur-of-the-moment. By his own account, this man who thrives on spontaneity had been planning it for months. He *chose* to ask me on the candy line. What does that say about him? What does it say about me?

23 September

Stephen and I have come up with a tentative guest list of seventy people, which I think is a nice intimate group for a meaningful experience. The last thing I want is one of those impersonal functions like Mandy's extravaganza where you're not sure whose wedding you're at.

'Did we take a wrong turn? Was it Ballroom Number One or Number Two?'

'Is this the Henson wedding or the Lieberman bar mitzvah?'

Size is especially important since *BB* says the bride and groom are expected to personally thank each guest for attending the wedding. Smile and shake hands. Smile and shake hands. This would explain why Mandy was wearing a wrist guard by the end of her wedding. But there's no way I'm spending my big day shaking two hundred and fifty hands. Not a chance. I won't have time to eat my pumpkin bisque.

Lobster risotto. Asparagus ravioli?

Our guest list includes friends and family, and allows everyone to bring their spouse or significant other. We decided that if someone's not seriously involved and they know other guests, they will be invited alone. There's no reason to subsidize someone's dating life. And, Lord knows, Stephen's got plenty of cheapo friends who would just love to bring their *gal du jour* to a fancy wedding with a fabulous meal and an open bar – all free of charge. Well, forget it. That's what Club Med is for. Go buy some beads.

Besides, being realistic, I know that our parents will want to include some of their friends in the list so we're bound to get up to eighty-five by the time all this is over.

Surprisingly, making the list – or, rather, agreeing on the list – was not as easy as I thought it would be. Stephen didn't want me to invite my friend Jane because he can't stand her so I volunteered to bump her from the list on the condition that he did not invite his ex-girlfriend Diane 'I'm a Big Pain in the Ass' Martin. But he didn't want to bump Diane since she invited him (without me!) to her wedding last year and he didn't want to seem petty. I also wasn't so crazy about him inviting the guys he plays softball with on the weekends. I've only met them once. After hours of arguing we finally compromised with him inviting Diane and her husband but not the softball gang, and my not inviting Jane but getting to seat Diane off in some corner with my cousin Eddie who suffers from chronic halitosis.

The one thing we immediately agreed on is that neither of us wants to invite Stephen's brother Tom.

24 September

I still slip occasionally and call Stephen my boyfriend. It's going to take a while to get used to calling him my fiancé. Especially without laughing. And by then it'll be time to call him my *husband*!

25 September

Today was crazy. We had an early-morning staff meeting to discuss the December issue. I came armed with story ideas but somehow forgot that December means holiday issue. I've been spending so much time thinking about next June that the holidays just seem like a minor inconvenience on the way to the rest of my life. Needless to say, my pitches on sanitation negligence, cabbie cover-ups, and a profile on a woman who recycles hypodermic needles were met with hesitance. And when I quickly suggested a profile on city caterers (slyly figuring that the research could be useful to my wedding) Barry gallantly praised my 'clever' idea, then side-swiped me by insisting that by the time the December issue hits the stands most the of the city's caterers will be booked for the holidays. Meanwhile his lengthy list of story ideas ranged from the ever-trite 'Who Are the Men Who Play Santa Claus' to a search for the perfect egg-nog.

Like anyone really drinks egg-nog.

In front of all the other editors, associates, and assistants, my boss Mr Spaulding made a point of asking me to submit a new list of holiday-oriented pitches by tomorrow. A serious blow to my image of authority. Besides, it's going to be near impossible to make that list by tomorrow since I looked at two potential reception venues after work today and have another scheduled before work tomorrow morning.

The venues I saw tonight, a famous hotel and a swanky nightclub, were all wrong. The hotel ballroom was too big and the nightclub was fine until you turned up the lights. Both were incredibly expensive.

And our time is quickly dwindling. Soon we'll be eight months away from our wedding. According to *BB* we may as well elope. So to expedite the process I've given Kate a list of thirty-five potential venues to call and make viewing appointments. After all, we really are open to anything.

Except boats and riverfront restaurants. Stephen has an aunt who's afraid of water.

26 September

This morning we saw a photographer's loft down in Chinatown. Very hip, open, and all white. The right size for a group of eighty-five and could easily be transformed into a romantic setting with some clever decorations. The photographer even offered to throw in a couple of backdrops for free. But the neighborhood was too seedy. It's one thing to step over restaurant trash on your way to a celebrity photo-shoot but for a wedding reception?

I composed my list of holiday-oriented story ideas on the bus ride to work.

Kate's gotten in touch with twenty-two of the reception sites I asked her to call. Half were already booked for our date. She scheduled appointments for the remaining eleven. Unfortunately Stephen's so busy with his project at work that it looks like I'll be seeing most of them myself. Hopefully Kate will be able to contact the remaining thirteen places.

As for the ceremony Stephen and I have chosen a church on the Upper East Side – First American Presbyterian. Since Stephen's family is Presbyterian and my family is only vaguely Protestant it makes the most sense. It's beautiful and classy and available for our date. We have an appointment to meet the minister next Saturday.

While Stephen thinks his mother will be disappointed that we're not being married by his family minister, Reverend MacKenzie, in the church that he attended as a child, he's fairly certain that she'll accept our decision to marry in the city. After all, First American is on the Upper East Side.

Besides, Stephen says Reverend MacKenzie gives him the creeps.

As for my parents, I'm certain they won't care. They didn't bat an eyelid when Nicole and Chet were married by Chet's renegade Baptist minister cousin who arrived five minutes before the ceremony after driving sixteen hours from Louisiana without stopping to shower. Trust me. The guy didn't shower.

I just hope my parents understand why I want to get married in the city instead of in their backyard. Unlike Nicole, who's permanently ensconced herself in our home town, I am no fan. Just going back to see my parents gives me the shakes. It's quiet, it's manicured, it's boring. It's like the whole place is on life support. Getting married there would be tantamount to running a lawn mower over my head.

Not to mention the fact that if we get married in the city our folks will be too far away to attempt a coup. I've seen *Betsy's Wedding* a thousand times on cable and I'm determined that this wedding be our personal expression, not some parental fantasy come true.

29 September

My mother and Gram came down to the city to do some shopping today. Before heading home they stopped by my office. While my mother was in the ladies' room I proudly held out my hand to show Gram my engagement ring. She took one look at it and clapped her hands in delight. 'Would you look at that! It's lovely!'

'Stephen gave it to me. It's my engagement ring.'

Gram's delight turned to concern. She looked me straight in the eye as if she was about to tell me I had male-pattern baldness, and said, 'But that's an emerald. Engagement rings are supposed to be diamond.'

'Typically yes, but there's no reason to be trapped by the shackles of tradition.'

Gram shook her head. 'Sure there is. Diamonds are tough as nails. They symbolize strength and fidelity. Emeralds are weak and unreliable. Liz Taylor wears them all the time.'

Weak and unreliable? Elizabeth Taylor? Was she kidding?

'Come on, Gram. You don't really believe that. Besides, this ring belonged to Stephen's great-grandmother.'

Gram clutched her heart 'You mean he didn't even buy it?'

'No. It's a family heirloom.'

'Heirloom? That means *free*. He should've spent some money on my beautiful granddaughter.'

Forget that this ring and I have bonded, and that it makes me smile every day. All of that meant nothing. Because in under thirty seconds Gram had somehow managed to turn my stunning emerald ring into a stinging source of shame. Like the magician pulling a rabbit from a hat – you don't know how it happens, but it does.

Just then my mother returned from the bathroom. I stuffed my hand in my pocket and quickly asked about their train schedule. I'd show her my ring some other time. Maybe in a year or ten. But right now, I'd had all the family support I could bear.

Minutes later I was putting them on the elevator as Barry was stepping out. 'What do we have here? Don't tell me. Three generations of Thomas women. No doubt in town to make wedding preparations. How exciting! You know, Amy, you never did tell me how your Dream Boy proposed.'

But before I could dodge the question Gram responded, 'On the candy line at the multiplex on Broadway. The one next to the adult bookstore.' I'm not sure whether I screamed or just felt like it.

Barry smiled. 'A "concession" proposal. That's original . . . *and* telling.' Then he and his shit-eating grin sashayed away, his howls of laughter ringing throughout the halls.

I turned to Gram in disbelief. But she was clueless: 'What's so funny? I'm certain that's what Stephen told me.' Looking at her sweet, innocent face I remember thinking that if she weren't such a kind old lady I would definitely kick her teeth in.

1 October

I saw five reception venues today as my lunch hour turned into a lunch afternoon. Two hotels – too expensive. One garden restaurant – affordable if I want to get married on a Tuesday night. A corporate-event space in the East-Asian Cultural Building. Too impersonal. Too cold. Too scary. Do I really want a bust of Chairman Mao spotlit during my wedding reception? And a SoHo art gallery. Great, except I'd have to buy a hefty insurance policy for the artwork, which would remain on the walls during my event. Scheduled for 2 June – 'High Heels and Hymens: Fetishistic Nude Photography'.

3 October

Stephen's just informed me that his friends Mitch and Larry are going to be his best man and groomsman.

Mitch and Larry, who might as well be called Beavis and Butthead, are like Mandy – only emotionally stunted. Unable to maintain their appearance, let alone jobs or relationships, they have little to do with who Stephen is now. They're more a part of his past than his future (God willing). They're his old fraternity brothers who have yet to realize that college is over, the frat house is gone, and those gray hairs in their goatee mean that forty-ounce beers are no longer for personal consumption.

I was really hoping that Stephen would choose one of his more interesting, *literate* friends. But no. He got all sentimental and clung to the gruesome twosome.

Marriage really is a package deal.

4 October

We met with Father Anderson today. He's the only minister I've ever seen who wears a Rolex and carries a cellphone. His broker called three times during our meeting. Apparently there was a rally on Seagrams. Anyway, First American Presbyterian is ours on 2 June. I just hope Father Anderson puts his phone on vibrate.

> Official THINGS TO DO List
> 1. Choose wedding date
> 2. Tell boss wedding date
> 3. Vacation time for honeymoon
> 4. Decide on honeymoon
> 5. Get minister/church
> 6. Choose reception venue
> 7. Make guest list
> 8. Choose maid of honor
> 9. Choose best man
> 10. Register for gifts
> 11. Arrange for engagement party
> 12. Buy engagement ring
> 13. Buy wedding rings
> 14. Buy wedding dress
> 15. Choose maid-of-honor dress
> 16. Order wedding cake

17. Hire caterer
18. Hire band for reception
19. Order flowers for ceremony
20. Buy shoes
21. Plan rehearsal dinner
22. Invites to rehearsal dinner
23. Hire musicians for ceremony
24. ~~Decide on dress code~~
25. Get marriage license
26. Hire videographer
27. Hire photographer
28. Order table flowers
29. Order bouquets
30. Order boutonnières for men
31. Order nosegays for women
32. Order invitations
33. Decide on wine selection
34. Postage for invitations
35. Choose hairstyle and makeup
36. Buy gifts for attendants
37. Buy thank-you notes
38. Announce wedding in newspaper
39. Buy headpiece
40. Buy travelers' checks for honeymoon
41. Apply for visas
42. Get shots and vaccinations
43. Order tent if necessary
44. Order chairs/tables if necessary
45. Make budget
46. Divide expenses
47. Make table-seating charts

48. Choose bridesmaid dress
49. Decide on menu
50. Decide on *hors d'oeuvres*
51. Decide on dinner service style
52. Decide on staff–guest ratio
53. Decide seated or buffet
54. Reserve vegetarian meals
55. Reserve band/photographer meals
56. Make photo list
57. Choose hotel for wedding night
58. Hire limo for church–reception transport
59. Buy guest book for reception
60. Find hotel for out-of-towners
61. Decide on liquor selection
62. Hire bartenders
63. Verify wheelchair accessibility
64. Choose processional music
65. Choose recessional music
66. Choose cocktail music
67. Choose reception music
68. Choose ceremony readings
69. Prepare birdseed instead of rice
70. Schedule manicure/pedicure/wax

5 October

Over a billion men on this planet and I found the one who puts the toilet seat down. It's like winning the lottery!

I am so in love.

6 October

I've seen seven more reception venues. None of them works. Of the remaining twenty-one, fifteen are booked for our date and I'm scheduled to see the last six next week. What a disaster.

I'm going upstate this weekend to spend some time with my parents and to determine how much money they're giving us for the wedding. Even before the food, liquor, and entertainment costs, these venues are more expensive than I ever imagined. We'll definitely have to cut corners here and there. But I can't worry too much. After all, does it really matter if we serve Californian wine instead of French?

7 October

Today is my thirtieth birthday. Everyone said I'd be disappointed, devastated, depressed . . . But I'm thrilled. I have friends, family, and Stephen. Not to mention (somewhat) meaningful employment. What more could I ask for?

9 October

Well I've had a RUDE awakening.

My parents are only giving us five thousand dollars for the wedding. That will barely pay for the food!

> DAD
> We're heading into retirement soon. If

you'd done this a few years back, like
your sister did, it would have been easier
for us.

ME
Well, forgive me for not jumping on the
first man I met just to ensure you'd pay
for my wedding.

DAD
Oh, sweetheart, we're glad you didn't
jump into marriage. Frankly we didn't
think you were the marrying kind.[17] It's
just that it's a little late.

ME
Late? I'm only thirty!

MOM
I had two children by the time I was
thirty.

ME
And look how we turned out!

MOM
You're getting hysterical.

ME
You bet I'm hysterical. I thought you'd

---

[17] Again with the Marrying Kind?

be more supportive of my marriage.

DAD
We're very supportive of your marriage.
Stephen's a nice, solid man. But our
accountant's advising us to be fiscally
conservative. You know Nicole was quite
pleased when she got five thousand
dollars for her wedding.

ME
First off, that was five years ago. If you
calculate the rate of inflation five
thousand dollars back then is like twenty
thousand today.

DAD
I guess that's New math.

ME
Second, Chet's family laid out twice as
much as that.

DAD
Then Stephen should ask his family for
the rest.

They were right. The only option is to ask the Stewarts
to shoulder the brunt of the cost. I hope they don't mind. It
could get as high as fifteen thousand dollars. But I suppose
that's just a drop in the bucket for them. After all, they've
got a four-car garage.

10 October

Stephen has just informed me that his family's willing to match my parents' five thousand dollars but that's it. Not a penny more. After I regained consciousness I reminded him that this isn't the Stone Age. The days of dowries, trousseaus and prized goats being offered by the bride's family are long gone. The groom's family is more than welcome to shoulder the financial burden of a wedding. Even *BB* says so. And Prudence agrees. I can see it in her eyes. Besides, the Stewarts are significantly more affluent than my family so it just makes sense.

> STEPHEN
> I understand that it makes sense to you.
> But my family is pretty traditional.

> ME
> Your mother keeps a miniature chihuahua
> in her handbag and your father's dating
> your lab partner from tenth grade.

> STEPHEN
> True. But we still go caroling at
> Christmas.

Yeah? Well, this year we may have to do it for profit because there's no way ten thousand dollars is paying for an elegant New York City wedding.

Stephen insists that we shouldn't worry. 'We'll work it out.' Sure, that's a terrific answer for a spontaneous person. But control freaks like me who can't sleep at night

92

without triple-checking their Things To Do list need a real *plan*. Besides, he's so distracted by his damn computer program that 'We'll work it out' is pass-the-buck language for 'You deal with it, Amy.'

11 October – 4 a.m.

I can't sleep. I keep reviewing the numbers in my head and there's no way to have an elegant wedding for ten thousand dollars. After all, this is America. Not Taiwan.

And for the record, if I could, I'd be more than willing to pay for this wedding myself. Except I work in magazines. It's a notoriously cheap industry. I do it for love, not money. Especially at *Round-Up*. So I can't pay for it out of my own pocket. I can barely afford clothes that have pockets. And despite Mandy's raving about how lucrative the software industry is, Stephen's at a start-up company, which is having trouble starting. He makes less than I do.

I'll just have to beg my parents for more money.

But what if they're being honest about their retirement fund? What if their accountant is right and they need to save now so they won't be in the street when it's time for pre-masticated foods and salt-water enemas? How selfish of me to bug them for more money. The very people who clothed and housed me and sent me to Girl Scout camp when I was twelve. Where do I get off deciding how they should spend their money?

On the other hand, it's not like they're impoverished. They both work, they both have pensions, and they own their house. They're debt-free: Nicole and I are repaying our college loans. And it's not like they'll starve – my dad's middle-management at a supermarket chain. They're even planning a trip to Europe next year for my mom's fifty-fifth birthday. So come on, people, ease up those purse strings!

And why is Stephen's family suddenly so tight-fisted? I thought they were delighted about this marriage. Why else would they give me the coveted emerald ring?

13 October

Barry interrupted our review of the December proofs to ask how many kids Stephen and I are going to have. Why's a guy I'd love to see sail the *Titanic* thinking about me procreating? He shouldn't even look at my briefcase let alone envision me splayed out on a hospital bed with another life spewing from my loins.

> ME
> It's not something we're thinking about
> yet. How long is your egg-nog piece
> going to be?

> BARRY
> A double-page spread. I've always felt
> that six children made a good-sized
> family. Very *Brady Bunch*.

> ME
> My writer covering the city's various
> religious celebrations says the piece is
> running over. He's going to need another

quarter-page. And having six children has been out of fashion since medical science perfected that smallpox vaccine. Besides, if Carol Brady actually birthed all six of those kids she wouldn't have had time to do the show.

BARRY
Why not? Shirley Partridge had five kids *and* a band. And with those hips you could have an entire litter if you wanted.

What the hell's wrong with my hips?

But before I could respond he was out the door and complimenting Mr Spaulding on his choice of tie.

14 October

I saw two more reception venues today.

The first was a veterans' administration party room. And they say war is hell. You should've seen this room. Throw a few late-night winos in there and it could pass for a bus terminal. No wonder vets are so depressed.

The second was the ballroom at the Marrion Hotel. It's where Stephen's ex-girlfriend Diane 'I'm a Big Pain in the Ass' Martin got married. Sure, that makes it a hand-me-down venue but I figured with ten thousand dollars I should just be happy it's not the Motel Six.

But even the Marrion wanted four thousand dollars just to rent the room. What are they? Crazy? They're barely above the Days Inn on the hotel food chain, and they want more than a third of my entire wedding budget? Forget it. That would leave a buck fifty for decorating and even I can't be creative on a buck fifty.

How the hell do people afford these things?

15 October

My parents are holding their position – no more money. Stephen's parents are taking their cue – no more money. Apparently the Stewarts are so busy arguing over the terms of their divorce that the mere mention of money sends shivers down their spines.

Well, they'll be sure to shiver when Stephen and I are married at the homeless shelter at Port Authority.

17 October

Kate expressed concern about my wedding today. She claims that it's consuming too much of her time. She's fallen behind on her filing, her typing, her inter-office memos ... And Barry's starting to complain that she isn't paying enough attention to *his* needs.

I don't get it. I'm an easy-going boss. She should be happy I'm not asking her to retype my file labels in a more 'stylish' font like Barry did last month. Besides, if she's got time to give herself a manicure in the middle of the day, then she's got time to call the Chambers of Commerce for all the metropolitan areas in the greater tri-state region in search of a potential reception venue.

I know how this sounds. I know it sounds bad.

The greater tri-state region? Who the hell wants to get married there? But I'm afraid it's come to this. No matter how creative I get there's just no way ten thousand dollars will pay for a unique and creative eighty-five-person wedding in New York City.

Stamford, Connecticut, still beats my hometown. Trust me.

20 October

Our parents have given us the names of people they want to invite to our wedding. All 135 of them! My parents had twenty-six, Mr Stewart had eighteen, and Mrs Stewart rang in with *ninety-one*. We don't even know most of these people. For instance, who the hell is Hans Lindstrom? And how are we supposed to pay for his lobster risotto with a budget of ten thousand dollars?

23 October

Mandy, who is still perfectly tan from her honeymoon in Hawaii, just told me that she and Jon exchanged engagement gifts. Who knew people even did this? Apparently *BB* discusses this custom in Chapter Sixteen. I'm still on Chapter Eight.

Well, there's no way Stephen and I can afford engagement gifts right now. He has to save money for his tuxedo, I have to save money for my stress-management seminar, and we both have to save money for Hans Lindstrom's lobster risotto.

I wonder if he'd like a subscription to *Round-Up*.

24 October

I had lunch with our staff writer, Julie Browning. She's spent the last two months doing an article on karaoke's impact on New York nightlife and we needed to hammer out a new angle since the latest issue of *Glamour* featured the exact same story. Did I mention that *Round-Up* is New York's least-read magazine?

While we were eating Julie noticed my engagement ring. Turns out emerald is her favorite stone. Classy lady. We started to talk about marriage and life and work. Julie used to be a senior editor at a magazine in D.C. I always assumed that she'd left because she preferred the freedom of a writer's lifestyle. *Wrong.* Seems that once her boss got wind of her plans to marry she was surreptitiously edged out of her job. She was no longer invited to big corporate meetings, she was left out of the loop on major issues, and her story ideas were routinely passed over.

I told her that I wasn't worried about that since, unlike her socially conservative magazine in D.C., *Round-Up* is a very liberal glossy. But Julie wouldn't waver. She kept warning me to watch my back: 'People assume that marriage, specifically being a WIFE, will affect your dedication to the job. They assume you'll devote your energies to your husband's career and turn your own to dilettantism. And, of course, they assume you'll be quitting any day to have six kids.'

I suddenly flashed to Barry, Carol Brady, and the arrangement of lilies. The flowers of death and funerals!

What a fool I'd been! And when I returned to the office there he was – Mr Bridal Booster himself – eyeing my corner office.

Rank with the stench of *coup d'état*.

25 October

Kate's had no luck with her search. She's called all the major metropolitan areas in the tri-state region in search of a reception venue in our price range that can accommodate anywhere from eighty-five to two hundred and twenty people (we've yet to settle this issue with our parents). Apparently she's come up empty-handed. Or, at least, she says she has. I doubt she truly applied herself to the task. I can't help but think that if I'd asked her to find the address of Ricky Martin's summer home or Brad Pitt's shoe size she would have had better luck.

But I can't complain too much. I've got to keep a low profile on my wedding. Julie's cautionary tale really spooked me and I don't want to provide anyone, especially Barry, with ammunition to take my job.

So I spent the rest of the day reworking an article on the efforts of hot-dog vendors to unionize.

27 October

Bianca Sheppard called me last night. I've known Bianca since the third day of college when she shoved me across the room while charging toward our handsome dorm advisor. To this day she swears she tripped. Since then she's been Bianca Sheppard, Douglas, Izzard, Santos, and Rabinowitz. Marriage seems to agree with her. Repeatedly. Hence her nickname 'Repeat Offender' or 'RP' for short. She marries, it lasts about two years, then she decides it's not what she wants and splits. A month later she's getting married again.

At a certain point, her weddings stopped feeling like romantic unions and started feeling like biennial wine tastings. Needless to say she was the last person I'd think of for wedding advice.

But a natural resource for wedding dresses. She knew exactly where to go. After all, she's already had four.

28 October – 12.30 a.m.

I've become an insomniac. Which is crazy because I've never had trouble sleeping. Back in college I had to chew espresso beans in order to stay awake. But now the minute my eyes shut my mind races – venues, menus, bridesmaid, bands. Bands! I've got to ask Stephen if he's started to look for a band.

Breathe. I must remember to breathe.

But not Stephen. Somehow he's managing to breathe *and* sleep. Ever since the engagement we've been trying to spend each night together. Usually at my house since I need more stuff in the morning. It's a strange sensation to see him lying next to me – his adorable little snores, the cute way he drapes his arm over my chest – and to realize that I'm going to spend the rest of my life with this man. Every night for the rest of my life I'll roll over and see him.

How the hell did I get so lucky?

1 November

Last night we went to Larry and Mitch's Hallowe'en party.
Larry went as a groom and Mitch went as a bride. They
did it to needle Stephen, who thought it was hysterical. I
thought it was totally obnoxious.

> STEPHEN
> Come on. He's even wearing a garter
> belt. You've got to admit it's pretty
> funny.

There was nothing funny about the fact that Mitch had
a wedding dress before I did. Besides, most brides wax
their backs for the big day.

> ME
> It'd be a whole lot funnier if Larry didn't
> have the word 'sucker' written across his
> forehead in lipstick.

> STEPHEN
> I admit that borders offensive, but you
> have to understand it's their way of
> showing support. They dressed up *for* us.

I could tell Stephen was trying to endear his Neanderthal
pals to me. But it wasn't working. They weren't freaks
passing through town in a travelling show.
The show's permanent. They're here to stay.
Stephen wrapped his arm around my waist and gave me
a hug.

STEPHEN
You have to remember, they've never
been wildly in love. Larry hasn't had a
date in over a year because he's too
nervous to call a woman. And Mitch is
so insecure that he'll sleep with anyone
with a futon.

That's half of New York. Suddenly the article we did
last May on the rise of venereal disease was starting to
make sense.

STEPHEN
Trust me. Once they're more comfortable
around you they'll start to relax and
show you their more interesting side. I
swear it's there.

ME
That'd be a lot easier to believe if Mitch
was wearing underwear.

As I pointed across the room, Stephen saw what I did –
the bride sitting on the sofa, straddling a giant bong,
giving everyone a glimpse at his full-frontal.

3 November

Today at the staff meeting Barry made a not-so-subtle
remark about the 'Faces In The City' issue being behind
schedule.

Which it's not. I've got it all in my head. I just need to commit it to paper, have Kate type it up, and get Mr Spaulding's approval before distributing it throughout the office.

The issue focuses on ten of the city's most influential and intriguing residents. So far I've come up with nine. I'm certain the last one will come to me any day now. I've done an enormous amount of research, but I've been stuck on number ten ever since the concessions-stand proposal. And since it's my first issue as editor I want it to shine. I want it to have my distinctive mark. Especially now that Barry's on the prowl.

I assured everyone that they'd have my complete list of ten 'Faces' within the week.

5 November

I couldn't stand it anymore. I've spent the last three months trying to pretend it didn't matter. But it does. So I finally broke down and asked Stephen why he chose the candy line of a stinky movie theater on Broadway to ask me the most important question of our entire lives.

The minute I asked I knew I'd done something horribly wrong. He looked like I'd told him the NBA Championships had been canceled.

> STEPHEN
> I was trying to be romantic. Don't you remember? We had our first kiss on the candy line of that stinky movie theater.

Oh, God. He's right.

STEPHEN
We were waiting to buy popcorn and all
of a sudden I couldn't stop myself. I just
had to kiss you. You were just so
beautiful.

I remember that kiss. Pure spontaneity. It made me
tingle from my head to my toes. It was the nicest kiss I ever
got. And I had entirely forgotten about it.

But not Stephen. He made the world's most romantic
gesture by proposing to me at the very same spot as that
fabulous kiss and I screwed it all up by complaining. My
fiancé may defy his gender's genetic coding with his
sensitivity, his tenderness and his affection, but I've
disgraced mine by acting like such a *guy*!

How can he ever forgive me? How can I ever forgive
myself?

6 November

I'm assuming Stephen still wants to marry me despite the
fact that I'm a heartless bitch because he's been arguing
with his parents about their outrageous guest lists for our
wedding. He's managed to get his dad's list down to ten
but his mom is still hovering at sixty-five – including the
ever-popular Hans Lindstrom. Who, it turns out, is her
optometrist *and* favorite client. She redid his cabin in the
Adirondacks last spring.

If I were the one doing the arguing I'd point out that five

thousand dollars buys a limited number of seats to our nuptial celebration. And that the only venue we'll be able to afford with that budget is the school auditorium in Love Canal.

But then that's me. Stephen's got a whole other way of handling things. Being a software developer/computer programmer he focuses on the 'logic' of the situation. Logically speaking, would Hans really be insulted if he weren't invited?

For the record – the answer was yes.

10 November

I presented my list of 'Faces' to Mr Spaulding today. He was thrilled with my choices. Particularly number ten – Reverend Dai-Jung Choi, a minister from the Unified Church who's married over four thousand New York-area couples in the last twenty years.[18]

11 November

The guest-list débâcle rages on. My parents are down to ten, Mrs Stewart's holding at twenty and Mr Stewart has stopped at five. Unfortunately those five include Misty and two of her relatives. Stephen is furious. He's argued all week with his father but Mr Stewart won't budge. To him, accepting Misty's relatives at our wedding is synonymous with accepting Misty as his lover.

---

[18] And who's cited in the index of *BB* as an authority on wedding legalities.

Well, Stephen doesn't accept Misty, and the mere act of Mr Stewart referring to her as his 'lover' made Stephen physically ill – and has set Mrs Stewart on a rampage. First she told Mr Stewart's college alumni magazine that he left her for a man. Now she's threatening to set fire to the wooden elf he spent years carving and which, being in the backyard, qualifies as her property. This was the first I'd heard about an elf statue. Stephen says it's beyond ugly but that his mother kept it all these years for sentimental reasons. Now she wants to torch it.

It reminded me of the ice rose/human brain that Stephen carved for me. Apparently a lack of artistic talent runs in the family. Thankfully Stephen's got the sense to work in a temporary medium.

And while I have to assume that our guest list won't come down much below the current 120, Chapter Nineteen of *BB* claims that an average of 25 per cent of invitees will be unable to attend the wedding. This leaves us at ninety, which is twenty more than we originally wanted but 130 fewer than when we started this debate so I won't complain.

Official THINGS TO DO List
1. ~~Choose wedding date~~
2. ~~Tell boss wedding date~~
3. ~~Vacation time for honeymoon~~
4. Decide on honeymoon
5. ~~Get minister/church~~
6. Choose reception venue
7. ~~Make guest list~~
8. ~~Choose maid of honor~~

9. ~~Choose best man~~
10. Register for gifts
11. Arrange for engagement party
12. ~~Buy engagement ring~~
13. Buy wedding rings
14. Buy wedding dress
15. Choose maid-of-honor dress
16. Order wedding cake
17. Hire caterer
18. Hire band for reception
19. Order flowers for ceremony
20. Buy shoes
21. Plan rehearsal dinner
22. Invites to rehearsal dinner
23. Hire musicians for ceremony
24. ~~Decide on dress code~~
25. Get marriage license
26. Hire videographer
27. Hire photographer
28. Order table flowers
29. Order bouquets
30. Order boutonnières for men
31. Order nosegays for women
32. Order invitations
33. Decide on wine selection
34. Postage for invitations
35. Choose hairstyle and makeup
36. Buy gifts for attendants
37. Buy thank-you notes
38. Announce wedding in newspaper
39. Buy headpiece

40. Buy travelers' checks for honeymoon
41. Apply for visas
42. Get shots and vaccinations
43. Order tent if necessary
44. Order chairs/tables if necessary
45. ~~Made budget~~
46. ~~Divide expenses~~
47. Make table-seating charts
48. Choose bridesmaid dress
49. Decide on menu
50. Decide on *hors d'oeuvres*
51. Decide on dinner service style
52. Decide on staff–guest ratio
53. Decide seated or buffet
54. Reserve vegetarian meals
55. Reserve band/photographer meals
56. Make photo list
57. Choose hotel for wedding night
58. Hire limo for church–reception transport
59. Buy guest book for reception
60. Find hotel for out-of-towners
61. Decide on liquor selection
62. Hire bartenders
63. Verify wheelchair accessibility
64. Choose processional music
65. Choose recessional music
66. Choose cocktail music
67. Choose reception music
68. Choose ceremony readings
69. Prepare birdseed instead of rice
70. Schedule manicure/pedicure/wax

14 November

We're less than seven months away from our wedding and we still don't have a venue. I'm afraid it's time to face the music. Even Prudence has that 'All right, already' look.

We'll have to get married at one of our parents' houses.

Since Mr Stewart now lives in a singles complex I'm ruling him out immediately. In theory we could get married at my parents' house but I don't see why we should since Mrs Stewart's house is bigger, more beautiful, and infinitely more comfortable for a wedding. After all, she's got a tennis court and two bathrooms on the first floor.

15 November

Stephen refuses to ask his mother if we can get married at her house. He said the last thing he wants to deal with is his mother's insanity. He's worried that she'll smother us with questions, concerns, and demands and that she'd make everyone, especially him, miserable.

Not to mention the fact that she'd sooner eat Chuffy with a knife and fork than allow Misty and two of her relatives into the house.

I reminded Stephen that we are now six months and eighteen days away from our wedding without a place to hold the reception. But he wouldn't budge.

Now I know how Joseph and Mary felt.

18 November

After combing through bridal magazines I decided to begin shopping for the most important, most photographed, most expensive item of clothing I will ever wear once in my life: my wedding dress.

Luckily *BB* has several tips on the subject:

(1) Make sure it's not too small, you may not lose those ten pounds.
(2) Make sure it's flattering from behind. The ceremony gives everyone a nice long look at your rear.
(3) Make sure you can raise your arms to dance. It'd be horrible to rip it during the reception.
(4) Make sure it photographs nicely.

I already knew that I didn't want any of that Cinderella-ballgown nonsense you see in the movies. My wedding dress will be elegant and fashionable. Like an evening gown you'd see at the Oscars. I want an ankle-length dress with a narrow silhouette in silk jersey and off-the-shoulder cap sleeves. Sure it'll be white, but it'll be sophisticated.

19 November

The only thing I look worse in than a bikini is a narrow-silhouette dress in silk jersey with off-the-shoulder cap sleeves.

First off, silk jersey has no shape of its own. It just falls where you do. Every bump, bulge and roll you've got is nicely highlighted. And underwear? Forget it. It's not going to happen.

Second, the narrow silhouette is seen so often on catwalks and at the Oscars because only supermodels and famous actors can afford the liposuction necessary to fit into it.

Third, cap sleeves were not designed for anyone with an upper arm thicker than a baguette. They draw your eye to the widest part of the arm and leave plenty of room beneath it for that extra roll of skin to flap freely in the wind.

Oh, and the last thing – either Bianca Sheppard's cleaning up in alimony or she's selling her internal organs to science because these dresses cost thousands of dollars.

Vera Wang must have a house for every season.

20 November

I'll be celebrating my wedding in the inner circle of hell.

Commonly known as my parents' backyard.

22 November

Stephen didn't seem to mind the idea of having our wedding reception in my parents' backyard until I mentioned that it meant swapping our cellphone-toting Father Anderson for his family minister Reverend MacKenzie. But what can we do? Nothing. Stephen will just have to get over his dislike of Reverend MacKenzie.

Trust me. In the 'Who's More Upset About the Way This Wedding's Turning Out' contest, I'm ahead by a mile.

23 November

After finally deciding to embrace my roots, to return to the homestead, to have my wedding reception in my parents' backyard . . .

They flat out refused.

When I reminded them that they'd been more than happy to host Nicole's wedding they reminded me that since then the house has been repainted and the backyard landscaped. My mom doesn't want dirty handprints all over the walls and my dad doesn't want people trampling the flower-beds. Not to mention the reseeded lawn.

Just as I was about to start yelling I thought, What would Stephen do in this situation? Logic. I calmly explained to my parents that their lovely backyard was the only choice Stephen and I had since we couldn't afford any place we liked in the city and because the Stewarts' acrimonious divorce currently precluded using their house. My mother mentioned that the local Lions' Club had a very 'pleasant' room, which was available for a reasonable fee. The image of a windowless basement crossed my mind. It took all my will-power not to cry.

Instead, I screamed. 'Nicole got everyone's enthusiasm! Nicole got plenty of money! Nicole got to use the backyard!'

I was now *begging* to celebrate my wedding in my parents' backyard.

Oh, how the mighty fall.

23 November – 9.30 p.m.

My mother called to suggest we scale back to a post-wedding celebration of cake and champagne on the church lawn.

Forget it.

There are Girl Scout meetings that are more substantial.

25 November

Thanksgiving was one long series of epiphanies.

Maybe those Pilgrims should've just stayed home.

It started with an early dinner at my parents' house. As we sat down to eat I noticed that my mother seated Nicole between my father and herself. I was seated at the other end of the table next to Stephen and Gram. It suddenly occurred to me that Nicole's been seated between our parents for every meal since 1973. They used to say it was because she needed help cutting her food. She's now twenty-seven years old. Trust me, she's mastered cutlery. But have the seating assignments been revised? *No*. And who was it who got all that money for her wedding? And who got to use the backyard? And who does my mother invite every summer to join her at the Tanglewood Crafts Fair? It was all beginning to make sense.

They liked Nicole better!

Sure they toasted my wedding and maybe they would have waxed sentimental a bit longer if Gram hadn't started to choke on a piece of turkey fat – but it doesn't matter.

It's just a drop in the bucket. Bud and Terry had chosen a favorite. No wonder I'd gotten the bottom bunk![19]

At least I know I'm Gram's favorite. She always pays special attention to me. And after we discussed the latest issue of *Round-Up*,[20] I began to tell her about my wedding. I was telling her all the difficulties we'd been having because Mrs Stewart didn't want Mr Stewart to invite his girlfriend when Gram suddenly interrupted me: 'You mean Stephen's parents are divorced?'

I could have sworn she knew that. 'Yeah. I told you that months ago.'

Clearly disturbed, Gram leaned forward and spoke in hushed tones: 'Call off the marriage.'

What?

'Stephen seems like a nice man, even if he does look like Dan Quayle. But everyone knows that children of divorced families are not as committed to their own marriages.'

Sweet Gram, always thinking of my best interests no matter how antiquated her ideas are. 'Don't worry, Gram. Stephen will take our marriage very seriously. Besides, they say almost half of all marriages end in divorce so chances of meeting someone whose parents are still married are pretty slim.'

'My point exactly. It's one of those cycles. Once you're in it, you're sucked up for good.' So charmingly old-fashioned.

'I appreciate your concern, Gram. But divorce isn't a contagious disease.'

'Sure it is. *20/20* said most people whose parents are divorced will have marriages that fail.'

---

[19] Despite the fact that Nicole was a bed-wetter.
[20] She's an avid fan. Perhaps the only one.

20/20 said that? 'Hugh Downs or Barbara Walters?'

'Barbara Walters, so you know it's true. And remember, we've never had any divorces in our family.' I was about to remind her that she and Grandpa would have gotten a divorce if they each hadn't been so determined to collect the other one's life insurance – but I didn't. I just smiled.

Note to self: have Kate verify Gram's sources.

After dinner Stephen and I drove an hour to his mom's house for dessert. I'd forgotten how beautiful it is. It makes me crazy to think that I'm begging to have my wedding reception in the dismal Americana of my parents' backyard when we could be celebrating in style at Mrs Stewart's Shangri-La.

My parents' house is functional and clean. My mom's always decorated like she taught: quick and to the point. If you need a chair somewhere – boom, you've got a chair. So what if it doesn't match anything else in the room? It's got four legs and a seat. Now sit. But Mrs Stewart treats her house like a showroom. Everything matches and shines and inspires a cozy sense of financial security and an endless supply of nourishing homemade meals. And the place is enormous. The three kids each had their own bed-*and* bathroom. Then there's the front lawn, the back lawn and the clay tennis court. If only!

But no.

Mrs Stewart served us homemade pecan pie and ice-cream. Stephen's sister Kimberly was there so we were four. But instead of sitting in the bright and happy breakfast nook we sat in the dining room at the huge formal table for twelve. The only light in the entire room was a single candle. It was like dining in the haunted mansion at Disney World.

115

I am beginning to understand Stephen's position about not having our reception at his mom's house. Mrs Stewart is clearly experiencing post-divorce depression. Some days she's up, up, up – but most of the time she's down and irritated. It's impossible to watch without feeling terribly sorry for her. Not to mention the fact that it's hardly a desirable temperament in the person whose space you're about to invade with caterers and ninety wedding guests – including the architect of her devastation and his perky young girlfriend. Yes, I was beginning to see Stephen's point.

As Mrs Stewart listlessly continued to feed her pie to Chuffy, Kimberly talked a blue streak about the new sofa she bought for her living room. Despite her self-absorbed monologue she managed to get in a few digs at me. A disparaging reference to *Round-Up* and a pointed comment about women who hit thirty and marry out of desperation. I've always politely suffered her vacuousness but her aggressive behavior really pissed me off.

So I called her on it as we were getting ready to leave: 'Is something wrong?'

Kimberly looked at me, surveyed the room for witnesses, then turned back with an expression I can only describe as what Amy Fisher must have looked like before shooting Mary Jo Buttafuoco in the head. 'Yeah.' She pointed an accusatory finger at my engagement ring. 'That's what's wrong. My grandmother must have been high on Citrucel to give it to you. That emerald belongs to me. It's been in our family for four generations. It's worth a *shitload* of money. And it should've been *mine*.'

I wanted to tell the Honda-driving brat to kiss my ass and then some, but just then Stephen appeared, forcing me

116

to smile and end our conversation with a terse, 'Tough luck, Kim.'

After all, how dare she?

Then, waving goodbye to Stephen's depressed mother, his bitter sister, and the sugar-high family pet, we drove across town to see his dad.

Mr Stewart and Misty had eaten Thanksgiving dinner at a local restaurant with Tom. By the time we arrived at the condo Mr Stewart and Tom were splayed on the couch in food comas while Misty was in the tiny galley kitchen brewing coffee. Not surprisingly, Stephen opted to join his father on the couch and steer clear of Misty.

I'd only met Misty once, a few months ago when Stephen and I dropped something off at Mr Stewart's apartment. But it had been brief and we certainly didn't have a conversation. So all I knew about Misty was what Stephen had told me – she was a sick, manipulative woman in search of a father figure and – which I could tell by looking at her – she was pretty in a Jewel sort of way. Not much to go on.

After she had congratulated me on the engagement, Misty and I stood in the kitchen talking for the next half-hour. Clearly she was in no hurry to join the Stewart men on the couch. And who could blame her? Tom's a pervert and Stephen's cold to her. She may not be a chess master but Misty isn't stupid. In fact, she's positively normal. Not exactly what you'd expect in a thirty-three-year-old woman who's romantically involved with a sixty-year-old man whose interests are limited to electrical wiring and golf. Mr Stewart himself does not play. He enjoys the sport from the comfort of his Ultrasuede recliner in a temperature-controlled environment.

Misty, on the other hand, can talk about everything from recent medical breakthroughs to Edith Wharton novels. *House of Mirth* is her favorite. Currently employed as a lab technician at a local hospital, she spent four years after college working on a cruise ship. They traveled ten months of the year and almost always in Europe. She spent the next two years in Madrid as a secretary for the European branch of an American clothing company. She moved back to her hometown when her sister had a baby, her nephew's birth rekindling her desire to be close to family.

Currently considering becoming a veterinarian, she wasn't my type, but she would have made a nice friend for Nicole. If it weren't for her bizarre relationship with my future father-in-law. A relationship which she *finally* mentioned at the end of our conversation. And *thank God*, because I was *dying* to know. After all, how does something like that happen? Don't you ever stop and think, Hey, this guy is old enough to be my father; He's got kids my age; He's got gray pubic hair? But Misty's story was short and sweet and void of salacious details.

They have the same auto mechanic and eight months ago they met at his garage.

That was it. No apologies and no explanations. Remorse is not what Misty is about.

When the coffee was ready I followed her out to the living room where she lovingly patted Mr Stewart's bulging belly as she handed him a cup. Stephen cringed at her affectionate gesture. And Tom misunderstood it. Slapping his father's gut he shouted, 'Yeah, Dad, you really packed it in tonight!' Mr Stewart just shook his head. Then he thanked Misty for the coffee, and made space for her alongside him on the sofa.

As I watched Mr Stewart and Misty together, snuggling on the sofa, I was surprised by how natural it all seemed. Sure, at first it looked like Misty was abnormally affectionate with her dad. And that her head should have been on Tom or Stephen's shoulder. But aside from the age disparity they seemed well suited and extremely content. And even though I felt guilty about not hating Misty on Mrs Stewart's behalf, the fact remains that I had seen the Stewarts' relationship, and it wasn't half as loving as this one.

Besides, isn't love what matters most? And who's to say what's appropriate? Jon and Mandy are the same age but I'd never say their relationship was appropriate. It's not even comprehensible.

26 November

My insomnia's getting worse. They say sleep deprivation can destroy your health with headaches, high blood pressure, and dementia – not to mention what it can do to your appearance.

And when I do manage to sleep it's generally accompanied by some horrible anxiety dream where I get married in an army bunker, or I walk down the aisle naked or, worse, half-way through the wedding reception I realize I've forgotten to invite someone I love like my great-aunt Lucy or my mother. In my dream I run to a payphone and call her. I try desperately to come up with some plausible, forgivable explanation as to why my wedding reception's in full swing and this is the first she's heard about it. I generally don't wake up before experiencing a torturous period of guilt and devastation. How will I ever make it up to her? How will I ever explain why I forgot to invite her to my wedding?

Clearly this wedding is getting the best of me. I'm *allowing* it to get the best of me. But no more! I'm bigger than this. I'm stronger than this. I can control this!

Breathe. I must remember to breathe.

27 November – 1 a.m.

My plan of action is set. I must lure Nicole over to my side, ally her with my cause, then send her into the enemy camp to negotiate on my behalf.

27 November

After reminding Nicole that I taught her how to feign illness in order to skip school, that I convinced our mother to allow her to wear a mini-skirt to her junior prom, and that I helped her avoid punishment in 1987 when she got caught sneaking out to a Debbie Gibson concert (like that wasn't punishment enough), Nicole agreed to speak with our parents about letting me use their backyard.

28 November

My parents have agreed to let us use their backyard for our wedding reception.

I beg for a month – zip. Nicole asks once – *voilà*! Apparently, whatever Nicole wants . . .

Official THINGS TO DO List

1. ~~Choose wedding date~~
2. ~~Tell boss wedding date~~
3. ~~Vacation time for honeymoon~~
4. Decide on honeymoon
5. ~~Get minister/church~~
6. ~~Choose reception venue~~
7. ~~Make guest list~~
8. ~~Choose maid of honor~~
9. ~~Choose best man~~
10. Register for gifts
11. Arrange for engagement party
12. ~~Buy engagement ring~~
13. Buy wedding rings
14. Buy wedding dress
15. Choose maid-of-honor dress
16. Order wedding cake
17. Hire caterer
18. Hire band for reception
19. Order flowers for ceremony
20. Buy shoes
21. Plan rehearsal dinner
22. Invites to rehearsal dinner
23. Hire musicians for ceremony
24. ~~Decide on dress code~~
25. Get marriage license
26. Hire videographer
27. Hire photographer
28. Order table flowers
29. Order bouquets
30. Order boutonnières for men
31. Order nosegays for women

32. Order invitations
33. Decide on wine selection
34. Postage for invitations
35. Choose hairstyle and makeup
36. Buy gifts for attendants
37. Buy thank-you notes
38. Announce wedding in newspaper
39. Buy headpiece
40. Buy travelers' checks for honeymoon
41. Apply for visas
42. Get shots and vaccinations
43. Order tent if necessary
44. Order chairs/tables if necessary
45. ~~Make budget~~
46. ~~Divide expenses~~
47. Make table-seating charts
48. Choose bridesmaid dress
49. Decide on menu
50. Decide on *hors d'oeuvres*
51. Decide on dinner service style
52. Decide on staff–guest ratio
53. Decide seated or buffet
54. Reserve vegetarian meals
55. Reserve band/photographer meals
56. Make photo list
57. Choose hotel for wedding night
58. Hire limo for church–reception transport
59. Buy guest book for reception
60. Find hotel for out-of-towners
61. Decide on liquor selection
62. Hire bartenders

63. Verify wheelchair accessibility
64. Choose processional music
65. Choose recessional music
66. Choose cocktail music
67. Choose reception music
68. Choose ceremony readings
69. Prepare birdseed instead of rice
70. Schedule manicure/pedicure/wax

30 November

Anita and I went to a symposium for women in journalism. As employees of *Teen Flair* and *Round-Up* we were seated in the back with a partially obstructed view.

Although the lectures were interesting I was hoping that the topic of married women in the workplace would be discussed. It wasn't. According to Anita it's old news: 'What's to discuss? It's the same as if you were single: keep office romances quiet or you'll be considered a slut, and don't let your personal life interfere with your work.'

What about discrimination? Hyphenated surnames? Spousal medical benefits?

During the cocktail reception, as Anita enjoyed the open bar, I spotted Janet Brearley. Janet profiles unique and noteworthy weddings for one of the city's biggest newspapers. I met her last year at the symposium but now I had something to talk about. 'Hi, Janet. I'm Amy Thomas from *Round-Up* magazine. We met last year.' Janet smiled and shook my hand. She had bits of duck confit wedged between her front teeth. 'So how's everything at the newspaper?' Blah, blah, blah. 'Did I mention that I'm getting married in June?' I tried to be subtle. To go for the soft touch. I guess Janet gets that a lot because her spine immediately stiffened.

'Is that so?' She rubbed her temples. 'Why don't you tell me all about it?' So I did. And she smiled the smile of pity. Like I was a dyslexic struggling to spell the word IMPORTANT. 'How lovely. It doesn't sound like the type of wedding *my* paper would cover but I wish you the best of luck.'

And there it was. Janet Brearley had confirmed what I'd long-suspected. My fiancé's in computers. I'm in second-rate publications. We're having our reception in my parents' backyard in upstate New York surrounded by Common Man. Neither poverty-stricken nor fabulously wealthy, we've never been arrested, broken a world record, nor been leaders of an extremist religious group. Our wedding was going to be a boring, connect-the-dots affair.

All in all, we're just another brick in the wall.

I joined Anita at the bar.

1 December

My great-aunt Lucy is back in the hospital. A new drug designed to increase her circulation gave her an incredibly high fever instead. And while it's not life-threatening, the doctors felt it was best to admit her. I called her room but a nurse said she was sleeping.

Why do good people have to deal with such horrible things?

Here I am running around, moaning about my ten-thousand-dollar wedding and Lucy's in Milwaukee General fighting a 100-degrees plus fever. Priorities, anyone?

2 December

I'm going to be a wife. I can't be a wife. That's RIDICULOUS! A wife is a chain-smoking, fifty-year-old woman who looks like Edith Bunker. I'm no wife. I'm too cute to be a wife! Not to mention the fact that I still crack up when I refer to Stephen as my fiancé. (Which I think he's beginning to take personally.)

3 December

Today was Stephen's thirty-second birthday. At six p.m. Mr Spontaneity decided he wanted to celebrate at a Russian restaurant in Brighton Beach, Brooklyn. Two hours later ten of us were knee-deep in frozen vodka.

I swear he's got some magic power to make things happen. Maybe it's his awkward charm. His tilted smile. His willingness to laugh . . .

It was a great evening. And I had a terrific time. But as I chewed my sturgeon, I couldn't help but wonder when Mr Spontaneity was going to apply his magic power toward procuring us a band for the wedding.

4 December

Mandy's agreed to go dress shopping with me later this week. After hearing Bianca's list she assured me we could do better. 'Oh, please. Saks? Barney's? Bergdorf's? Those are Flash and Cash stores. They provide the flash, you hand over all your cash. Only bozos and tourists pay retail. The real bargains are in the outer boroughs and on Long Island. You'd be amazed at the deals you can find in Queens.'

I have to admit I was impressed. This was not the whiny pampered bride of months gone by. This was Superhero Mandy – frugal, irreverent, and sensible. 'Is that where you bought your dress?' I asked hesitantly. 'Of course. At Helman's in Forest Hills, Queens. They have fabulous sales on discontinued styles. *And* they negotiate.'

So even the rich economize? Even the rich haggle over dollars and cents? I find this incredibly comforting.

Now I just have to find a dress that brings out my inner beauty – and hides my saddlebags like Houdini. If nothing else, at least I know it will be white.

5 December

The *Round-Up* holiday issue has only been out for a week and already we've gotten six complaints from readers who have actually made Barry's choice for the 'best' egg-nog in New York. The recipe came from a small pub on Staten Island named Scotty's. It appears Scotty's egg-nog recipe tastes great but has a significant expulsive – read laxative – side-effect. Sure, it's got nutmeg and egg yolks but that's not holiday cheer you're feeling. Two people have already gone to the hospital through dehydration.

A good editor would have tested the recipe before sending it to the printers. But this is Barry we're talking about. So instead he spent the whole day with the legal department hammering out a defense strategy.

I bet my rejected-story idea on caterers seems like a real winner just about now.

6 December

Anita and I are going to the revival house to see Steve McQueen flex his wild thing in *The Getaway*. It seems like forever since I've seen Anita and even longer since we made a public spectacle of ourselves. I can't wait. I view the evening as an unofficial celebration of Barry's week-long suspension without pay. Yip-peee!!!

7 December

Finally some frivolity!
My mom's decided to invite Stephen's family for a big Christmas Eve buffet in celebration of our engagement. Obviously this is the result of her conversation with Nicole. And while I'm thrilled at the prospect of an engagement party it's further proof that Nicole's her favorite. I can't believe it took me this long to notice.

8 December

Mandy and I dress-shopped for ten hours today – and zip. Over sixty dresses later I'm still naked at the ball. Who knew there were so many shades of white?
I even followed all of *BB*'s helpful hints on the topic of 'Shopping For Your Bridal Gown' (Chapter Twenty-two):

I wore pantyhose, slip-on shoes, and an easily removable outfit. I brought a pair of pumps whose heel is similar to the heel I want on my bridal shoes, assuming I ever find any. And I sucked on hard candy all throughout the day, just to keep my energy up.

But no matter how much candy I sucked, I just couldn't get my blood sugar high enough to buy anything I saw. There were ugly dresses, atrocious dresses, flammable dresses and dresses that were okay and passable, and even some that were very beautiful. But the very beautiful dresses weren't flattering on me and if I'm bothering to get married, it better be 'very beautiful'.

Mandy found a skirt.

10 December

It just dawned on me that Christmas is in two weeks and I still haven't shopped for presents. What rock have I been under? Oh, yeah. That wedding boulder.

11 December

Stephen discussed our wedding date with those brain-surgeon friends of his, Larry and Mitch. Together the Three Stooges decided that 2 June is 'not a great idea' because it might conflict with the basketball play-offs. Stephen doesn't want to make anyone choose between our wedding and a game.

I really thought he was kidding. I kept expecting him to

say, 'Gotcha!' But he was dead serious. After four months of being engaged he suddenly wants to change the date? This is no time for spontaneity. I couldn't believe it. A basketball game or someone's wedding – is it really *that* difficult a choice? I know my friends wouldn't have a problem with it. And somehow I don't see Mrs Stewart running out to the sports arena. So what he's really saying is that Larry and Mitch might have a 'conflict'. Boo-hoo. I'll weep later.

As an alternative date Stephen proposed 2 March – the middle of the basketball season but way before the play-offs. I needed no time to consider it.

'Have you ever heard of anyone getting married in March?'

'No.'

'Well, that's because March is a horrible month. It's cold and it's gloomy.'

'But that's the great part. It's off-season. We'll get great bargains.'

Thank you, Homer Simpson. But I'm not getting married outside in three feet of snow unless someone pays *me*.

13 December

We are now getting married on 22 June at which point, I've been assured, there is little chance of any professional sport being in the play-off, finals or trophy stage of their season.

I must really love this guy.

15 December

Mr Spaulding and I met today to discuss assigning the ten 'Faces' profiles. Since they are in-depth looks into the way these people live, work, and think, it's imperative that the writers have plenty of time to study their subjects. We spent an hour going through a list of possible writers. I lobbied hard for Julie Browning. In addition to Julie being a talented journalist, the karaoke story got killed because *Glamour* did it first, and I think anyone who gets edged out of a job for getting married deserves all the opportunities she can get. And, while I didn't say anything, I secretly longed to profile the Unified wedding minister myself. But who am I kidding? I barely had time to buy Christmas gifts.

But not so for Barry. He made a big scene of presenting Kate with a cashmere sweater. He made certain that the whole office heard about his generosity, knew it was *two-ply* cashmere, and was aware of his close ties to the 'support staff'. Kate was so thrilled by her new sweater that she wore it for the rest of the day.

It really was nice.

Note to self: exchange Kate's designer peanut brittle for nicer gift.

16 December

The company Stephen works for had their Christmas party last night. Not bad for a bunch of computer nerds pinning all their financial hopes on Stephen's ability to perfect a program that enables one type of computer to talk to another type of computer when something else is also going on. He's explained it to me thirty times and that's as much as I understand. But he can barely write a letter let alone a magazine article so in the end we're well matched.

The company rented a Mexican restaurant in mid-town and hired a live band whose upbeat salsa music I was really enjoying until I heard Stephen talk about hiring them for our wedding reception.

'That was a joke. Right, honey?' His fleeting nod did little to inspire my confidence. But it was more than enough to get Louise, one of Stephen's co-workers, to start talking about her own wedding plans.

Louise is like Central Casting's idea of a successful computer programmer. Barely in her twenties she's five-nine, 130 pounds, blonde and beautiful. Nicole Kidman would play her in the movie. And despite what the packaging may lead you to suspect she's also extremely intelligent and hard-working. I breathed a long sigh of relief when I learned of her engagement. Irrational as it may be, ever since she joined the company I've harbored a deeply rooted fear that Louise and Stephen would fall madly in love and run off to beget some dippy, albeit outrageously attractive colony of computer geeks named Byte, Ram, and Mouse. But no. Louise is marrying some guy she met in an on-line chat room.

Which is good because she's recently been assigned to help Stephen develop his computer program. This means that every night Stephen's working late, he's working late with Louise.

Thank God for cyber-love.

Over one too many margaritas Louise told me about her mother, who was so distraught at the thought of 'losing her baby' that she had channeled her grief into collecting an enormous trousseau of all the nightgowns, robes, and lingerie Louise will need for the *rest of her life*. Louise was getting a friggin' trousseau!

My envy was only vaguely tempered by the fact that the thought of my mother buying me lingerie makes me queasy.

17 December

It's official. I've seen every wedding dress on Long Island. And Mandy now has bunions.

18 December

I forced myself to brave the holiday crowds and shop for wedding shoes after work. Result: nothing. I know I should wait until after New Year. I might even catch some sales that way. But I can't. I'm desperate to feel some sense of accomplishment. Of progress. It's barely six months from our wedding day and all I've got is a backyard with a newly reseeded lawn.

Thank God I've got a groom. But he doesn't count. I had him before all this started.

According to the schedule in Chapter Three of *BB*, I should be spending this time planning the menu with my caterer and engraving gifts for our attendants. But I don't have a caterer, a menu, or gifts.

At this rate I'll be walking down the aisle in a plastic trash bag and a pair of rubber flip-flops.

23 December

I must have been crazy to let my mother invite both our families for Christmas Eve. It's the first time I'll be meeting Stephen's grandparents. I want them to think I'm charming and beautiful and worthy of their grandson. Not to mention their heirloom emerald ring. I should have bought a new outfit.

Then there's the issue of Stephen's parents getting along with my parents. Not to mention with each other, since Mr Stewart insists on bringing Misty. I'll have to put Nicole on the look-out to ensure that Mrs Stewart doesn't quietly slash Misty's throat with a cake knife. That would just fuel Gram's argument about Stephen's genetic predisposition toward disastrous marriages. And I should probably watch my own back lest Kimberly decides to reclaim her precious emerald ring while my finger's still in it.

And then there's Tom. Maybe Chet can regal him with tales of suburban life. Or dish the dirt about seventh-grade social studies – the secret life of Pilgrims, why Columbus really sailed the ocean blue . . . Anything to keep Tom away from my relatives.

Trust me, they don't need to know how highly sexed he is.

24 December

Where do I begin?

I had intended to arrive at my parents' house early this afternoon to help my mother prepare for the party. But I got there two hours later than planned because I missed my train at Grand Central Station. I missed the train because I was busy laboring over an extremely tricky and elaborate recipe for Sachertorte. At three in the morning I woke up and realized that although this engagement party is in honor of me and Stephen it was also the perfect opportunity for me to make a good impression on my future in-laws. I decided to accomplish that by making a Sachertorte – the traditional celebratory dessert of Austria.

By 7 a.m. I was at the grocery store getting the necessary ingredients. I'd never made a Sachertorte, in fact I hate cooking, but that didn't discourage me. I'd found a detailed recipe in my *New York Times Cookbook*. Everything was fine except that my oven must cook at a particularly slow pace because it took a full hour longer for the torte to bake than was indicated in the book. But it looked great. Stephen went ahead to meet his parents as I waited patiently for my torte to come into its own.

By the time I arrived at my parents' house everything was ready. Thankfully Nicole and Chet had come early that morning to help. After they had all praised my culinary efforts we exchanged gifts since we had all agreed that my engagement party would also serve as our Christmas celebration. We swapped the usual – sweaters, books and CDs – but Gram didn't give me my annual Christmas check. Gram's given me a Christmas check for the last thirty years. And even though the amount – generally between twenty-five and fifty dollars – isn't going to change my life, I find the gesture comforting.

Gram must have sensed my distress because she winked at me and said, with a smile, 'Christmas checks are for little girls. Not grown-up women who have decided to get married.' What? I failed to see how my marital status impacted on my ability to receive my beloved Christmas check. Am I any less worthy this year than last? Does getting married mean that I'm no longer Gram's little girl? After all, aren't I her favorite?

Separation. Confusion. Abandonment. Suddenly I felt every one of them. That Christmas check represented a bond that would never be broken. And yet now it was. But what could I say? Gram's from a different generation. She probably feels like I belong to Stephen's family now. Swapped like a goat or some prized chickens.

The Stewarts arrived in two waves. First, Stephen came with his mother, his sister, Chuffy and his grandparents, the Brocktons who drove in from New Jersey. After all the introductions were made and people had got drinks in their hands, everyone relaxed and got to know one another. It was fabulous – even though my mother momentarily lapsed into teacher mode when she had us go around the room and say our names.

Mrs Stewart and my parents immediately hit it off (with my dad scoring big with his comment about loving dogs) while Nicole worked overtime to make Kimberly feel welcome. But it was the Brocktons who won the award for the most incredible couple ever. They showered me with kisses and raved about how happy they are about our engagement. Keeping an eye out for Kim, I proudly displayed the emerald ring and thanked them for their generosity.

Mr Stewart arrived half an hour late with Tom, Misty, and April – a cousin of Stephen's who's enrolled at NYU and had chosen not to go home to California for the holidays. A palpable chill went through the room, although we all tried to act normal. As Stephen informed me *after* the party, it was the first time the Brocktons had seen Mr Stewart since he left Mrs Stewart. And it was the first time Mrs Stewart had seen Misty since Misty and Tom graduated high school together. *This* he neglects to mention?

Accustomed to manipulating the attention of large groups, my mother the schoolteacher made quick introductions then immediately announced dinner. Overwhelmed by the sudden need for comfort and security, people ran to the buffet table like deer during hunting season. Soon we were all face-deep in plates piled high with food. Except for Mrs Stewart, who ate just enough to be polite to my parents and to deny Misty the satisfaction of knowing that she had ruined her appetite. Although I doubt Misty noticed. She was far too busy chatting with Chet. Apparently she had been a counsellor at his sleep-away camp.

Since Gram was already seated with Nicole, I chose a seat next to Stephen and the Brocktons. After fifty-six years of marriage the Brocktons, who still hold hands, can finish each other's sentences and practically read each other's minds. Simultaneously they both began to tell me about their wedding. Mr Brockton deferred to Mrs Brockton, who went on to recall their ceremony in the back of her mother's house in Philadelphia. She sewed her own dress and each of her twenty guests made food for the reception. Mr Brockton had surprised her that morning with a bouquet of roses to carry down the aisle. For her part, Mrs Brockton was eternally grateful that her husband had remembered to remove the thorns. It was an incredibly romantic story and as she finished telling it Mrs Brockton gave Mr Brockton a kiss. 'He still buys me roses.'

The Brocktons are truly wonderful. 'So, when are you two going to have kids?' And *pushy*. I thought for sure the ink on our marriage license would dry before the push toward procreation came. Hell, as far as the Brocktons are concerned we still haven't had sex. Keeping his grandparents blissfully ignorant of our rabid pre-marital sex life is one of the reasons Stephen and I have never lived together. But Mrs Brockton wouldn't let it rest: 'You know, back in our day people got married to have babies.'

Regretfully Misty chose that moment to join in our conversation: 'That's just a euphemism. Back then people got married to have sex. These days, people don't wait for a license. They're much more liberated. Aren't they?' And she turned to look at *me*.

A tortured, gurgling noise erupted at the base of my throat. It was the sound of my innocent façade – drowning.

The Brocktons fell silent, Stephen changed the topic to his mother's new hairdo, and I swiftly escorted Misty across the room to Mr Stewart's side. She knew she'd screwed up. 'Oh, my God, Amy. I'm so sorry! It never occurred to me that they didn't know you and Stephen were sleeping together. After all, you're *adults*.'

Yes, yes, I'm a wimpy hypocrite who cowers in the face of octogenarian expectations. Sue me.

I ran to the bar for a glass of wine.

My grandmother no longer considers me her little girl, my future grandparents-in-law think I'm a tramp, and from where I stood it looked like Tom was putting the moves on Nicole. I was suddenly overwhelmed with the urge to run and hide in my childhood bedroom.

Desperate, I turned my attention to Stephen's cousin

April. When Mr Stewart asked if he could bring April he neglected to mention that she'd be dressed like a refugee from a Kiss concert. Wearing black from head to toe, including her eyeliner, her lipstick and her nail polish, April was the type of person who made you want to bathe. It was something about her nose ring. But since she was Stephen's cousin and just barely a freshman at college I struggled to find some compassion for her naïveté. Someday she'd look back at pictures of herself and feel appropriately ashamed. We all do.

Besides, April is a student at NYU Film School and has agreed to videotape our wedding for free with the school's equipment. I was duty bound to be patient with her. 'How's school, April?'

April adjusted her nose ring. 'Pretty cool. I'm minoring in women's studies.' Oh, please. How can you minor in women's studies? It's a lifelong field of inquiry to any woman. 'So why'd you and Stevie decide to get married?' *Stevie?*

'Because we're in love.'

'So what? That doesn't mean you need a piece of paper from the government.'

Great. The last thing I need is some brash college freshman doing her Gloria Steinem impression at my engagement party. 'Stephen and I want to celebrate our joy.'

April shrugged. 'Well you don't need the State for that.'

This is where I SNAPPED.

'True, but you do need them for the medical benefits and the bequeathment rights. Now, don't think I'm not happy that you just completed your first semester of women's studies. But reading a few Erica Jong books and mastering that Martina Navratilova hairdo of yours hardly qualify you as an authority on female liberation, let alone a spokeswoman for everyone with a vagina. So why don't you relax and soak up some holiday cheer before I kick your PC ass into the street. Okey-dokey?'

April was stunned. 'Jesus Christ, I'm gonna be your cousin. You can't get all aggressive with me.' And as she scurried across the room in search of a friendly face, I realized she was right. This Goth-attired, pain-in-the-ass, amateur feminist would soon be part of my family.

I looked around the room at all these people talking, eating, sharing, laughing, avoiding one another, and realized that in only five months and twenty-nine days we would all be related. We would all be next of kin, able to verify one another's identity in the morgue, ride in each other's ambulance, turn off life-support.

All these people had come to celebrate our engagement. To celebrate *us*. How outrageously gracious and kind!

Just then my mother brought out my Sachertorte 'And here's a little something Amy made for the occasion.' Everyone oohed and aahed. Turns out Sachertorte is the Brocktons' favorite cake. I began to relax. I was being ridiculous. I was overreacting. I was becoming a Mandy.

As my mother walked around serving the torte my father raised his beer and offered a toast: 'I'd like to welcome you all to our house and to our family. Terry and I are very happy that Amy and Stephen found each other. Stephen's a wonderful man. Any father would be thrilled to have him marry their daughter. And Amy has grown from a little girl who used to teach her sister cuss words to a wonderful, intelligent . . .' It was a heartwarming speech. And as Stephen and I basked in the limelight of family love, it happened.

'Good Lord, how long did this torte bake? It's like a rock! I think I broke my bridge!' And there was Gram, hunched over and clutching her jaw in pain.

Suddenly everyone was converging upon her, running for ice, offering amateur dental assistance, *setting aside their Sachertorte*. My father's speech forever left unfinished as Gram soaked up all the attention.

That's when it hit me. Every time we start to celebrate my wedding Gram mysteriously injures herself. Tripping over the electrical cable when I first announced my engagement, choking on the turkey fat at Thanksgiving, and now this. The old woman was sticking it to me!

Christmas Day

After the excitement and chaos of yesterday Stephen and I decided to spend today cuddled in bed. We rented some movies (*Stagedoor* for me, *North Dallas Forty* for him) and ordered in Chinese food.

We also exchanged Christmas gifts. I gave him a twelve-pack of toilet paper. Each roll had the entire history of basketball printed on it – statistics and all. He *loved* it so much he practically unfurled a whole roll just reading it. Then he gave me a silver bracelet with a single charm. He said that every Christmas for the rest of our lives he's going to add a charm to the bracelet. The first one, a heart with a key.

It was the most romantic gesture. I cried straight through my wonton soup and well into my egg roll.

27 December

I've got to do something about Gram. The more I think about her outrageous behavior the more I realize that my once-beloved grandmother is plotting a hostile takeover of my wedding glory.

- She tripped over the television cable when I announced my engagement.
- She insists my engagement ring symbolizes wantonness.
- She squealed about my cut-rate marriage proposal to *Barry*.
- She choked on turkey fat the minute my parents got sentimental about the wedding.
- She force-fed me divorce statistics.
- She maintains that my fiancé looks like Dan Quayle.
- And she humiliated me in front of my entire family, old and new, by claiming to have chipped her tooth on my Sachertorte!

Stephen thinks I'm overreacting. Anita thinks Gram's brilliant. Mandy suggested we institutionalize Gram until after the ceremony: 'I told you families get nuts around weddings.' And my mother says I'm paranoid: 'Don't be ridiculous. She's an old woman.'

Well, I've got this old woman's number! *666!*

29 December

Lucy's back home from the hospital. I called to thank her for the blue enamel barrette she sent me as an engagement gift. It's belonged to Lucy since she was a child. She figured by 22 June I'd have plenty of things which were old, new and borrowed but that I might have difficulty finding something blue. I was amazed that despite her illness she'd found time to send me a gift, let alone something so thoughtful.

And for the record, it was the *only* engagement gift we got. All those freeloaders at the engagement party came empty-handed. Don't they know 'no gifts' is just a euphemism for 'We know it's tacky to ask but bring something anyway'?

I'd been fantasizing about Lucy flying out for the party but I knew it was unrealistic. Between the cost and her health it just wasn't going to happen. But since Lucy loves gossip (she subscribes to the *National Enquirer*, *Star*, and *People* magazine) I did my best to give her the gory details – Misty, the Brocktons, the Sachertorte and most of all Gram.

Lucy loved hearing every high and low point of the event. And she backed me up completely on the 'Gram Is An Attention-stealing Octogenarian' theory. She said Gram's been a junkie for public adoration ever since 1956 when she appeared on the *Queen For A Day* show. Well, Gram will just have to face facts –

There's a new queen in town.

30 December

At 1 p.m. this afternoon Stephen suddenly suggested we go sledding. Except there was no snow in the city and we didn't have a sled.

Stephen didn't bat an eyelid.

We ran to Grand Central Station, hopped a train, went to his mother's house, searched the attic, found his childhood sled, and spent the next four hours jockeying for the best runs with the local pre-teen set at the neighborhood park. It was a blast.

If only he'd apply that same sense of mission to planning our wedding.

New Year's Eve – 9 p.m.

This is the last New Year's Eve that I will ever be single. Exciting, yet somehow extremely unnerving.

1 January

New Year's Resolutions:

1. Be a better person.
2. Lose 10 lbs.
3. Remember how lucky I am to have met Stephen.

4. Enjoy the wedding plans. (Don't
   become a Mandy.)
5. Stop making fun of Mandy.
6. Call Lucy twice a month.
7. Work harder at the magazine.
8. Be a more tolerant boss to Kate.
9. Resolve difficulties with Gram.
10. Keep my New Year's resolutions.

4 January

Kate came back from the holidays in a major snit.
Apparently she 'evaluated the situation' and doesn't like
the way my wedding 'has imposed upon her work
environment'. Where does a twenty-one-year-old with a
secretarial degree come up with this crap?

Too much *Oprah*. Or *Barry*.

And to think I gave her a real Kate Spade handbag for
Christmas. Maybe I should have given her that designer
peanut brittle and kept the handbag for myself. Lord
knows, I could use a new handbag.

WAIT! It's only four days into the new year and I'll be
damned if I abandon my resolutions so soon. No. 8: Be a
more tolerant boss to Kate. Tolerance.

Maybe Kate's having trouble at home. Maybe Barry
scolded her for not placing his story ideas at the top of the
distribution packet. Or maybe she's just cranky because
that mangy Backstreet Boy still hasn't answered her fan
letters. Who knows? But whatever it is I must try to
understand her position and respect her feelings. Besides,
what if my wedding really has become a burden to her?

5 January

I couldn't sleep last night. At 4.39 a.m. I broke down and called the Psychic Phone Line. A woman with an oddly calm voice advised me to abandon all romantic plans. Apparently Venus has descended into the House of Aquarius where she's been shackled and held captive. Does anyone else find this alarming, or is it just me?

On a lighter note, my lucky numbers are two and thirty-six.

6 January

'Face' number two, Murray Coleman, New York's 'Bagel King', has refused to be profiled in our annual issue.

Stephen tripped in a pothole on his way to work. After falling face first on to the sidewalk he was taken to St Luke's Hospital where he received thirty-six stitches above his left eye.

I will never call the Psychic Phone Line again.

7 January

Mandy reached into her bag of tricks (a.k.a. her bottom-less pit of well-informed wannabe-chic women) and located a dress shop known for its reasonably priced copies of famous designer wedding gowns. After a cab ride down to the Bowery then a harrowing walk into a neighborhood generally reserved for drug-dealers and Mafias of various ethnicities, we finally reached an old tenement building. In the basement window a handwritten sign read:

DRESES

Okay. I'm not a snob. And I certainly don't consider myself easily flustered. But the minute I caught sight of that misspelled sign through a dirty glass window in the bowels of a dilapidated tenement building, in the middle of a neighborhood that clearly God and the agents of gentrification had chosen to forget, I had only one thing to say – 'TAXI!'

I was certain Mandy was already on her cellphone calling a cab.

But no. This was Superhero Mandy – able to go where no bride has gone before. She was marching down the basement stairs. Unwilling to be outbraved by *Mandy* I followed anxiously behind.

The basement store was filled with racks of wedding gowns covered in plastic. Five young women sat hunched over sewing machines and before you could say, 'Sweatshop', a burly middle-aged woman with a thick neck and hairy forearms brusquely introduced herself as Gayle. She wore a Yankees T-shirt and culottes. I hadn't seen a pair of culottes since fifth grade. Anxiety constricted my esophagus as Mandy took it upon herself to inform Gayle that I was looking for a wedding dress, preferably a Carolina Herrera or Vera Wang knock-off.

Gayle blanched. Then bellowed, 'Knock-off? I don't have any knock-offs. Only high-quality merchandise. All original!' A quick glance around the shop revealed bins filled with clothing labels marked 'Escada', 'Armani', 'Vera Wang'.

As the seamstresses frantically debated whether or not we were Immigration, Gayle continued to protest and wave her arms in the air. I gasped, certain I'd seen a pistol stuffed into the waistband of her culottes. Gayle was packing heat! Mandy rebuttoned her Anne Klein jacket and stood her ground. 'Originals, designer imposters, whatever you like to call them, Gayle, is fine with us. But I think we both know what we're talking about. So, how about showing us something nice in a cream silk satin with a princess neckline?'

But Gayle was having none of it. 'What are you two anyway? Cops? Well forget it, Charlie's Angels. We're closed.'

Charlie's Angels? God, I hope I'm not Sabrina.

Mandy impatiently tapped her heel 'Look, Gayle. I didn't come down here after a long day's work just to be sent home.'

Did I mention that Mandy sells residential real estate? In *Manhattan*. She does not take negotiations lightly. 'Now, my friend would like to see some dresses, wouldn't you, Amy?'

Quick! Which is more important – finding the dress of my dreams or living to see my wedding day? Luckily Gayle made the choice for me. 'Like I said, we're closed.' She threw open the front door. And when Mandy strutted toward the exit, hissing, 'I cancelled an aromatherapy session to come here,' Gayle just stared blankly.

During the cab ride home Mandy carped about the lack of professionalism in the garment industry while I thought wistfully about the chiffon dress with the basque bodice hanging in the back of Gayle's shop.

Wasn't this supposed to be fun?

8 January

If you can get past the whole 'staples in your face' thing, Stephen actually looks pretty handsome with his stitches. Sort of a young Charles Bronson.

> Official THINGS TO DO List
> 1. ~~Choose wedding date~~
> 2. ~~Tell boss wedding date~~
> 3. ~~Vacation time for honeymoon~~
> 4. Decide on honeymoon
> 5. ~~Get minister/church~~
> 6. ~~Choose reception venue~~
> 7. ~~Make guest list~~
> 8. ~~Choose maid of honor~~
> 9. ~~Choose best man~~
> 10. Register for gifts
> 11. ~~Arrange for engagement party~~
> 12. ~~Buy engagement ring~~
> 13. Buy wedding rings
> 14. Buy wedding dress
> 15. Choose maid-of-honor dress
> 16. Order wedding cake
> 17. Hire caterer
> 18. Hire band for reception
> 19. Order flowers for ceremony
> 20. Buy shoes

21. Plan rehearsal dinner
22. Invites to rehearsal dinner
23. Hire musicians for ceremony
24. ~~Decide on dress code~~
25. Get marriage license
26. ~~Hire videographer~~
27. Hire photographer
28. Order table flowers
29. Order bouquets
30. Order boutonnières for men
31. Order nosegays for women
32. Order invitations
33. Decide on wine selection
34. Postage for invitations
35. Choose hairstyle and makeup
36. Buy gifts for attendants
37. Buy thank-you notes
38. Announce wedding in newspaper
39. Buy headpiece
40. Buy travelers' checks for honeymoon
41. Apply for visas
42. Get shots and vaccinations
43. Order tent if necessary
44. Order chairs/tables if necessary
45. ~~Make budget~~
46. ~~Divide expenses~~
47. Make table-seating charts
48. Choose bridesmaid dress
49. Decide on menu
50. Decide on *hors d'oeuvres*
51. Decide on dinner service style
52. Decide on staff–guest ratio

53. Decide seated or buffet
54. Reserve vegetarian meals
55. Reserve band/photographer meals
56. Make photo list
57. Choose hotel for wedding night
58. Hire limo for church–reception transport
59. Buy guest book for reception
60. Find hotel for out-of-towners
61. Decide on liquor selection
62. Hire bartenders
63. Verify wheelchair accessibility
64. Choose processional music
65. Choose recessional music
66. Choose cocktail music
67. Choose reception music
68. Choose ceremony readings
69. Prepare birdseed instead of rice
70. Schedule manicure/pedicure/wax

9 January

Invigorated from the holidays Barry swept into my office and inquired about the status of my wedding plans. Was there anything he could do?

Not in the mood for his crap I decided to taunt him by saying that Stephen and I were reconsidering the whole marriage thing. Maybe we'd just keep dating. Barry looked sick. He begged me not to make a rash decision that I'd undoubtedly live to regret. 'Good men are so hard to find!'

So are good jobs and I'm keeping mine. Now, step away from my desk, Barry.

Agitated and anxious he exited my office. I couldn't help but smile. Then I began to wonder: of all the possible ways to taunt Barry why had I chosen that one?

10 January

I tracked down some of my long-lost married friends to ask them for information about photographers. No one had any recommendations. But they all had plenty of complaints. The photographers were late to show up, failed to show up, got drunk at the reception, were intrusive and distracting during the ceremony . . .

And they were all outrageously expensive. We're talking thousands of dollars.[21] It seems that in addition to the film, the processing, and the photographer's hourly rate, you pay for the prints and the photo albums. Sure you don't want to develop your wedding photos at the Quickie Foto stand in the mall, but do you really need to pay fifteen dollars per photo? Who cares if it's printed on archival paper that's guaranteed to last for a hundred years? I'm not guaranteed to last for a hundred years. And most of these photographers insist on owning, or at least maintaining possession of, your negatives so you couldn't bring them to the Quickie Foto even if you wanted.

Then there's the issue of the photo albums. The book for your parents, your maid-of-honor, your sister . . .

Sure I could forgo a real photographer and just buy a

---

[21] The official monetary denomination of the wedding industry.

bunch of those disposable cameras and set them on the tables for guests to take pictures, but even that will cost a couple hundred dollars. And I still won't have a formal portrait, suitable for framing, of Stephen and me and our families. The kind of photo that you see on the walls of old-style Italian restaurants with the bride and groom flanked by fifty of their closest relatives and the family pet.

You bet Chuffy can join in the fun but will she help pay for it?

11 January

The more time I spend with Prudence the more I wish she was the chatty type. She seems so level-headed.

12 January

Since Nicole is the family *darling* I decided to talk to her about Gram. I told her Gram was going out of her way to draw attention to herself at the expense of my wedding. That she was purposely manipulating people and that, in short, she was plotting outright sabotage.

Nicole looked at me like I was crazy. 'You're kidding, right?'

I wish. 'Look, I know she does the sweet-old-lady routine, but behind that façade lurks a woman with some bizarre chip on her shoulder and a selfish plan in her heart.'

Nicole remained unconvinced. 'The woman who sewed our Hallowe'en costumes, who gave us fudge when we were sick, and who still shows a vital interest in our lives is secretly plotting to sabotage your wedding?'

'I told you that sweet-old-lady bit is just a front.'

'A front? For God's sake, Amy, she can barely walk.'

'She may be slow, but she's sly. Why else would she act so strange?'

'I don't know. Maybe she's lonely. Maybe she's come to depend on the family's attention. Or maybe you're just completely *paranoid*.'

'Have you been talking to Mom?'

'See! You are paranoid. And no, I haven't talked to Mom. I may not be some big magazine editor but I'm smart enough to realize how ridiculous this whole thing is.'

Maybe Nicole was right. Maybe I am overreacting. Maybe this is like me thinking more about myself than Lucy. Selfish. New Year's resolution No. 1: Be a better person. And worse yet, resolution No. 9: Resolve difficulties with Gram. What if Gram's behavior is just a desperate attempt to cling to her family's love? After all, she actually reads *Round-Up*. Could I be such a chump?

'All right. Maybe I am overreacting. But it's only because I haven't felt a lot of familial support for my wedding.'

'What about the engagement party last month?'

'That was great but I have to be honest. I really expected more sustained enthusiasm from everyone. Including you.'

'Me?'

'Yeah, you. I would have been happy with a lousy thumbs-up but you've barely shown any interest at all.'

'You mean like the interest you showed in my wedding?'

'What are you talking about? I was in Europe until the day before.'

'Exactly. You didn't help or support or enthuse anything at my wedding. You just popped in a few hours before the ceremony.'

And the problem would be . . . ? 'You had all your girlfriends here. You didn't need me. Besides, I assumed you wouldn't want me there. I'm not the marrying kind, remember? Weddings just aren't my thing.'

'Sure. Until now. How convenient.'

So there it was. Nicole's pent-up rage released five years after the fact. No screaming or crying. No thrown objects or spewed invectives. That's not Nicole's style. She's reserved. Repressed. Suburban.

We'd never make the talk-show circuit.

15 January

Citing bunions, swollen ankles and migraine headaches, Mandy refuses to shop for any more wedding dresses with me. The indefatigable wedding fanatic has declared me impossible to please. 'I'll throw you a bridal shower, help you choose flowers, and give you a Valium before the ceremony – but no more dresses.'

How can she abandon me like this? She's my maid-of-honor. My right-hand gal. My *yin*! What about fealty?

17 January

Paula and Kathy went dress-shopping with me today. Big mistake. Paula kept pushing me toward the tarty dresses generally reserved for child brides from Tennessee. Skin-tight, sleeveless, backless, frontless, adhered to your body with a piece of double-sided tape. And Kathy, no fan of the Super Tramp collection, went right for the Elizabethan fantasy. High-collared, corseted, billowing poet-sleeves with a twenty-foot train. Give me a chastity belt and a leg of mutton and to the throne I go.

18 January

My mother called to remind me not to forget my sister's birthday. Nicole's birthday has been on the same day for the last twenty-seven years. Trust me, I've memorized it by now. She was really calling to badger me into buying Nicole a gift: 'I know she'd like some new gloves.'

Well, la-de-dah. 'Mom, do you harass Nicole about buying me birthday gifts?'

'No. But your birthday isn't three weeks after Christmas. Everyone always forgets Nicole's birthday.'

'No one forgets Nicole's birthday, Mom. You do it because she's your favorite.'

Well the cat's out of the bag now.

'Don't be ridiculous, Amy. I love you both the same.'

How many times have I heard *that* line? 'Oh, yeah? Who sits between you and Dad at every family meal?'

'We're all lefties. We sit together so we don't bump elbows.'

Isn't that convenient? 'And who got to use the backyard for their wedding?'

'Have you forgotten where you'll be on June twenty-second?'

Sure, but I had to beg. 'And who goes with you to the

155

Tanglewood Crafts Fair every summer?'

'Nicole does because she *enjoys* crafts. The time I took you, you told one vendor to keep her day job and another to shave her armpits.'

She's right. I hate crafts. And underarm hair. I'm being a complete idiot.

Breathe.

19 January

After careful scrutiny of *BB*'s index I've concluded that there are no formal guidelines for elopement.

Just checking.

21 January

I met Mandy and Jon at Frutto di Sole last night. Stephen had to work late with Louise so it was just the three of us. Between their wedding and now the planning for my wedding it'd been a long time since we'd gotten together. Thankfully Jon couldn't pressure me about marriage anymore.

So he chose a new topic: 'You lucked out. "Amy Stewart" sounds pretty good. Very British royalty.'[22]

'Actually I'm not sure I'll be changing my name.'

Jon rolled his eyes. 'Don't tell me you're going to hyphenate?'

'No, I may just keep my maiden name. It's who I am. It's part of my identity.'

---

[22] That would be 'Stuart', you moron.

Jon shook his head. 'It'd be one thing if you came from a famous family, or had something named after you.[23] But you don't. So what's the difference if you're a Stewart instead of a Thomas?'[24]

Mandy smiled and held Jon's hand. 'Trust me, Amy. A shared name brings a greater sense of union.'

Great. In order to join that union Mandy Alexander had to become Mandy Skepperman. *And* she has to sleep with Jon.

22 January

The word must be out because no one will go dress-shopping with me. Work commitments, family obligations, flu-like symptoms, poor circulation and flatulence. The list of excuses goes on and on . . .

And the timing couldn't be worse. The wedding 'high season' is just around the corner and new dresses are arriving in the stores every day. I just know my dress is out there. Somewhere.

But I can't go by myself. Shopping alone for a wedding dress is like confiding your first sexual experience to a pet rock. *BB* suggests going with a friend. Did that. Or a female relative. You couldn't pay me to do that.

I wonder who Prudence went shopping with.

---

[23] You mean like a toilet? Oh, sorry. That would be 'jo*h*n.'

[24] Forgive me. I forgot that only the rich and famous are entitled to a sense of personal identity. What a pinhead this guy is. I don't know how Mandy refrains from smacking him. If he were my husband I'd smack him every ten seconds. On second thought, if he were my husband, I'd just hang myself.

23 January

Stephen and I ordered our wedding rings at Lancaster Jewelers near Rockefeller Center. Two simple, matching fourteen-karat gold bands.

It was really exciting, not just because it's the first big wedding task we've done together, but because these rings symbolize the depth of our commitment. We'll be wearing these rings until the day we *die*. I could tell Stephen was nervous. He kept commenting on how strange it would be to wear a ring all the time. He isn't accustomed to wearing jewelry. Not a class ring, and sometimes not even a watch. Although some married men choose not to wear wedding bands, Stephen feels pretty strongly about it. In fact it was his idea to have them engraved

Bytes Infinitum

It's computer-ese for 'Forever'.

25 January

Stephen, Mr Spontaneity, wants us to start looking for a new apartment. Now.

According to Chapter Twenty-five of *BB*, weddings, moving, and death are the three most stressful events in a person's life. I'm already neck-deep in the first. If I do the second then how far behind can the third be?

And while I can understand Stephen's desire to get this task out of the way, he's so busy at work that he can't even plan his own wedding. Lord knows, I haven't heard a peep about that band for our wedding he was so eager to find.

And how easy will it be to find an affordable one-bedroom apartment on a safe block with at least two windows and no rodents? After all, this is Manhattan we're talking about. It took me eight months just to find my crummy studio *and* I had to pay a broker's fee. Not to mention all the delicate negotiations that will have to take place regarding the disposal of Stephen's 'less than attractive' possessions.

Under no circumstances am I starting my marriage with a plaid couch in a fifth floor walk-up.

As far as I'm concerned we can wait until after the wedding to find our new apartment. A love nest for Stephen, me, and Miss Pamela Anderson – 1990 Playmate of the Year.

27 January

Not sleeping has certainly been educational. Who knew that infomercials fill the airwaves from 1 to 5 a. m.? Whatever happened to the shot of the American flag waving in the wind? So proud, so brave, so stoic.

Screw it. I'm getting one of those Fatbuster 2000 grills. It's endorsed by four celebrity housewives and that's good enough for me.

29 January

It started very innocently. I was flipping through the newspaper on the bus ride to work when I noticed an advertisement for Élan Bridal Salon on Madison Avenue. They were having a one-day preview of Dalia Dolan's new bridal collection. *Preview*. The collection isn't due out for another month but this preview would enable you to find your dress and place an order now. As in a.s.a.p. As in, I'm getting married in four months and twenty-five days and need to act quick.

I love Dalia Dolan dresses. And she always has a 'special' dress that is priced under a thousand dollars. Last year's was cut on the bias so I couldn't get it past my hips. But somehow I knew this collection would be different. This year's 'special' dress would have an A-line skirt. It would look ravishing on me.

One problem: The preview was scheduled for 11 a.m. I had an editorial meeting at 10.30 a.m. There was no way I could see the dress. Or was there?

Kate arrived for work fifteen minutes late. I told her not to worry about it. She spilled Diet Coke on my presentation packet. I told her just to print a new one. She accidentally erased part of yesterday's dictation. I told her we'd do it again. Then I sweetly asked her to do me a *favor*. If I gave her an extra-long lunch break and spending money would she buy a disposable camera, take a cab to Élan's and photograph Dalia Dolan's 'special' dress?

After squeezing me for an additional twenty bucks she finally agreed. It cost me another ten to ensure that Barry wouldn't find out.

Who knew Élan strictly prohibits photography in their store? Something to do with design infringement and people making knock-offs: Gayle with her pistol and culottes. And no doubt Kate was anything but subtle with her task. So is it *my* fault that they confiscated the camera?

160

Am *I* to blame that she was strip-searched by security then physically escorted out of the store?

Kate thinks so. She's filed for a stress-related leave of absence. Barry is livid. I am going to need a ton of Kate Spade handbags to fix this one.

30 January

People keep asking if I'm going to change my name. As if my decision will help them to define who I am. If I change my name I'm a family-oriented wife. If I keep my name I'm an aggressive professional with a frosty interior. And if I hyphenate? I'm just plain stupid. It sounds old-fashioned but you'd be amazed by how we cling, consciously or not, to these stereotypes.

So what's a girl to do? On the one hand everyone in this industry knows me as Amy Thomas.[25] But, on the other hand, Stephen thinks it'd be nice for our kids to share the same name as their parents.

I'm assuming he doesn't mean Thomas.

31 January

It was parent-teacher conference day so my mom was free by 1 p.m. After she did some shopping in the city we met for dinner at T.G.I. Friday's. We always eat at T.G.I. Friday's because it's well priced and the portions are large.

---

[25] Okay, maybe not everyone. I doubt anyone at Condé Nast has ever heard of me, regardless of what my name is. But the fifty or so people I do know *definitely* know me as Amy Thomas.

My mother's criteria for a good meal. Value and size. This explains so much about my wedding dilemmas.

Unwilling to appear paranoid or selfish I went out of my way not to mention Gram. Instead we talked about the parents who refused to believe that their kids are nose-pickers, chronic potty mouths or attention deficit. Inevitably the parents themselves are nose-pickers, potty mouths or attention deficit. This always fascinates my mother so she was in a particularly good mood. In fact, she was downright effusive. She even brought up my wedding.

Over Cobb salad and minestrone soup she asked if I'd found a caterer (I haven't), if I'd chosen a florist (I haven't), and if I had a dress yet (I don't). 'You know, Amy, this may sound old-fashioned to you but I still have the dress I wore when I married your father.' News to me.

'The day you were born I did two things. I decided to name you Amy after my favorite of all the Little Women – well, actually Beth was my favorite but she dies in the end and that didn't seem right – then I packed my wedding dress into a box in case the day came when you'd want to wear it. I saved it especially for you.'

Finally some mother-daughter bonding! It was my *Terms of Endearment* moment.[26] I was shocked. 'I'd *love* to wear your wedding dress!'

1 February

I actually slept well last night. Since my mother offered me her wedding dress I feel like an enormous weight has been lifted from my shoulders. Her very own wedding dress. It's

---

[26] But without the whole death thing.

a token of her affection, it's family history. And it's a lucky charm – my parents have been happily married for over thirty years.

May we all be so fortunate.

And there's even more good news. One of Stephen's co-workers has a brother who's a freelance newspaper photographer but wants to expand into wedding photography. Since he needs to build his portfolio he's agreed to shoot our wedding for free! All we pay for is the film and the processing and the printing! No overly precious, able-to-withstand-nuclear-fall-out fifteen-dollar prints, and he'll give us the negatives!

A wedding dress. A photographer. Next thing you know I'll find shoes!

3 February

I went shoe-shopping at Bendel's after work. I found nothing

Official THINGS TO DO List
1. ~~Choose wedding date~~
2. ~~Tell boss wedding date~~
3. ~~Vacation time for honeymoon~~
4. Decide on honeymoon
5. ~~Get minister/church~~
6. ~~Choose reception venue~~
7. ~~Make guest list~~
8. ~~Choose maid of honor~~
9. ~~Choose best man~~

10. Register for gifts
11. ~~Arrange for engagement party~~
12. ~~Buy engagement ring~~
13. ~~Buy wedding rings~~
14. ~~Buy wedding dress~~
15. Choose maid-of-honor dress
16. Order wedding cake
17. Hire caterer
18. Hire band for reception
19. Order flowers for ceremony
20. Buy shoes
21. Plan rehearsal dinner
22. Invites to rehearsal dinner
23. Hire musicians for ceremony
24. ~~Decide on dress code~~
25. Get marriage license
26. ~~Hire videographer~~
27. ~~Hire photographer~~
28. Order table flowers
29. Order bouquets
30. Order boutonnières for men
31. Order nosegays for women
32. Order invitations
33. Decide on wine selection
34. Postage for invitations
35. Choose hairstyle and makeup
36. Buy gifts for attendants
37. Buy thank-you notes
38. Announce wedding in newspaper
39. Buy headpiece
40. Buy travelers' checks for honeymoon

41. Apply for visas
42. Get shots and vaccinations
43. Order tent if necessary
44. Order chairs/tables if necessary
45. ~~Make budget~~
46. ~~Divide expenses~~
47. Make table-seating charts
48. Choose bridesmaid dress
49. Decide on menu
50. Decide on *hors d'oeuvres*
51. Decide on dinner service style
52. Decide on staff–guest ratio
53. Decide seated or buffet
54. Reserve vegetarian meals
55. Reserve band/photographer meals
56. Make photo list
57. Choose hotel for wedding night
58. Hire limo for church–reception transport
59. Buy guest book for reception
60. Find hotel for out-of-towners
61. Decide on liquor selection
62. Hire bartenders
63. Verify wheelchair accessibility
64. Choose processional music
65. Choose recessional music
66. Choose cocktail music
67. Choose reception music
68. Choose ceremony readings
69. Prepare birdseed instead of rice
70. Schedule manicure/pedicure/wax

4 February

I took the train upstate right after work to go see my mom's – my – wedding dress. I'd originally planned to go tomorrow morning but I couldn't wait. I was on the 7 p.m. train.

I found my parents sitting down to watch a rerun of *Diagnosis Murder*. My father had already slipped into his pajamas. But that didn't matter. This moment was about us girls. It was a female thing.

Bursting with excitement I followed my mother to her bedroom and into her closet – a place forever off-limits to my sister and me. Consequently a place forever filled with mystery and intrigue. As kids, Nicole and I spent hours speculating about what lay behind that closet door: boxes brimming with dazzling jewels, a safe filled with the family fortune, love letters from my mother's *previous* husband – a tall, dark figure whom my sister and I had inexplicably conjured up. A man who looked like Humphrey Bogart and took my mother to smoky bars where they swore. Even as adults we weren't allowed into that closet. And yet here I was, being shepherded in by my mother herself.

Shepherded into what had to be the world's most claustrophobic space. Crammed with shoes, clothing, old luggage and forgotten sporting gear, it was poorly lit and smelled like mothballs. It was, indeed, our family's fortune. And from the back, under a pile of ancient *Good Housekeeping* magazines and some knit jumpers from the early eighties, my mom unearthed an enormous cardboard box. It was the box in which she'd kept her wedding dress, for decades, in hopes that one day *I* might wear it.

Together we carried the box to her bed. My heart was

pounding. My mother lifted the lid and began gently to pull back layer upon layer of yellowed tissue paper.

Then, when the final layer of tissue paper was finally removed, I saw my wedding dress – and wept. Really wept. Not delicate girlie tears but the kind of tears reserved for occasions of monumental joy. And horror. It was the ugliest thing I'd ever seen in my entire life. And it was all mine.

Not wishing to insult my mother I quickly repacked the dress in its enormous cardboard box and took the next train home. Maybe, if I was lucky, I'd be robbed at gunpoint.

5 February – 2 a.m.

I can't sleep. When I close my eyes all I can see is that horrible dress – the high collar, the flowing sleeves, the pinafore front and the hoop-like skirt. I look like a cross between a *Little House on the Prairie* extra and a cast member from the road company of *Godspell*.

It suddenly occurs to me that the photos of my mother at her wedding are shot exclusively in close-up.

Is there any way to get out of this without forever destroying the mother-daughter bond?

5 February

I left a desperate message for Mandy this morning. She still hasn't called me back.

Meanwhile I returned home to a message on my

answering-machine from Gram. We haven't spoken since my engagement party and I'm not sure whether anyone's told her about my suspicions. In either event her message was very sweet. Or was it?

'Amy, your mother's just told me that you're going to wear her wedding dress. I'm so pleased. I thought of that dress the minute I heard about your engagement. That's why I urged her to offer it to you.'

So that's how all this started. My mom assumed I wouldn't want her dress but *Gram* convinced her to offer it to me.

A well-intentioned bad idea or a set-up? Should I worry, or seek psychiatric attention for advanced stages of paranoia? It's so hard to tell these days.

7 February

I'm falling behind at work. Two of my writers are late with their assignments for the April issue and I haven't even begun to think about May.

The good news is that, after begging and pleading, I think I've convinced Kate not to take a leave of absence. This is a difficult time for me. I need her more than ever. She knows where everything is filed, is familiar with the job, and she can read my handwriting. Sure, groveling at her feet was pathetic but I think it tipped the scales in my favor. Few secretaries have the pleasure of bringing their bosses to their knees.

9 February

Kate presented me with a typed list of demands ranging from her refusal to make phone calls or written inquiries relating to my wedding, to her request that wedding vendors be transferred directly to my voicemail thereby relieving her of the apparently odious task of taking their messages. And then there's that little matter of my not discussing the wedding between the hours of 9 a.m. and 6 p.m. And though I sensed Barry's evil influence behind these demands, I readily agreed. What else could I do?

Meanwhile Stephen has become smitten with a woodwind band from Ecuador. He 'discovered' them playing in the subway station by his apartment. He's just dying for them to play at our wedding.

I fully support breaking with tradition. Soprano? Harpsichordist? String quartet? Forget 'em. Bring on the bamboo flute and bells. But shouldn't our band at least be familiar with American standards? If someone makes a musical request, shouldn't the band-leader be able to respond in English?

You bet. But this band issue is Stephen's domain. I'm not getting involved. No way. I'm keeping my mouth shut. Whatever he decides is fine. And he's decided on these Ecuadorian woodwind people. He says their music soothes him.

How nice.

But isn't that what *wives* are for? And how the hell do you play 'Brick House' on a recorder? You don't.

Yet why quibble about that when my mother's just laid down the 'ground rules' for my wedding reception – in both the figurative and literal sense. Leave it to an elementary-school teacher to be so clever.

Apparently the wedding reception must be wholly

contained in the backyard and the first floor of the house. No one will be allowed upstairs. This means all ninety-five quests will have to share one bathroom since Bud and Terry don't want a Porta-potty stationed in the backyard. Something about septic fluid and germs.

10 February

Mandy finally came to my apartment to see the dress. She was furious. 'You drag me all over the city and this is the dress you choose?'

Who chose? This isn't free will. This is a horrible mistake.

Her suggestion: start a fire in my apartment then use the dress to snuff the flames. What could possibly please my mother more than to know her cherished wedding dress had saved my life?

10 February – 11 p.m.

No matter how long I hold the dress over the lit stovetop it still won't ignite. I've singed my hair and melted my nail polish but the damn dress *will not die*.

Lucky me. An asbestos wedding dress. What next? A poison-ivy bouquet?

11 February

On a lark I proposed James Royce as Face number two for

our annual issue. Royce is a best-selling crime novelist who's lived in and written about New York for the last twenty-eight years. He's also notorious for refusing interviews. Until now. Apparently he's ready to talk and is willing to do it in *my* 'Faces In The City' issue of *Round-Up*!

Mr Spaulding was thrilled. Barry was apoplectic. Stephen and I splurged on a fabulous steak dinner to celebrate. Who knew losing Murray Coleman as Face number two was a stroke of enormous luck?

12 February

It's hopeless. There is no acceptable reason why I can't wear my mother's wedding dress. It's in pristine condition and fits perfectly. Like a glove. Like a huge dishwashing glove soaking in a big vat of ugly. And how can I tell her *that* when she saved it especially for me?

13 February

Stephen and I went upstate for the requisite 'pre-marital counseling' with Reverend MacKenzie. Stephen complained the entire way there. 'I can't believe we're letting MacKenzie counsel us, let alone join us in holy matrimony. If he asks about our sex life just ignore him. If he pressures you, talk exclusively in generalizations. Under no circumstances should you divulge details.'

'Would you relax? The guy can't be that bad. Your mother adores him.'

Stephen held his ground. 'Just wait until you meet him. You'll know exactly what I'm talking about.'

'Is he forgetful? Rude? Verbally abusive?'

'No. It's more subtle. Like a bad vibe.'

A bad vibe? He's a minister, not a pawnbroker. How ridiculous. I was certain Stephen's feelings for Reverend MacKenzie were colored by recollections of interminable church sermons about sacrifice and shame. As far as I was concerned, so long as Reverend MacKenzie didn't carry a cellphone we had no problems. We could talk loyalty, respect and fidelity until the sun set. Then confirm my wedding date, speak highly of me to my mother-in-law, and I'll be on my way.

Stephen just continued to pout.

The United Presbyterian Church, to which Stephen's family has belonged for the last twenty years, is like the country club of churches. It makes First American on the Upper East Side of Manhattan look like a Pentecostal store-front. Built in the early 1920s it gleams from its spotless whitewashed exterior to its over-polished red oak interior. The hymn books are covered in full-grain leather, and every carved pew boasts a fluffy seat pad to cushion the strain of religious devotion. It's elegant, classy and luxe.

As was Reverend MacKenzie, an affable albeit reserved man in his mid-sixties with a firm handshake and natty wingtips under his ministerial robe. Direct and expedient, he asked about our thoughts on marriage – what we expected from it, what it meant to us – then scheduled another meeting for the month of May. No inappropriate sexual questions and no shady solicitation of funds. Just the facts.

The minute we exited the church Stephen was on a roll: 'See what I mean. He's creepy.' But how creepy could the guy be? His nails were clean and his breath smelled like Listerine. The minty kind.

14 February

Love is about compromise.

The day started with Stephen sending a dozen long-stem roses to my office. Then ended with the two of us at his favorite video arcade.[27] We converted thirty dollars into a bucket of quarters and went wild. He's sharp with Kung Fu Kick Fighter II but I can still whoop his butt at Mission Control Stun Gun III.

Next Valentine's Day I'll be a WIFE.

18 February

I cannot wear this hateful dress.

I must wear this hateful dress.

Thank goodness for friends.

Having heard about my disastrous wedding dress Paula

---

[27] Yes, my thirty-two-year-old fiancé has a *favorite* video arcade. It's his secret shame. Okay, so it's *my* secret shame about *him*. He's a rabid arcade junkie. He prances when he wins free games and yells when the pre-teens hog the machines. Thankfully, like a fondness for airline food or a sincere appreciation for Elvis impersonators, the opportunity to indulge in this obsession is limited. It's not so easy to find a good video arcade in Manhattan. Which is the *only* reason I'm in the game room of the Summit (read: Slum It) Hotel on Valentine's Day.

called to tell me about her friend Katrina – a clothing designer who's got her own studio in Greenwich Village. Apparently Katrina's agreed to take a look at Mom's dress and see if there's any way to redesign it. Who knows? I may end up with a custom-made wedding dress.

19 February

It seems I hold only two points of interest: either you're wondering why my engagement ring's not a diamond, or you want to know if I'll be keeping my last name. So what's my answer?

I DON'T KNOW!

I've been Amy Sarah Thomas for the last thirty years. It's not like it's some TV character I've been playing. It's my real-life identity. And getting married doesn't change that. But part of me likes the idea of sharing a name with Stephen. Sure I know that love is the tie that binds but the same name can't hurt. And on a practical level it will make things a lot easier – restaurant reservations, legal documents, airline tickets . . .

Then there's the whole hyphenate thing. Mrs Amy Jacob-Jingleheimer-Schmidt. Stupid? Damn straight. Yet suddenly it makes a little more sense. You get to keep your identity while publicly declaring your relationship to your spouse. But Amy Sarah Thomas-Stewart? It sounds like roll call at a white Anglo-Saxon Protestant support group.

And it will never fit on a credit card.

20 February

Katrina howled with laughter when she saw my dress. None of the giggles or titters generally reserved for velour cowl necks or outdated swimwear. No, sir. My goddamn wedding dress brought down the house.

Coincidentally, my insomnia has returned.

21 February

Anita loves the idea of having an Ecuadorian woodwind band at our wedding: 'Finally a wedding band that doesn't play "Unforgettable".' Give me a little credit. 'Unforgettable' won't be played at my wedding no matter who the band is. I'm more concerned with getting some classic seventies disco. But Anita's delight went beyond music. 'You know, Ecuadorian men are really sexy. Great skin. I'm definitely going to want an introduction.'

Sure. What better reason to hire a wedding band than to procure dates for your friends?

Mandy, on the other hand, was horrified by the idea. 'Those men in the subway? Playing at your *wedding*? This is a disaster! Do they even have waltzes in Ecuador? You can't do this! Their music doesn't have downbeats!'[28]

But what can I do? The music was the one thing Stephen really cared about. I'm making all the other decisions. Shouldn't he at least make this one? No matter how completely stupid it is?

---

[28] A musical impossibility? Who knows? But why quibble?

22 February

I called our photographer to arrange for a meeting. I wanted him to come see the church and my parents' house and talk with us about portraits. After all, doesn't he need to assess the lighting conditions?

Yes. But not now. It seems that winter is low-season for brutal crimes and fires, which means to a freelance newspaper photographer that times are tough. He's got to stay glued to his police scanner in case something good – *bad* – comes up. He'll get back to us in spring.

23 February

Stephen is planning to sue the city for his pothole injury.

After spending the last six years attending law school and failing the bar exam three times, Larry's finally a *bona fide* personal-injury attorney. He has big plans to advertise his services on buses and public-access cable. *This* is the source of Stephen's decision to sue.

According to Larry, Stephen has a solid case: a wretched pothole, a police report, eyewitnesses – and thirty-six staples in his head. Luckily Larry's graciously volunteered to represent Stephen free of charge. It's his *wedding present* to us.

Cheap bastard.

Meanwhile Katrina's decided that it'll cost five hundred dollars to redesign my dress and even then she can only promise that it will be 'okay'.

Five hundred dollars for a dress that's 'okay'? That's obscene. But what could I do? I *have* to wear this dress. It's my familial cross to bear. Besides, five hundred dollars is still cheaper than a new dress and I can use the extra money to rent a tent for the reception.

I gave Katrina my blessing. Cut the thing to shreds. My check's in the mail.

25 February

I spoke with Lucy last night. I filled her in on my latest disasters. She advised me to follow my heart but I think it's too late to elope.

28 February

I knew I couldn't afford a big-time caterer. And I knew that none of the city caterers would travel upstate for a ten-thousand-dollar wedding. So I acted responsibly. I aimed low.

Apparently not low enough.

Karry, of Karry's Kitchen, a nice little caterer located two towns over from my folks, took one look at my budget, then packed up her display book. 'I'm afraid there's no way I can do dinner for ninety in your price range.' I was mortified. Ticked off. Alarmed. 'Well, do you have any suggestions? Is there anyone else I should call?'

'Yes. Chef Boyardie and Little Debbie.'

Nice. Real nice.

With such monetary realities in mind, Stephen and I have decided to honeymoon in South Carolina. This way we don't need to worry about passports, visas, or shots. And we can actually afford to sleep in a hotel instead of the back seat of our rental car. Besides, Stephen's got this incredibly romantic notion about the beach: 'It's so warm and relaxing. How could you not want to go there? Unless, of course, you've seen *Jaws*.'

Oh, and for the record, I've officially decided to take Stephen's last name.

2 March

After picking up my wedding ring from Lancaster's I spent the entire night strutting around my apartment with it on my finger. Imagine me, Ms Costume Jewelry that comes on little plastic squares from the twirling display racks at Macy's, all decked out with a gold band and an emerald ring. Sure I've got nothing on those Indian brides who wear so much gold it looks like lamé, but I do feel special. Like a princess. Or a syndicated talk-show host.

I'm well aware of all the antiquated reasons why married women are decorated in precious metals and stones: to display their husband's wealth, to ensure them monetary compensation for their soiled purity should their fiancé/ husband suddenly dump them, to publicize their husband's ownership of them, and lastly, to highlight their worth – like giving a prized pig the biggest pen. But screw it. My husband's not wealthy. We paid for our rings with *our* money. My 'purity' was soiled long before we met. And the only thing about me that Stephen possesses is my love.

And if this is about highlighting my worth, then forget the rings. Bust out my crown and scepter because I'm a damn good person with good intentions – most of the time. But for now I'm putting my wedding ring back in its box. I once heard that wearing your ring before the ceremony is bad luck and I've got enough to worry about without some hex hanging over my head

Bytes Infinitum.

3 March

Anita came over last night to watch bad TV. During a commercial break I told her I was changing my name to Amy Sarah Stewart. I expected her to rant. To accuse me of being a sell-out, a Stepford wife, a Mandy.

Instead she dissolved into hysterics.

> ANITA
> That's priceless! Your new initials will be A.S.S.!

Maybe I won't take Stephen's last name.

4 March

I've called eight caterers and none of them will do our wedding. Between date conflicts, budget restrictions and outright disinterest I've come up empty-handed.

For all its billions of chapters *BB* never once mentions how to handle being turned down by everyone you ask. I guess the answer is obvious. Forge on. Grin and bear it.

No wonder Prudence smiles so much.

6 March

Not being able to sleep has given me plenty of time for reflection. I spent all last night thinking about the first time Stephen and I met at our friend James's party. Who would've guessed that almost two years later we'd be getting married. How bizarre. If you had told me back then, I would've said you were crazy. But here we are.

And what if I hadn't gone to the party? What if I hadn't met Stephen? What if I hadn't heard the warm, embracing laugh that won my heart?

I'd probably be dating a sociopath. A freeloader. A white-collar criminal. Or (D), all of the above. But never again. I won't ever date another man. I'll never have a romantic dinner with anyone else. I will never see another man naked. I will never have sex with another man. Stephen is the only man I will ever date, see naked, have sex and eat with for the rest of my life. For the remainder of my mortal existence I will be exclusively with Stephen.

Is that humanly possible? Am I genetically capable of this? Sure Stephen's great but is he THE ONE?

7 March

The more I look at Prudence the more convinced I am that she's trying to tell me something.

8 March

To comfort myself from the painful realization that my

wedding dress will undoubtedly have a frontier theme I decided to shop for shoes. Again.

Having gone to all the department stores, bridal boutiques and specialty shops I could think of, I finally braved the Bridal Building in Queens.

To my mind the Bridal Building is where dreams go to die. It's filled with wholesalers and a handful of retailers who make a living off bridal misfortunes. What's that? You say you've got almost no money? Fear not. People without the ability to utter complete sentences will sell you the cheapest, tackiest, most grotesque wedding accessories that child laborers in Malaysia, Taiwan, and the Dominican Republic can make. And in an effort not to discriminate there's a healthy showing of products manufactured domestically by pre-teens in Mississippi and the Bronx.

Needless to say I brought my *own* nylon footsocks. The last thing I need is some crusty foot fungus – international or domestic.

The Bridal Building is truly bad to the bone. The architect must have been a sadist because there are virtually no windows. Just like in casinos on the Vegas strip, your internal clock is set by the buzz of fluorescent lights. Is it day or night outside? Who the hell knows? You're stuck in the land of stale, recycled air and permanent noon. But unlike the lush, albeit tacky décor of Vegas, the Bridal Building is stark and clinical. Its hallways of cheap Formica and yellowed linoleum floors lead you to an endless number of unmarked doors – like an old medical building with unlicensed doctors lurking around every corner. Is this periodontistry or organ donation?

I spent hours wandering into single-room stores filled with progressively less attractive merchandise. Plastic bridal bouquets, fuchsia garter belts, and cubic zirconia engagement rings with adjustable bands. On an up-note I did see wedding dresses uglier than my own but there was no time to gloat. I have three months and fourteen days to find wedding shoes.

So I forged on. Through rows of stiletto-heeled white pumps and bubblegum-pink sling-backs adorned with tiny plastic angels. I saw open-toed mules with fur appliqué, and white sandals with long leather laces that tied all the way up your thigh. If it hadn't been *my* wedding I would have laughed. But it was. So I was just about to cry when I happened to catch sight of some rhinestone hair combs in Mrs Cho's Bridal Accessory Shoppe.

I made my way to the cabinet. Was that really an attractive object in the bastion of all that is cheap and flammable? Yes! The hair combs were darling – and could be used to highlight a fabulous hairstyle without causing radio-wave disturbances like Prudence's massive head-piece. Suddenly my mind was racing. I'd never considered wearing anything other than fresh flowers in my hair.[29] But these hair combs were so delicate, so sparkly, so special. Just the thing to add a touch of class to my cowgirl bridal ensemble.

But as I took the comb from the display cabinet and brought it to my head, Mrs Cho – a diminutive Korean woman with a piercing voice – shouted, 'No! Fa kids.'

---

[29] A veil was too old-fashioned, not to mention virginal, for this Big City gal. Besides, if everything goes right, you only get married once so who's got time for modesty?

ME
Excuse me?

MRS CHO
Not fa adults. Too little.
It's fa children.

ME
Sure. But couldn't a grown-up wear these
hair combs if she wanted to?

MRS CHO
It's not hair comb. It's tiara. Like
princess. Fa little kid princess. You too
old.

And tearing it from my hand she swiftly returned it to
the display case.

Since when do hair accessories have age limits?

9 March – 3 a.m.

I once saw a *Nightline* report about a woman who went
insane from sleep deprivation. Not nutty, or irritable, or
cranky, but full out INSANE from lack of sleep. For anyone
who's remotely skeptical let me tell you now.

Oh, yeah, it could happen. *Just keep me in your
crosshairs.*

Every night I get a bit closer – sleep-deprivation
extremis. And Stephen's certainly no help with his damn
'little' snores and the way he throws his arm across my

lungs. Even if he doesn't sever my oxygen supply with his bony elbow I'm sure to go deaf from those foghorn snores. Deviated septum my ass!

How can *this* be the man I'm going to spend the rest of my life with? *What the hell am I thinking?*

I must be insane. I can't be insane.

I'm too well dressed!

Maybe I should bail. Maybe that's what Prudence has been trying to tell me.

10 March

It's been several weeks since I heard from Gram. Nothing but silence. Silence isn't good. Silence means something bad is brewing. Now, as I lie awake at night, I'm waiting for the other shoe to fall.

11 March

I'm screwed. I need to edit an exposé on sanitation disposal, reassign an article on computer-related joint diseases, and come up with a complete list of summer-stories ideas for the June issue by *tomorrow*. Sure I could have done these things yesterday. Or last week. But no. I've been running around with my head cut off looking for a caterer and a florist and a loophole in my medical plan that will qualify me for mental-health benefits!

All this because of a wedding that I'm no longer certain I should be having.

Stephen is refusing to sleep over anymore. He says I make him nervous. How could I possibly make him nervous? I'm the one doing everything so it's not like I'm asking him to participate beyond his one task of finding a band, which he's doing slowly and poorly and I'm beginning to worry he won't complete until two weeks before the wedding. So let's be real. I'm the one who's got an unrelenting list of things to do, not to mention find a pair of wedding shoes!

And how difficult can it be to find shoes? I'm not asking for a miracle. Just something classy, comfy, and afford-able, which I can walk in without breaking my neck and he says I'm making *him* nervous? *Oh, please.*

Let him try being a BRIDE!

Official THINGS TO DO List
1. ~~Choose wedding date~~
2. ~~Tell boss wedding date~~
3. ~~Vacation time for honeymoon~~
4. ~~Decide on honeymoon~~
5. ~~Get minister/church~~
6. Choose ~~reception venue~~
7. ~~Make guest list~~
8. ~~Choose maid of honor~~
9. ~~Choose best man~~
10. Register for gifts
11. ~~Arrange for engagement party~~
12. ~~Buy engagement ring~~
13. ~~Buy wedding rings~~
14. ~~Buy wedding dress~~

15. Choose maid-of-honor dress
16. Order wedding cake
17. Hire caterer
18. Hire band for reception
19. Order flowers for ceremony
20. Buy shoes
21. Plan rehearsal dinner
22. Invites to rehearsal dinner
23. Hire musicians for ceremony
24. ~~Decide on dress code~~
25. Get marriage license
26. ~~Hire videographer~~
27. ~~Hire photographer~~
28. Order table flowers
29. Order bouquets
30. Order boutonnières for men
31. Order nosegays for women
32. Order invitations
33. Decide on wine selection
34. Postage for invitations
35. Choose hairstyle and makeup
36. Buy gifts for attendants
37. Buy thank-you notes
38. Announce wedding in newspaper
39. Buy headpiece
40. ~~Buy travelers' checks for honeymoon~~
41. ~~Apply for visas~~
42. ~~Get shots and vaccinations~~
43. Order tent if necessary
44. Order chairs/tables if necessary
45. ~~Make budget~~
46. ~~Divide expenses~~

47. Make table-seating charts
48. Choose bridesmaid dress
49. Decide on menu
50. Decide on *hors d'oeuvres*
51. Decide on dinner service style
52. Decide on staff–guest ratio
53. Decide seated or buffet
54. Reserve vegetarian meals
55. Reserve band/photographer meals
56. Make photo list
57. Choose hotel for wedding night
58. Hire limo for church–reception transport
59. Buy guest book for reception
60. Find hotel for out-of-towners
61. Decide on liquor selection
62. Hire bartenders
63. Verify wheelchair accessibility
64. Choose processional music
65. Choose recessional music
66. Choose cocktail music
67. Choose reception music
68. Choose ceremony readings
69. Prepare birdseed instead of rice
70. Schedule manicure/pedicure/wax

13 March – 1.37 a.m.

Just when I thought things couldn't get any more complicated, overwhelming or confusing . . .

I HAVE A SEX DREAM ABOUT MY CONGA

DRUM-PLAYING, EXCEEDINGLY HANDSOME, EX-BOYFRIEND RICK!

In exactly three months and ten days I'm committing to be with Stephen for the rest of my natural life and here I am dreaming about Rick playing my bare bottom like a conga drum of love *while riding a Ferris wheel at Coney Island*?

13 March

I am totally freaked by my Rick sex dream. After he played my bare bottom he played the rest of me. For *hours*.

Really well.

I don't know what to do. I have to talk to someone about this but who can I tell? I feel so dirty and guilty and ugh!

I can't stop calling Stephen.

> ME
> Hi, honey. It's me. I love you. I love you
> so much. I really, really do.

> STEPHEN
> Is something wrong?

> ME
> No! Why would you say that? How
> could anything ever be wrong between
> us?

STEPHEN
I didn't necessarily mean between us.

ME
Oh. Well, nothing's wrong.

STEPHEN
Then why have you called me thirteen
times today?

ME
No reason. I just want you to know I
love you. Very much. More than any
other man in the entire world.

STEPHEN
Is it 'that' time of the month?

ME
No!

STEPHEN
Then tell me what's going on. If our
marriage is going to work we'll have to
learn to communicate. Clearly
something's bothering you.

ME
Ah—

STEPHEN
Wait a minute. I know what this is
about.

ME
You do?

STEPHEN
This is about sleeping arrangements, isn't it?

ME
Ohmygod! It's meaningless. I swear!

STEPHEN
Amy, relax. If I'd known that my not sleeping over would upset you this much I never would have done it.

ME
Huh?

STEPHEN
I just wanted a few nights of solid sleep without you tossing and turning every twenty minutes. But forget it. It's not worth putting you through all this agony.

ME
Ooh. Yeah. The agony.

STEPHEN
I'll just start sleeping over again.

ME

Great. Wait. No! I'm still having trouble sleeping. Let's wait until I figure things out.

14 March

What am I going to do? The last thing I want is to have sex dreams about other guys while I'm in bed with Stephen.

Ewwwee.

After months of insomnia and praying for sleep I'm now terrified to close my eyes lest some silken ex-lover suddenly appears. What if these dreams never stop? Do Stephen and I sleep separately for the rest of our lives? Do I buy twin beds? That means new sheets. Sheets are expensive!

15 March

Last night it was Anthony. The abstract-expressionist. He was working with oils and I was his canvas. He didn't stop working until he got it right. *Really* right. And to think I was upset by those dreams where I forgot to invite my mother to the wedding. Those were Disney productions compared to these EXTRAVAGANZAS OF THE FLESH!

Needless to say, Barry was the last person I wanted to see when I arrived at the office. 'Are your articles ready? The division meeting's in less than ten minutes and we still have to distribute your proofs.'

I couldn't take it. 'Bite me, Barry! Just bite me!' The entire office went silent. Even Barry was speechless.

I think it's time to seek help.

16 March

I'm calling Mandy and Anita. Somewhere between *yin* and *yang* there must be a voice of reason. Or at least knowledge of how to procure strong pharmaceutical drugs without a prescription.

17 March

I convened an emergency meeting at Frutto di Sole.

> ME
> There's something important I need to talk about. But first you have to swear that you won't repeat a word of this conversation.

> MANDY
> Sounds exciting. Is that why you've gone incognito?

> ME
> What?

> MANDY
> Your outfit. The quiet black suit, the silk scarf wrapped around your neck, the dark sunglasses. Hello! Amy, we're indoors.

ANITA
You don't like it? I think it's sexy. Very
Sophia Loren.[30]

ME
That's great. Now will you both shut up
and swear to secrecy so I can get on
with it?[31]

ANITA
I swear.

MANDY
So do I.

ME
This means total secrecy. No telling your
hairdresser or co-workers no matter how
much they plead. And under no
circumstances may you ever mention this
to your significant other.

MANDY
I assume you're referring to Jon.[32]

---

[30] Sophia Loren? Sure she's stunning and classy but she's like 110 now.
At least cut me a break and stay in my century. Isabelle Adjani, anyone?

[31] Does everyone have friends like this? Here I am with two of my
closest friends and they're more interested in my 'look' than my state of
mind. If a friend of yours showed up to a restaurant dressed like a spy
wouldn't you be more concerned about her mental health than whether
or not it's a viable fashion alternative? Can't anyone see I'm dyin' here?

[32] Well, duh.

ME
Yes.

MANDY
And exactly what do you have against
Jon?

ME
Nothing.[33] It's just a formality. Now
swear.

MANDY
I swear. But this better be good.

I hunched down and lowered my voice. You never know
who might be listening.

ME
I've been having sex dreams about old
boyfriends.

MANDY
That's horrible!

ANITA
Are you kidding? That's great!

ME
Anita, I'm getting married in three

---

[33] Nothing we can talk about.

months. I'm not supposed to be having sex dreams about other men. What am I going to do?

ANITA
You're going to sleep as much as humanly possible. Just because you're getting married doesn't mean you shut your mind off. And these dreams don't mean you don't love Stephen. After all, haven't you agreed to subjugate your entire existence to him on June twenty-second?

MANDY
Oh, please. Amy's right to be worried. It's a dangerous thing when a woman dreams about having sex in a sauna with a man other than her husband.

ME
Who said anything about a sauna?

MANDY
Oh . . . Well, I was just illustrating what type of sex dream a person *might* have were she dreaming on a fairly regular basis about adulterous encounters.

ME
I see.

ANITA

I can't believe you guys are being so
puritanical about this.

MANDY

It's not puritanical. It's practical. You
can't fully give yourself to one man
when you're dreaming about another.

ANITA

But dreams are harmless. Besides, maybe
those dreams weren't really about sex.
Maybe they were a symbolic gesture. A
way of saying goodbye to past lovers.

MANDY

I never thought about that![34]

ME

Terrific. But how many times do I have
to say goodbye?

18 March – 3 a.m.

I had another sex dream. About *Jon*.

And I was *into* it. Now, in addition to being unfaithful,
I'm desperate!

---

[34] Why does she sound so relieved?

Yuck!

18 March

My first dress fitting with Katrina. She's straightened and cropped the sleeves to a three-quarter length, which has eliminated all traces of *Godspell*.

But I still look like Nellie Olsen after a nasty tumble down a well.

Katrina kept shaking her head mournfully as if the situation were terminal. You'd think for five hundred dollars she'd have a better bedside manner.

I'm finally beginning to understand why the Moonies opt for massive group weddings. No caterer, no band, no bridesmaids. And in a group of a thousand brides who's going to notice your dress?

20 March

My day was going so well. I'd only had a brief sex dream about my eleventh-grade boyfriend Denny, found a florist, and gotten a compliment on my June-story ideas from Mr Spaulding. Then Barry opened his mouth: 'So what type of invitations are you sending out? Modern or traditional?'

The kind that doesn't have your name on it, *Barry*. Poor moron. Like getting rid of me is going to be that easy. 'One day she got married and *poof*! She was gone.' I wish he'd give it a rest.

'I really haven't thought about it.'

'You mean you haven't ordered them?'

'Nope.'

'But you're getting married in three months and two days.[35] When my friend Denise got married she ordered her invitations months in advance. And f.y.i. – they were stunning. Dusty rose, thirty-two-pound linen-bond paper printed with apple-red ink and tissue inserts. I'd be happy to get the printer's name and number if you'd like.'

Great. And how about pushing me into oncoming traffic while you're at it? 'Thanks, but no thanks, Barry. I'll be fine.'

Or will I? Maybe Barry was on to something.[36]

I immediately called Mandy, who flipped out. 'What do you mean you haven't ordered your invitations? Didn't you read Chapter Thirty-four of *Beautiful Bride*?'

'I started to skim around Thirty-one.'

'This is your wedding! You can't skim. There's no skimming in matrimony!'

I was a basket case for the rest of the day. What had I done? Here I thought the scales of bridal calamity had finally balanced out. Maybe all wasn't great, but at least it was placid. And now this.

I ran home after work and turned to Chapter Thirty-four. The more I read the quicker my pulse raced. According to *BB* invitations must be sent out approximately six weeks before the wedding: not so far in advance that people forget, but early enough for them to clear their schedule. Add to that an average of two months to print invitations, make the necessary corrections, address and

---

[35] Not that he's counting.

[36] Quick! Someone smack me. Next I'll be saying Jon's a Rhodes Scholar.

mail them. Six weeks plus two months. At this rate my wedding invitations have to be ordered *last* week!

The apocalypse must be near – because Barry was right.

21 March

Panicked about our invitation dilemma, I decided to call Stephen at work. It was only 5 p.m. but he'd been working since seven in the morning and I could tell he was tired and distracted. So it was no surprise when, instead of offering some advice, he suggested lamely I ask my mother for help.

Pass the buck much, *Stevie?*

21 March – 10.30 p.m.

Although I'd been civil to Stephen during our earlier phone call I felt bad about all the hostile things I'd said in my head. After all, he's been working like a dog. Of course he's distracted. I decided to call him at home and tell him how much I love him. Between his late nights at the office, my being overwhelmed with wedding details, and our current separate sleeping arrangements, we'd barely seen each other this month.

But Stephen wasn't home. So I called his office.

After six rings he finally answered the phone. But before I could say hello I heard Louise giggling in the background. It was almost midnight and they'd been in that office together since 7 a.m. What the hell was she *giggling* about?

Unable to come up with an acceptable answer I hung up.

22 March – 1 a.m.

I can't get Louise's damn giggling out of my head. She was too pleased. Like a kid sneaking an extra slice of cake when no one was looking.

Well, it better not be *my* cake that Louise is munching on!

Wait a minute! How can I even think this way? Stephen and I are about to get married. Shouldn't I trust him implicitly?

22 March – 2 a.m.

MANDY
I can't believe you're calling me at two
in the morning.

ME
If it makes you feel any better I called
Anita first but she hung up on me.

MANDY
Actually that makes this even more
annoying.

ME
Sorry, but it's an emergency.

MANDY
No, it's not. You heard some woman

giggling. They've been working for a thousand hours. She was probably just giddy from exhaustion. Like me. Tee-hee, tee-hee, tee-hee. See? I'm giddy from exhaustion, too.

ME
Come on, Mandy. What if my sex dreams have driven Stephen away?

MANDY
Did you tell him about them?

ME
Of course not. But what if he *sensed* them?

MANDY
Listen to me, Amy. Men sense almost nothing. It's their best and worst trait. Now, go to bed. I'll tell you when it's time to worry.

22 March

Against my better judgment I took Mandy's advice. Twice. First, I decided not to worry about Stephen and Louise. Although I did ask him to start sleeping over again. And, for the record, he was very pleased.

Second, I went to Mandy's printers. Berington Stationer's is located just around the corner from Tiffany's. It's filled with 'sales associates' seated in Louis the Schmooey chairs behind Louis the Schmooey desks. Each desktop is oddly devoid of any office supplies, save a single pad of linen paper embossed with the store's name. The sales associates, all of whom are women, wear conservative blue dresses and a single strand of pearls.

The woman I dealt with was so uptight and brittle I was afraid she'd snap in two. Ms Handel must have sensed I wasn't the typical Berington customer because during our five-minute conversation she mentioned six times that Berington uses only the highest quality paper and engraving, both of which are quite 'precious'. Read: expensive. Or more likely: overpriced.

Disgusted by her wealthier-than-thou attitude, and horrified to discover that her attempts to shame me were in fact working, I thoughtfully shook my head and sighed. 'I'll have my driver bring my secretary over tomorrow morning. She'll give you the necessary details and choose the paper.' Uncertain as to how to reply, Ms Handel asked cagily for my name and phone number – ostensibly to schedule an appointment for the following day.

I happily complied. 'Miss Astrid Rockefeller. 555–5633.'

My one regret upon leaving Berington Stationer's was that I wouldn't see Ms Handel's face when she called the Leather Fetishists' Chat Line.[37]

---

[37] Yes, I have the Leather Fetishists' Chat Line number committed to memory. It has something to do with a college dorm room, day-old pizza and the guy who delivered it – but that's all I'll ever admit to.

23 March – 1.45 a.m.

Jonas the inventor. I'd forgotten how good he looked wet.

23 March

Stephen may actually have a case against the city.
According to Larry, the pothole Stephen tripped on is six
months overdue for repair. It's a clear example of
municipal negligence. They're filing a complaint next
week.

Terrific. Now he'll never deal with the band issue.

24 March

I can't stop thinking about that rhinestone comb at the
Bridal Building. It would look great alongside Lucy's
enamel barrette. Except I'll have to find some twelve-year-
old to buy it for me. How nuts is that? It's like some
cosmic payback for all those high-school years I spent
convincing adults to buy me beer.

25 March

After deciding to use my free time to make my own
wedding invitations with a computer, I remembered that I
have no free time. So I went to Bunny's Printing Emporium
in Chinatown. I chose Bunny's based on her well-worded
advertisement in the *Yellow Pages* – 'Nice, Speedy, Cheap'.
Located between a dumpling house and a porn shop,
Bunny's was about as far from Berington Stationer's as

you could get. Anywhere between sixty and seventy-five years old, Bunny herself stood behind the counter dressed in a nylon jogging suit. Her overflowing ashtray and the garbage can filled with Budweiser empties revealed that she smoked almost as much as she drank. Stranded on a deserted island without food, Bunny would have Ms Handel for lunch, then pick her teeth clean with the remains.

After listening to Bunny's tale about how her printing shop was there 'long before the Chinks came to town', I explained my desperate situation. It turns out that, in addition to being racist, Bunny is also fully knowledgeable about her industry. Willing to inform and ready to haggle, Bunny provided me with a quick education about wedding invitations which boils down to: colored paper, illustrated designs, special enclosures, calligraphy and engraving all cost more.

I settled on a medium weight, cream-colored paper, thermal printing and standard RSVP enclosures. I personally would address the envelopes using my laser printer at work. On Bunny's advice the invitation's distinctive touch would come from its clever wording. As Bunny reminded me, 'Talk is cheap.'

26 March

Stephen's grandparents sent me a present. Although the gesture was incredibly thoughtful I suspect Mrs Brockton hasn't bonded with my decision to keep my maiden name. The present was a throw pillow with the name 'Mrs Stephen Stewart' embroidered on both sides.

Now I don't have a new identity. I have *no* identity.

29 March

I asked Anita to use her twelve-year-old niece Molly as a front and buy the hair comb from Mrs Cho at the Bridal Building.

Sure it would mean Anita taking the train out to Queens. But she's my best friend. I'd do it for her. And Molly lives in Queens. So it really could be viewed as a nice family outing for the two of them.

Besides, I *need* that hair comb.

After I begged and pleaded she finally gave me a half-hearted, 'Yes.' Which was fine since she also gave me a handful of sleeping pills that she'd pirated from the health editor at *Teen Flair*.

30 March

Anita's sleeping pills knocked me out cold. Not a sex dream in sight. Unfortunately they also left me groggy and gullible.

When my mother asked how the wedding plans were going – why wasn't the florist coming to see the site? why wasn't the caterer coming to see the kitchen? – I actually answered her. *Honestly*. I told her I was having trouble finding a caterer. That our florist was dragging his feet. But that I did have a photographer and as soon as he got a break from chasing fires, knifings and shootouts he'd surely stop by to say hi.

She offered to help.

I may have been overly medicated but I wasn't stupid. I know her offer was well intentioned *but* the best-laid plans . . . I could just see it: I let her help with some small task and before I know it she's wiping everyone's nose, handing out multiplication flashcards, and ordering ninety hot lunches from the school cafeteria. With value and size as her main objectives, *taste* is destined to be overlooked.

Despite Stephen's insistence that it might be a good idea, I politely declined.

31 March

Stephen was panicked because the computer program he's been working on was almost complete when they found a flaw in it. His company's future is depending on the success of this program. If the program fails or isn't released by early September he's out of a job. So I understand that he's under a lot of pressure.

But does that mean we have to get *plaid* dishes?

No joke. There we were, standing in the middle of Bloomingdale's trying to register for wedding gifts and Stephen decides he wants the plaid dishes. Plaid. Like that damn couch isn't enough for him. He wants to see plaid at every meal for the rest of our lives because you know we're keeping these dishes until the day we die. They're *bone china*, for Christ's sake. We'll never spend the money on another set.

It was our first real fight since the engagement. He refused to budge and I refused to give in. We were at a complete impasse. And then it hit me: how can we get married if we can't even agree on a china pattern?

So I broke down in tears.

1 April

Prudence doesn't want to get married. That's what her expression's all about. Trapped against her will in *BB*'s glossy cover Prudence is straining to warn me, 'Don't do it, Amy. You can still turn back!'

2 April – 2 a.m.

If I burn my hateful Things To Do list will it wash away my woes?

Official THINGS TO DO List
1. ~~Choose wedding date~~
2. ~~Tell boss wedding date~~
3. ~~Vacation time for honeymoon~~
4. ~~Decide on honeymoon~~
5. ~~Get minister/church~~
6. ~~Choose reception venue~~
7. ~~Make guest list~~
8. ~~Choose maid of honor~~
9. ~~Choose best man~~
10. Register for gifts
11. ~~Arrange for engagement party~~
12. ~~Buy engagement ring~~
13. ~~Buy wedding rings~~
14. ~~Buy wedding dress~~

15. Choose maid-of-honor dress
16. Order wedding cake
17. Hire caterer
18. Hire band for reception
19. Order flowers for ceremony
20. Buy shoes
21. Plan rehearsal dinner
22. Invites to rehearsal dinner
23. Hire musicians for ceremony
24. ~~Decide on dress code~~
25. Get marriage license
26. ~~Hire videographer~~
27. ~~Hire photographer~~
28. Order table flowers
29. Order bouquets
30. Order boutonnières for men
31. Order nosegays for women
32. ~~Order invitations~~
33. Decide on wine selection
34. Postage for invitations
35. Choose hairstyle and makeup
36. Buy gifts for attendants
37. Buy thank-you notes
38. Announce wedding in newspaper
39. Buy headpiece
40. ~~Buy travelers' checks for honeymoon~~
41. ~~Apply for visas~~
42. ~~Get shots and vaccinations~~
43. Order tent if necessary
44. Order chairs/tables if necessary
45. ~~Make budget~~
46. ~~Divide expenses~~

47. Make table-seating charts
48. Choose bridesmaid dress
49. Decide on menu
50. Decide on *hors d'oeuvres*
51. Decide on dinner service style
52. Decide on staff–guest ratio
53. Decide seated or buffet
54. Reserve vegetarian meals
55. Reserve band/photographer meals
56. Make photo list
57. Choose hotel for wedding night
58. Hire limo for church–reception transport
59. Buy guest book for reception
60. Find hotel for out-of-towners
61. Decide on liquor selection
62. Hire bartenders
63. Verify wheelchair accessibility
64. Choose processional music
65. Choose recessional music
66. Choose cocktail music
67. Choose reception music
68. Choose ceremony readings
69. Prepare birdseed instead of rice
70. Schedule manicure/pedicure/wax

2 April

My second fitting with Katrina. It took every ounce of strength not to burst into tears. The dress was five inches too long and three inches too tight in the hips.

I can't believe I'm paying for this.

Meanwhile Backstabbing Barry has begun to work overtime on a regular basis. Needless to say, he's taking pains to publicize this fact. I can only guess he's doing it to make me look bad. But since he seems to accomplish less work in sixty hours than I do in forty-five I'm not going to worry.

Too much.

Does anyone know when Martha Stewart's *Weddings* magazine comes out?

3 April

I don't know how it happened. One minute everything was fine, sort of, then suddenly things were spinning out of control and—

But I should start at the beginning.

Due to some bizarre cosmic alignment Stephen left work early enough to join me at the florist's. It was during this visit that the florist finally decided to mention that the tropical flowers I want for the wedding, the very flowers we'd been discussing for the last three weeks, would have to be specially shipped from the Pacific. At a cost so astronomical I swear I thought he was calculating in yen.

I was furious. Why had we wasted all this time talking about tropical flowers if they were going to cost more than a new kidney? I immediately threw a fit.

It was around here that Stephen decided to pay some attention. Gently putting his hand on my shoulder, Stephen, my knight in shining armor, my hero, looked that idiot florist straight in the eye and said, 'Would you please excuse us a minute?'

Huh?

And before I could express my disbelief he was dragging me out of the store. 'Amy, you've got to relax. You're acting like a complete lunatic because lotus blossoms are indigenous to the Pacific.'

'It's ginger blossoms, *not* lotus blossoms. Now what's your point?'

'My point is that it's a reality that precedes your birth and will far outlast your lifetime. So who cares? It's just a bunch of flowers.'

Just a bunch of flowers? How dare he be so cavalier about all the energy and time I'd spent trying to create a moving and memorable wedding on an anorexic budget while he's been sitting in front of a souped-up television monitor scratching his ass with a programming manual?

'Gee, Stephen. Let's think – who cares? Hmmm . . . That's a toughie, but wait, I think I know the answer . . . *I care*!'[38]

It was around here that I noticed people on the sidewalk edging away from us. Like we might be dangerous or, even worse, contagious. In a matter of seconds we'd become that bickering couple you hurry past on the street and feel really sorry for. Then you feel really happy it's not you. Except now it was *me*. My day had come.

---

[38] And let's be real – so does he, the Big Faker. He may not care about the flowers, but trust me he's got *his* issues. Or have we forgotten who whined about not wanting Reverend MacKenzie because he was 'creepy'? And who insisted on no finger foods. And who made us *reschedule our entire wedding* in order to accommodate the National Basketball Association!

'You're right, Amy. I understand that you care. And that's real touching . . .'

Wait! Is that sarcasm I hear sneaking into this heartfelt reply?

'. . . but it's not that big a deal. We'll get something else. Something cheaper. Now, relax. You're starting to sound like Mandy.'

'What's that supposed to mean?'

'You know exactly what it means. Mandy went nuts over that crazy wedding of hers.'

(Here's where it got really good.)

'The flowers, the carriage, the cake . . .' Then, with the world's most pathetic expression of sorrow he shook his head. 'Poor Jon.'

Poor *JON*!

'Are you kidding me? That loser would be lucky to get bitch-slapped by someone as great as Mandy. That she actually *married* him is fucking unbelievable. You can't possibly take his side.'

'This isn't about sides, Amy. It's about perspective. And you've completely lost yours. First the bridal registry. Now these flowers . . . I didn't think I was marrying someone like this.'

STOP. EVERYTHING.

What the hell did that mean? It suddenly occurred to me that I hadn't heard Stephen's warm, embracing laugh in a *very* long time.

'Is that a threat?'

'Don't be ridiculous.'

'Well, it sounded like a threat. Like maybe if you'd known I was someone like *this*, you wouldn't have proposed.'

'That's not what I meant.'

'Then why'd you say it? You could have said, "Gee, I think Skipper is a nice name for a dog." Or "Wow, the vegetarian lasagna is delish!" But no. You *chose* to say you didn't think you were marrying someone like *this*!'

'You know what? You're right. I said it and I meant it! You're running around screaming about lotus blossoms—'

'Ginger blossoms!'

'Whatever! It might as well be daisies! I like daisies. But did you ever ask me what I like? No! Instead you're being a total pain in the ass, which is really disappointing, not to mention a *gigantic* turn-off!'

'Oh, yeah? Well, the hell with you!'

And I stormed away. Never once looking back. That was five hours ago. And I still haven't heard a word from Stephen.

I don't think we're getting married anymore.

4 April – 1 a.m.

What am I going to do? How am I going to tell my parents? My friends? *Barry?*

I've already called in sick for work tomorrow. I left a message on Kate's voicemail. There's just no way I can face the world. There's no way I can get out of this bed.

I am completely numb.

Part of me wants to call Stephen, part of me wants him to call me, and part of me never wants to speak to him again. I don't know what to do. What to think. What to feel.

All I do know is that every time I look at my emerald engagement ring, I cry.

4 April

My apartment has never seemed so hollow. With the exception of an occasional car horn or squeaky bus brake from the street below, it is as silent and still as a tomb. As if it's been sealed off from the rest of the world. Forgotten. I feel forgotten.

I wish the phone would ring.

To remind myself that I'm still alive I've decided to keep a steady stream of food entering my body. Except that after four boxes of Kraft macaroni and cheese the only thing I can taste is doubt. Am I relieved or completely devastated?

If I thought planning a wedding was tough, I can't imagine how difficult it is to unplan one.

I finally called Anita around noon. Except she's out of town on a business trip – some profile of a thirteen-year-old boy who recorded a top-ten single in his uncle's root cellar – and won't be back until tomorrow. So I called Mandy. Because I really needed a hug.

Within the hour Mandy stormed my apartment brandishing a basket filled with comfort food and self-help tapes, determined to put Humpty-Dumpty back together again.

     MANDY
     Oh, my God!

Wrapping her arms around me she hugged me like a solider returning from war. I sank into her embrace.

> ME
> Thanks for coming over.

> MANDY
> Of course I came over. You need me.
> Besides, my two o'clock showing got
> canceled. Now, how *are* you?

> ME
> I think I'm numb.

Mandy glanced with disapproval at the mountain of Kraft mac and cheese boxes littering my floor.

> MANDY
> No wonder. Now, tell me what
> happened.

Well, it all started when Stephen accused me of being like you . . .

> ME
> I don't know. First we were talking
> about flowers then he was talking about
> my behavior and then I was storming
> off.

Mandy popped a self-help CD into my stereo. Suddenly some woman with clogged nasal passages was bleating in

syncopated rhythms over a tambourine track. I climbed
back into bed.

>MANDY
>I don't understand. I thought things were
>going so well – you ordered those
>invitations, didn't you?

>ME
>Yes. In only five weeks I'll have a
>hundred and twenty invitations to a
>wedding that's not happening. I've got a
>lifelong supply of scrap paper.

>MANDY
>Don't be ridiculous. This is just a bump
>in the road. Things will smooth out.

Then she looked at me. Panic in her eyes.

>MANDY
>Please tell me you haven't told anyone
>about this.

>ME
>I left a message for Anita, but that's it.

>MANDY
>Thank goodness. The last thing you want
>is to hear this story repeated at some
>cocktail party next year . . . Which
>makes me think. We should definitely

remind Anita to keep her trap shut.
Now, really, how *are* you?

ME
I'm mad. I'm sad. I'm relieved . . .

Mandy removed two spoons and a pint of reduced-fat
Ben and Jerry's ice cream from her goody basket and
climbed into bed with me.

MANDY
Here, have some ice cream.

I obeyed.

ME
I'm serious, Mandy. It's like I can't think
straight. And when I do, I just get so
angry! You had to hear him. He couldn't
give a damn about all the work I've
done for this wedding.

MANDY
Men are so spoiled. They want things
their way, but they don't want to work
for it and they certainly don't want to
hear the gory details.

ME
Exactly!

Mandy yanked the ice cream away from me.

MANDY
Don't hog.

I had forgotten that I was still eating it.

ME
Honestly, I'm beginning to see how this
could all be for the best.

MANDY
If by 'best' you mean a sure-fire way to
grow old alone, then yes, breaking up
with Stephen is a grand idea.

ME
He said I was a turn-off!

MANDY
Heat of the moment, inflamed passions
. . . Isn't he part Greek?

ME
No.

MANDY
Well, anyway, you're very emotional
right now. You and Stephen just had a
little tiff. You love him. He loves you.
That's all that matters.

ME
Mandy, you're not listening. It wasn't a

little tiff. He called me a *pain in the ass*.
We had a huge, make-a-scene-in-broad-
daylight blow-out.

MANDY
You argued in *public*?

She shivered.

ME
Yes! I'm telling you, it's over. The whole
thing is finished!

I couldn't help myself, I was crying again. Mandy
wrapped her arms around me.

MANDY
Nothing's finished. I've got a plan that
will fix everything. First we put a new
outgoing message on your answering-
machine. You'll sound happy and peppy
like someone who's having a lot of
casual sex. That way if Stephen calls,
he'll panic and apologize immediately.
But if he doesn't call I'll get Jon to call
him about some silly computer question.
Jon will get the scoop and report back to
us and . . .

Comforted by hugs and plied with reduced-fat dairy
products, I continued to listen as Mandy outlined her
calculated plan to reunite me with Stephen. And though I

was uncertain it would work, and even more uncertain that I wanted it to work, it did occur to me that Mandy had missed her calling. She really should have gone into the military.

> MANDY
> Don't worry. We'll have you walking
> down that aisle if it kills me.

4 April – 10 p.m.

After spending the entire day in my apartment I was overwhelmed by the need to see people. To make contact with the outside world. To breathe the semi-polluted air of car exhaust and dry-cleaning fumes. So I threw a long coat over my sweats and went to the newsstand. Just because my life had ground to a halt didn't mean the rest of the world had.

Even at 10 p.m. the streets were well populated. And everywhere I looked I saw men. Men with women, men with men, men by themselves. Men leaving restaurants, going to bars, walking their dogs, talking to themselves and scratching their balls. That's when it occurred to me that I could flirt with these men. That as a single woman I could introduce myself, chat them up, and even bring them home.[39] The hell with Stephen. Let's see if any of these fine young gentlemen thought I was a *turn-off*.

---

[39] Not that I've ever brought a complete stranger home. (At least not since college.) After all, they could be psychotics with hacksaw fantasies or cross-dressers who look better in lingerie than I do.

So when I caught the newsstand guy checking me out I stood tall and proud – shoulders back, boobs forward – until I remembered that I hadn't showered today and that perhaps he wasn't so much enamored with my looks as disgusted by the oily clump of hair matted to my scalp. Or my face, which was bloated from sobs and high-sodium snack foods. And just as my boobs were falling back and my shoulders were slumping forward, I noticed the display of bridal magazines behind the counter.

I bought *People* and called it a night.

5 April

I took another sick day from work. And to be honest, I really do feel sick. I may have lost Stephen but between the fine folks at Kraft and Mandy's goody basket, I've eaten his weight in foodstuffs. Unlike those thin girls who get depressed and can't eat, I'm biologically driven to drown my sorrows in cheese dip.

And for the record, I've officially forgone bathing for forty-eight hours. A fact that did not escape Anita when she came to my apartment – straight from the airport.

> ANITA
> Filthy really isn't a good look for you.

> ME
> It's part of my angry phase – I'm the
> anti-bride. Thanks for coming.

She gave me a hug.

ANITA
I knew you couldn't have one of those
normal, repressed weddings. I knew
you'd delve into hysterics.

ME
I didn't delve. If anything, it was only a
dabble. And it was wholly justified. He
said I was a *pain in the ass*.

Anita laughed.

ME
What are you laughing about?

ANITA
Nothing.

Opening her suitcase Anita removed an eight-by-ten
glossy of Bobby Flax – the thirteen-year-old whose root-
cellar recording was burning up the pop charts.

ANITA
Here. I thought this would cheer you up.

Bobby had scribbled 'Love Ya, Babe' in red ink.

ANITA
I know it's not a solution to your
immediate problem. But in four years
he'll be at his sexual peak. And those
braces are coming off next summer.

She poured us some cheap white wine she found in my refrigerator. I climbed back into bed.

ANITA
So, do you want to talk about it?

ME
It's pretty simple. I was struggling, as usual, to plan our wedding and he was entirely unhelpful and unappreciative and unsympathetic. And then he said he didn't realize he was marrying someone like 'this' and that I was a *turn-off*!

ANITA
Harsh! What'd you do?

ME
I told him to go to hell, then I came back here and began my crusade of food and filth.

ANITA
Very mature.

ME
Thank you.

Anita sipped her wine. It was clear she was trying to find a way to say something that I wouldn't want to hear. After two false starts, she finally got it out.

ANITA

Look, I don't mean to sound
unsympathetic. And I certainly don't like
seeing you so upset. But on an
intellectual level, as well as a personal
level, I've always felt that matrimony was
a losing proposition. Anything that
involves monogamy is unnatural. We're
not supposed to be with one person
forever. Even most married people aren't
with one person forever.

I thought of Bianca Sheppard. And Donald Trump. And my cousin Paul who'd had a 'mistress' for six years before anyone found out. Yes, Anita was definitely on to something. And it wasn't necessarily a bad thing. It was simply a reality. People had urges. Why deny them? Just look at my sex dreams. Besides, I never wanted to get married. I never wanted to be a wife. I just wanted to love someone for longer than a calendar year.

ME

Maybe you're right. Maybe canceling this
wedding is the best thing that could
happen to me. Stephen's a wonderful guy
but do I really want to spend eternity
with him? Especially now that I've gotten
a glimpse of the future – me doing all
the work, all the planning, and him
sitting back and criticizing and, oh, my
God!

Unable to sit still I jumped up and grabbed Anita by the shoulders.

>ME
>What was I thinking? I don't want to be *married*!

>ANITA
>Like I've always said, marriage is a societal ill.

>ME
>No wonder I've felt so miserable! I've been ill!

It was as if I'd suddenly been released from some horrible burden and I could finally see sun peeking through the clouds. It was hope. It was freedom. It was my life reclaimed!

>ANITA
>Not to mention a total farce.

>ME
>You're absolutely right!

>ANITA
>I know. Now get the hell out of this bed and make up with your fiancé.

>ME
>*What?*

ANITA

You heard me. Shake a leg. You can't
get married without some sucker to say,
'I do.'

ME

But you just said that marriage is a
societal ill. You said it was a farce!

ANITA

It is. But I've never seen you so happy as
when you're with Stephen. So for you,
I'm thinking maybe marriage won't be so
pathetic. Maybe.

ME

So you think I *should* get married?

Anita averted her eyes and mumbled.

ANITA

Yeah. Just don't tell anyone. Especially
that troll Jon.

I clutched her tightly to my bosom.

ME

Thank God! Because I *really* want to
marry him!

And before you could say, 'Hello, Sybil,' I was sobbing
again.

ME
I miss him so much! I miss his tilted
smile, and his laugh, and—

ANITA
I know, I know. You miss his smile, his
laugh, his knobby knees—

ME
You think his knees are knobby?

ANITA
Forget I said it.

I continued to cry.

ME
I wanna get married!

Anita poured herself another glass of wine.

ANITA
Before you launch into your 'I Love
Stephen' show tunes, there's something I
need to say. He's a fool for calling you a
turn-off, and he's got no business
complaining about all the work you've
done, but as far as his not helping goes –
that's your fault.

Excuse me, but when did the Tough Love seminar start?

> **ANITA**
> You told him it'd be okay if he did
> nothing. You're an enabler.

I was so shocked that I stopped crying. Could I really be an *enabler*? It was like discovering I was tone-deaf. Or had really bad breath. If you hadn't cringed the minute I opened my mouth, I never would have known.

But what if Anita was right? Lord knows, she's right about Stephen being an idiot. Maybe I am responsible for this mess. And all for what? A wedding? Well, like Anita says, you can't have a wedding without some sucker to say, 'I do.'

But where's my sucker?

> **ANITA**
> Now, please, mellow out. It's just a
> wedding. You can always have another
> one.

5 April – 11.30 p.m.

What have I been thinking? My fiancé's petrified about losing his job and I pick fights with him about dishware and flowers. I abuse my position of authority and turn my secretary into a serf. I forget to call my favorite relative when she's got chronic health problems. I resent my mother for saddling me with the world's ugliest wedding dress. And my own grandmother hates me. Stephen's right! I have become a pain in the ass!

Who still hasn't found wedding shoes!

I swore I'd never let my wedding get the best of me. New Year resolutions Nos 4, 5, and 10. But suddenly here I am. Pulling a Mandy. My nerves are shot, I haven't slept in months, and I've got the onset of back acne. Yick. Somewhere along the line I became what I've always hated – A BRIDE!

So, despite Anita's pleas, now is not the time for me to 'mellow out'. Now's the time for me to tell Stephen how incredibly sorry I am for totally losing perspective, for being a pain in the ass, for enabling his bad behavior and for jeopardizing the very thing that means most to me – my love for him! Or, more accurately, his love for me.

From now on I keep my priorities straight and my head screwed on properly. I'm getting a clue. And buying a vowel. 'A U please, Vanna.' For *u*nder control.

The hell with tropical flowers and unique presentations. Daisies, carnations, and bud vases for all!

But first, I need to get my fiancé back.

6 April

I spent all night trying to figure out how to reconcile with Stephen – assuming he even wanted to, which looked unlikely since our last exchange ended with me telling him to go to hell.

But I had to try. Our flower-shop fall-out had driven home how much I love him. Yes, he was insensitive and, yes, he was unappreciative but for that I had to assume part of the blame.[40]

---

[40] A fractional part – say, between a quarter and a third.

And yet I couldn't bring myself to pick up the phone. I was just too scared. What if he hung up? Or told me that it was over? It felt so odd – less than a week earlier this was someone to whom I could tell anything and now I was literally too nervous to call him. So I decided to take a less-direct approach. One that involved neither face-to-face contact nor linguistic interaction. In fact, the crux of my plan was rooted in his total absence.

At eleven o'clock in the morning, when I was certain he'd be at work, I went to Stephen's apartment. Using my key I let myself in and, hoping to convey the depth of my affection, put a vase full of daisies on top of his big-screen TV. After all, hadn't he vehemently declared his appreciation for daisies?

But in the middle of this heartfelt, conciliatory gesture I realized that unlike my apartment, which was littered with the remains of my bingeing bacchanal, Stephen's apartment was positively tidy. Sure, men grieve in a different way, more machismo than melancholy, but a close inspection revealed that the garbage was void of sob-filled tissues, and stacks of our relationship mementos – amassed for grieving purposes – were nowhere to be found. It was like we'd never fought. And like I'd never existed.

Stephen had already moved on.

Faced with the obvious, I locked the apartment and slid the key under the door.

I walked home. Over thirty-six blocks in the freezing cold, chiding myself for being so careless with something so precious. I had sabotaged my own happiness. Even Mandy could do nothing to save it. By the time I was opening my own apartment door I was too exhausted to cry.

Or so I thought . . .

Until I saw that my entire living room was filled with ginger blossoms. While I was putting daisies in Stephen's living room, he – assuming I was at my office – was filling my living room with ginger blossoms. It was like 'The Gift of the Magi' by O. Henry.

Seconds later the phone rang. It was Stephen calling from his apartment. Daisies in his hand. I didn't know where to start so I just spewed, 'The flowers are beautiful and you were right I have become a pain in the ass but I've been so overwhelmed and everything just seemed so important and I'm so sorry and—'

'No, I'm the one who's sorry. I love you so much. You've been terrific about handling all the wedding arrangements and I've been a complete dolt. I've been so wrapped up with work that I haven't stopped to thank you. I never should have complained and I promise that I'll deal with the music and, Amy, you're the biggest turn-on in the entire world.'

Now *that*'s what a girl likes to hear.

6 April – 8 p.m.

Considering my own emotional rollercoaster, I feel like I should personally apologize to all the brides whom I mocked or ridiculed about their wedding hysteria.

But time's tight. And that could take all week. So I left an apology on Mandy's answering-machine. She can be symbolic of everyone I taunted. Besides, I mocked her the most. Whether she's aware of it or not.

7 April

I called Lucy today. Resolution No. 6 – call Lucy twice a month – has bitten the dust hard. It's been over six weeks. I know she doesn't hold it against me, she's far too gracious. But I hold it against myself. Especially since a new problem concerning her sugar levels has landed her in the hospital twice since our last conversation. I tell myself that I don't have enough time to call her. But that's a lie. The truth is I don't make the time.

As usual, Lucy was far more interested in hearing about my life than talking about her own. Aware that for a housebound woman obsessed with tabloid news I often function like an issue of the *National Enquirer* I did my best to recount the highs and lows of my life – including the infamous flower-shop fall-out – with as much dramatic flair as possible.

I was alarmed by how little embellishment was needed.

8 April

Round two at the bridal registry.

This time we had a hearty meal beforehand and wore sensible shoes. As for the plaid dishes, we compromised and decided to skip china altogether. Instead we're registering for two sets of casual tableware. This way, if a piece breaks, we can afford to replace it.

As for the rest of the registry, we made sure only to ask for things we'd really use. Have you noticed that every married couple has either a pasta machine or a bread-maker stuffed in the back of their kitchen cabinet? Used only once, if at all. And the cappuccino-maker. Oh, *please*. Do you really see yourself slaving away over steamed milk when a cup of freshly brewed Colombian takes less than three minutes? Not to mention the fact that those cappuccino makers have about 1,005 parts, which need to be individually dismantled and cleaned after each use.

But, most importantly, we registered for gifts in *every* price range. When Bianca Sheppard got married the third time she registered at Tiffany's. The cheapest thing on her registry was a $125 sterling-silver lemonade stirrer. I'm not kidding. I couldn't afford to eat out for the next month. And I haven't had lemonade since.

10 April

I couldn't wait to tell Mandy the great news.

> ME
> Great news! Stephen just told me that
> the Ecuadorian woodwind band is
> already booked on June twenty-second!

> MANDY
> I know.

> ME
> What do you mean you know?

> MANDY
> They'll be playing at my cousin

233

Whitney's birthday party in the
Hamptons. You can thank me later.

Wow. Sometimes Mandy's *really* scary.

11 April

Stephen must have told his mother that I was having
difficulty finding a caterer because Mrs Stewart called me
at 7.15 a.m. to offer some assistance. She recommended
Betsy's Banquets. I thanked her for her help, and meant it
sincerely until she mentioned that Betsy's Banquets caters
for the Upstate Kennel Association. I've seen Mrs Stewart
feed Chuffy right off her plate too many times not to
wonder if Betsy feeds the dogs or their owners. Or both.

Don't get me wrong. I've got nothing against dogs.
Heck, I saw *Benji* six times. But that doesn't mean I want
to eat his food.

12 April

And people say I'm paranoid.

Last night Stephen and I went upstate for dinner. The
purpose of the evening was for us to bond as a family and
to review some issues regarding the wedding reception.

It was also the first time I'd seen Gram since her
unfortunate dental incident with my Sachertorte.

But the minute we arrived Gram was headed for the
door with bingo chips in one hand and a wad of singles in
the other. When I reminded her that the whole evening was
designed to enable Stephen to get to know the family she

just laughed. 'Oh, sweetheart. I don't need to be here for that. Besides, disappointment's a hard thing to witness.'

Excuse me?

Then as she exited the house I distinctly heard her whisper in Stephen's ear, 'Too bad you didn't marry up. Maybe next time.'

Stephen just laughed. He says every family's got a character and that Gram is ours. That's a real embracing, non-judgmental way of looking at things, and it certainly makes me more comfortable about the idea of introducing him to my Uncle Rudy who believes excessive belching to be a sign of appreciation. But what Stephen doesn't seem to understand is that Gram's no character. She's sharp as a tack.

That's not goofy talk she's spouting, it's venom.

13 April

The Wedding Cake. The culinary representation of our nuptial love. It had better be *really* good.

Wedding cakes from caterers tend to look great but taste like cardboard. The caterers are assuming that by the end of the festivities your eyesight will be sharp but your tastebuds will be catatonic from heavy drinking. In a perfect world I'd ask some gifted relative to bake us a towering *tour de force* of strawberry shortcake. But alas. My family specializes in Moist 'N Easy. The kind you microwave, not bake.

So I called Bianca Sheppard. The cakes have been delicious at every one of her weddings. Moist, creamy, and beautiful. Bianca says she gets all her wedding cakes from

Piece-A-Cake down in Little Italy. And, unlike her wedding dress recommendations, she swears Piece-A-Cake is reasonably priced.

Let's hope so. Otherwise it's my dear friend Mr Kipling.

14 April

We had an inter-office meeting today about the 'Faces In The City' issue. *My* issue.

In front of the entire staff I reviewed the progress we've made with our ten 'Faces'. I discussed the focus of each profile and what our writers had come up with thus far. That Face number five, Ingrid Narez, an infamous performance artist from Spanish Harlem, had insisted on doing most of her interviews wearing an eyepiece and no shirt was of particular interest to everyone.

After my formal presentation I took suggestions for the issue's sidebars. Kate proposed a survey about employee satisfaction with bosses. On a scale of one to ten, ten would be 'highly satisfied' and one was 'hoping for terminal illness'. Everyone laughed. Barry laughed the loudest.

Nice. Real nice. Besides, she *could* have been referring to him.

15 April

Finally we're getting something accomplished!

Lucy called with the name of the niece of a friend of hers in Wisconsin who is married to a caterer in upstate New

York. Confusing? Yes. But at least it works in my favor. Jeb is a graduate of the American Culinary Arts School and he's willing to work within our budget.

All hail, Lucy!

16 April

Mrs Stewart has invited me to join her and Kimberly next weekend at the annual Kennel Club Invitational. Chuffy's showing in the 'Open Bitch' category. Whatever that means.

Reasons to go
Nice to bond with future mother-in-law.

Reasons NOT to go
Afraid to bond with future mother-in-law.
Don't like Kimberly.
Don't like dogs *that* much.

Reasons why I HAVE to go
Mother-in-law will never forgive me if I say no.

What do you wear to a dog show?

17 April

I went upstate today to meet with Jeb the caterer. His house is like a glorified log cabin tucked deep in the woods so I expected he'd be a Grizzly Adams pioneer type. But no. He's this middle-aged white guy with dreadlocks. Standing in his huge commercial kitchen, he was busy slicing raw onions into a salad for a local horticulture club. His eyes were so bloodshot he could barely see but he cut straight to the chase.

'Here's the 411, Amy. No way we're doing lobster risotto and pumpkin bisque for ninety people with your budget. End of story. But I appreciate you're not wanting to go the traditional route of chicken, beef medallions, etc. So my suggestion is to go ethnic. Mix things up. Do some couscous, stewed vegetables, seared fruits, then throw a little lamb in there to sate everyone's carnal needs. I know that your group isn't accustomed to feasting on nuts and berries but these things are cheap. Besides, it'll enable you to put your money into some top-quality lamb. It'll *seem* expensive but it won't be. We'll craft a visual presentation so sensual it'll look like Manet on a plate.'

My mom, Mrs Stewart and Mandy are going to hate this guy. I gave him a deposit on the spot.

18 April

Mr and Mrs Stewart are struggling to establish a vaguely civil relationship for the sake of their children. How thoughtful. Unfortunately they've decided to use our wedding as Part One of the peace process.

Their first point of agreement in a year and a half: they will jointly host (read: pay for) our rehearsal dinner the night before the wedding. Mrs Stewart will select the restaurant. Mr Stewart will split the cost.

Their second point of agreement in a year and a half:

Stephen's brother Tom can't be a guest at the wedding. He must be a groomsman.

Stephen is furious. I'm incredulous. Tom is delighted. He's already called Stephen twice to say he won't wear a cummerbund.

Tom, Mitch and Larry. It's like having the Three Stooges at our wedding. So why pay for live entertainment when I can just shoot myself instead?

19 April

Now that Tom's a groomsman I need another bridesmaid. I thought about asking Kathy or Paula but I just kept coming back to Anita. It's simply the right thing to do – whether she knows it or not.

So after forty-five minutes of begging her to see things from my perspective, and ultimately invoking her poetic endorsement of my marriage to Stephen,[41] Anita finally agreed: 'Well if I'm going to be at the circus, I might as well be one of the clowns.'

Ain't love grand?

20 April

My third fitting with Katrina. It's barely two months away from the most important fashion day of my life and I still look like I should be birthing livestock rather than getting married.

---

[41] 'Maybe it won't be so pathetic.'

As God is my witness I'm going to bury this dress the minute my wedding is over.

Meanwhile Mandy wants to know if I've chosen the bridesmaids' dresses. She's worried about having enough time to properly accessorize. The bride won't have shoes but the maid-of-honor will have a stunning handbag.

Since I can barely dress myself for this event I've decided to relinquish all issues concerning bridesmaids' dresses to Mandy. I don't even care if she, Nicole and Anita wear the same style. Let them choose something they like and will wear again. As long as it's ankle-length and sleeveless I'll be happy.

That should please Anita. She's got fabulous upper arms.

21 April

I finally got a chance to call Piece-A-Cake. They scheduled a tasting for 6 June. Stephen's promised to come with me. Since I view the cake as a symbol of our union it needs to be something we both like. But since I'm allergic to hazelnuts (I break out in hives) and mocha gives him migraines (it reminds him of a particularly stressful childhood vacation his family took in Zurich), we've got to be careful. Luckily we both like strawberry.

22 April

The Kennel Club Invitational was today. Who knew dogs used hairspray? Chuffy herself wore more Aqua Net than all the geriatric women of south Florida. Sure she was sticky but she looked good.

And when's the last time you heard a bunch of well-dressed people say things like 'She's a delightful bitch.' Can't remember? Well, welcome to Thousand Pines Country Club in upstate New York! Sure they allow blacks and Jews, but half-breed mutts without pedigree? Forget it. The local pound's down the road.

The fact is, these pooches are worth more than I am. It's humbling. Not to mention educational. Among the many things I learned today:

- If the ship were sinking and Mrs Stewart could save only one family member, she'd choose Chuffy.
- Kimberly has an unrelenting obsession with expensive jewelry. Particularly that which now belongs to me.
- Never wear open-toe shoes to a dog show.

23 April

Bianca Sheppard's getting married again. Who knew she was even dating? I called Mandy the minute I got the invitation. Apparently Bianca met George Carson a few weeks ago at the dermatologist's office. She had heat rash. He had eczema. Love was a foregone conclusion.

And who knows? Maybe the fifth time's a charm. I hope so – for George's sake.

They're getting married here in the city in the Markson Hotel ballroom (where I happen to know the basic venue charge starts at twelve thousand dollars). And even though it's just two weeks before our wedding I think we'll go anyway. By that point I'll be thrilled to think about a wedding other than my own.

24 April

It's been more than three weeks since my last sex dream. At this rate I'll be off Anita's sleeping meds any day now. And, though I'm enormously relieved, it's also begun to strike me as a bit depressing that getting married means denying yourself the right to such pleasures. Maybe Anita's right. Maybe these dreams are harmless. After all, I am marrying Stephen. What greater commitment could I offer another human being? Does dreaming of lustful sex with someone else take anything away from that? Do I love Stephen any less? Of course not. And I bet Stephen would agree. After all he's free to have sex dreams, too, if he wants. It wouldn't bother me a bit. Unless, of course, he were dreaming about Louise. I mean, come on, she's built like friggin' Barbie. But it doesn't matter. Stephen wouldn't have sex dreams. Sure he likes sex. A lot, actually. But he's not the type to dream about it.

Is he?

25 April

The shit has officially hit the fan.

I got a phone call at 1.30 this afternoon from George Harriman of Harriman Carpets, one of the 'Faces In The

City' profiles. He'd been sitting at the Park Avenue Café for over an hour waiting for me to show up to a lunch meeting that I didn't even know was scheduled. He was understandably ticked off. I apologized profusely for the mix-up, promised to reschedule with his secretary, then stormed out of my office and gave Kate a scolding that she'd never forget. I reminded her that Mr Harriman's profile was a focal point of the issue, that Mr Harriman's time was incredibly valuable as he's on the board of directors for over twelve different charitable organizations, was the regional spokesperson for the Urban Children's League and ran one of the biggest carpet companies in the country. Then I told her the next time she wanted to forget to inform me about a meeting she should choose someone less important.

That's when Kate stood up and informed *me* that she had told me about the meeting, that it was written in my appointment book, and that she had included it on today's itinerary – a copy of which was sitting on top of my desk.

I looked at my appointment book. She was absolutely right. The meeting was right there. The whole thing was my fault. And everyone in the office knew it.

26 April – 2 a.m.

I can't sleep. I keep thinking about that girl in my freshman literature class. The one who married the guy with chronic dandruff. She was so desperate to marry and there were hundreds of guys to choose from – wealthy, handsome, pre-med, pre-law, well groomed. But she chose the one with decent tennis skills and dandruff.

I used to think it was an act of desperation but now I think maybe it was love.

26 April

I broke down today in the office bathroom. Tears of appreciation all over the place. Because things aren't good. They're *great*.

When all this fighting, negotiating, and planning is over I am going to spend the rest of my life with the world's most incredible man. Someone who may not be perfect but who understands me, accepts my faults, loves my strengths and keeps me smiling no matter how many foolish ideas he has about the wedding band.

I don't ever want another wet and wild sex dream again. Not about Rick or Anthony or Jon or Denny or Jonas or Tim or Dylan. All I want is Stephen. My wonderfully boring Stephen!

Overwhelmed by emotion, I decided to call Stephen's office and share my love. Louise answered his phone. Apparently Stephen had stepped away from his desk. After offering to take a message she mentioned how sorry she was that the Ecuadorian woodwind band had fallen through. It seems she's a fan.

But if the band plays in the subway station near Stephen's house and Louise lives all the way across town how does she know what they sound like?

Breathe. I must remember to breathe.

And then I called Anita.

ME

This is a warning. Louise is a sign. I've
been inconsiderate, self-centered, and I
enjoyed my sex dreams. I'm being
punished.

ANITA

By whom?

ME

By God!

ANITA

God? I thought you were an agnostic.

ME

I am. I was. Maybe I'm reconsidering.

ANITA

Don't tell me you found God while
planning your wedding. Where was She?
Hiding in the flatware department?

ME

I'm being serious, Anita.

ANITA

That's what worries me. Look, this is
why I didn't want you to get married.
It's turning you into an idiot. Besides,
assuming there is a God, don't you think
She'd be more merciful than to pit one
woman against another?

ME
You've got a point.

ANITA
That's the first intelligent thing you've
said in months. Now remember, if you
start hearing strange voices, it's not God
– it's your Inner Bride. So unless she's
telling you to serve premium liquors at
your reception, silence her immediately.
She's *insane*.

27 April

The good news and the bad news.

The good news: I went upstate tonight to sample the
menu Jeb is proposing for our wedding reception. Lamb
with almonds and currants, couscous and glazed yams . . .
It was fabulous! As is Jeb, who continues to be the most
pleasant, easy-going man despite his on-going battle with
hayfever. I may not be having a fancy New York City
wedding in some elegant ballroom but you can be damn
sure the food will be KICK ASS. No beef medallions for this
gal.

The bad news: on the way back to the train station I
stopped in the mall to buy a twelve-pack of nylons. A man
was taking a leak against the side of the building. It was
Reverend MacKenzie.

WHILE YOU WERE OUT   4/29 11.05 AM
From: Your Wedding Photographer
Message: Has a last-minute double
suicide to photograph. Needs to
reschedule this afternoon's meeting about
portraits.

WHILE YOU WERE OUT   4/29 11.06 AM
From: Kate
Message: Your voicemail box is too full
to accept messages. Please empty it
IMMEDIATELY.

WHILE YOU WERE OUT   4/29 11.15 AM
From: Mandy
Message: Has chosen an ankle-length
sleeveless dress made of Asian nubby silk
in an elegant cherub pink with a hint of
silver for the bridesmaids. Will this co-
ordinate with your tablecloths?

WHILE YOU WERE OUT   4/29 11.25 AM
From: Julie Browning
Message: Anne von Trier wants a
guarantee that her profile will be ahead
of James Royce's. Can she do that?

WHILE YOU WERE OUT   4/29 11.35 AM
From: Anita
Message: What the hell is 'Asian nubby
silk in an elegant cherub pink with a

hint of silver' and why does she have to
wear it?

WHILE YOU WERE OUT   4/29 11.43 AM
From: Jeb the caterer
Message: Has forgotten how many
people he's supposed to be feeding at
your wedding.

WHILE YOU WERE OUT   4/29 11.45 AM
From: Mr Spaulding
Message: Bring the article drafts for the
June issue to the 12.30 meeting.

WHILE YOU WERE OUT   4/29 11.49 AM
From: Mandy
Message: Please inform Anita that verbal
abuse is an inappropriate mode of
communication among civilized human
beings. Especially since cherub pink will
help to offset her sallow undertones.

WHILE YOU WERE OUT   4/29 12.04 PM
From: Anita
Message: The entire concept of
bridesmaids and bridesmaids' dresses is
hateful and barbaric. Could she tend bar
instead?

WHILE YOU WERE OUT   4/29 12.15 PM
From: Stephen
Message: Has to work late again. Don't
wait up.

WHILE YOU WERE OUT   4/29 12.25 PM
From: Rick
Message: 'Long time no see.' Back in
town. Has a conga-drum gig at the
China Club tonight. Wants to catch up.

WHILE YOU WERE OUT   4/29 12.35 PM
From: Mr Spaulding
Message: They're waiting for you in the
12.30 meeting.

WHILE YOU WERE OUT   4/29 12.48 PM
From: Kate
Message: Payroll doesn't have my check.
You never signed my time sheet. My rent
is due TOMORROW.

WHILE YOU WERE OUT   4/29 12.53 PM
From: Mr Spaulding
Message: Where are you?

WHILE YOU WERE OUT   4/29 1.05 PM
From: Mr Spaulding
Message: Wants to see you in his office
immediately.

WHILE YOU WERE OUT   4/29 1.06 PM
From: Macy's Linen Department
Message: Your grandmother-in-law has
purchased monogrammed towels for you.
The store needs to confirm the spelling of
your name. Is it 'Stewart' or 'Stuart'?

From: Kate
Message: I quit.

30 April

Mr Spaulding called me into his office to discuss my ability to see my 'Faces In The City' issue through to completion. Perhaps *Barry* should take over. The weasel! I adamantly assured him that wouldn't be necessary. He's giving me one more – read: LAST – chance.

Meanwhile Kate has really gone. Poof! Like a cloud of angry smoke. She requested her final paycheck and COBRA medical extension. She even took her Backstreet Boys screen-saver. Barry is livid.

And I feel horrible. About Kate. Not Barry. My life has become this huge mass of scary – that spews. I'd run from me too, if I could. But I can't.

30 April – 10 p.m.

If a man who is prone to spontaneous gestures suddenly proposes marriage what are the chances that he really means it? Sure he planned my proposal. Sort of. But it's not like he ever mentioned marriage before that.

30 April – 10.30 p.m.

MANDY
Well, at least this time you had the
decency to have your panic attack *before*
my bedtime.

ME
I'm serious, Mandy. Do you think he
regrets proposing?

MANDY
Did he actually go with you to register
for sheets?

ME
Yes.

MANDY
Then what greater sign of commitment
do you expect from a man? Now, relax.
There's no reason to worry.

2 May

The first step in solving a problem is admitting you have
one: I can't plan this wedding alone.

There, I said it. Ugly but true – I need *help*.

I'd ask Stephen but he's too consumed with his
computer program. He can barely get dressed in the
morning let alone help plan a wedding reception. As for
the band he's supposed to hire . . . I figure we'll be firing up
my dad's eight-track and poppin' in some Pat Boone.

Then there's Mandy who, despite her pledge of fealty, has basically retreated into the matrimonial black hole with Jon.

It's time for desperate measures.

3 May

I asked my mother for help.

I chose five specific tasks for her to handle. Things I can't possibly do and she can't possibly screw up. I feel better already. It was the best decision I've ever made. And she was delighted.

Who knows? Maybe it was a mistake not to ask for her help from the start.

I'm such an idiot.

4 May

Nicole called this evening. She wanted to talk. (Okay.) She wanted to come over right away. (Curious.) Alone. (Ding-ding-ding!) That's when I knew something was wrong. The last time my sister came over to my apartment alone was four years ago when I got stuck in a bustier that I bought on a whim. It was the kind that slips over your head. Getting it on was a quiet struggle but as I fought to get out of it the metal stays caught my hair and left me naked from the waist up with my arms trapped above my head and the bustier wrapped around my face. Dialing the telephone necessitated a whole new yoga position. And since unlocking the door was physically impossible, I called Nicole who had an extra set of my keys. It was that or my dad and there simply wasn't enough therapy in the world that could have enabled us to recover from that experience.

But tonight as I waited for Nicole it occurred to me that perhaps she was attempting some type of pre-wedding sisterly bonding. The kind of thing Jane Austen characters did. But when she walked through the door I knew something was wrong. She looked anxious and tired. Like she hadn't slept in weeks.

> ME
> Are you all right?

> NICOLE
> Yes and no. I need to talk to you about
> something. Something important.

As she sat down on the sofa Nicole took a cigarette out of her purse. My sister hasn't smoked since she was twenty-one and Chet made quitting a condition of their marriage. She glanced around the apartment and chuckled.

> NICOLE
> Hey, do you remember the time I came
> over here to rescue you from that crazy
> push-up bra—

> ME
> Yeah, yeah. It was a bustier and that's
> not why you came here. Now, what's
> going on?

NICOLE
Chet and I are splitting up.

It was like someone punched me in the stomach, then banged my head against the wall. I don't remember sitting down but suddenly I was.

ME
Are you kidding me?

NICOLE
No. It's real and it's final.

ME
What happened?

NICOLE
A lot of things. It's been coming for a while.

ME
I had no idea.

NICOLE
We didn't advertise.

ME
But I mean, there's got to be a reason
... Oh, God, is there someone else?

She looked at me in shock.

NICOLE
How did you know that?

ME
Sonofabitch! I always suspected Chet was
too good to be true. Under that Perfect
Man façade was a dirtbag having an
affair with some tramp!

NICOLE
Actually, I'm the dirtbag having the
affair.

ME
Excuse me?

NICOLE
I said I'm the one who's having the
affair. And Pablo's no tramp.

ME
Who the hell is Pablo?

NICOLE
Pablo's the guy I've been seeing for the
last six months.

ME
Six months!!!!

NICOLE
I know how it sounds. But it's for the

best. Chet and I haven't been happy for
a while.

Nicole spent the next two hours telling me how her marriage was a mistake from the beginning. How she and Chet were so used to being together after all those years in college and how they were afraid of the uncertainty which their post-college future held that they had married out of fear and complacency. The first year was fine but after that things just got bad. They simply weren't happy. And while Chet was willing to spend the rest of his life in denial, Nicole wasn't. She wanted to be happy. She wanted a chance to find her true self.

As I listened to Nicole's story, and wondered how some guy named Pablo who works for the cable company could help my sister find her true self, I began to feel increasingly sick. I know it sounds selfish – my sister and her husband get divorced and *I* have a nervous breakdown – but I couldn't help it. I'd always considered their relationship to be the gold standard for a healthy marriage. One where the participants were blissfully in love and whose inner workings seemed harmonious. I'd thought if I was really lucky I could have a marriage like hers. Now I'd learned that the ideal to which I aspired didn't really exist. What did that mean for me?

Nicole stood up to go.

NICOLE
Thanks for listening.

Hey, if I couldn't be there to support her wedding, I might as well be there to support her divorce.

NICOLE
I guess I just wanted to practice on you
before telling Mom and Dad. I know
they're going to be devastated. I just
hope they remember that it's my
happiness which counts most.

Yeah, right. That's what I was hoping for and look what
happened there – value, size and frontier wedding attire.

NICOLE
Oh, and thanks for giving me the
courage to end my marriage.

ME
Why me?

NICOLE
It was listening to your wedding plans
that made me realize I had to leave Chet.

Excuse me, *what*?
But it was too late. She was already out the door.

5 May

CHET AND NICOLE ARE DIVORCING.
CHET AND NICOLE ARE DIVORCING.
CHET AND NICOLE ARE DIVORCING.

6 May – 2 a.m.

Just when I'd gotten used to the idea of me being married Chet and Nicole are breaking up. It's like the whole world's flipped inside-out.

Or maybe things have been backward from the start. Maybe it's Nicole who's not the marrying kind.

6 May

I went down to Chinatown and picked up the invitations from Bunny. It was the first really hot day we've had this year and Bunny's shop hasn't got air-conditioning. One would think the case of Budweiser chilling in a Styrofoam cooler by the cash register would help Bunny beat the heat. But no. To relieve her discomfort, and add to everyone else's, seventy-something Bunny was wearing hot pants and a halter top. It wasn't pretty.

But the invitations are. Crisp, clean, and pristine, they're beautiful.

As I turned to exit the shop Bunny hacked up some smoker's phlegm and offered a nugget of wisdom: 'Listen, kid, marriage can be great or it can stink. My first two were disasters. But the third was a keeper. We had twenty-six terrific years, right up to the minute he kicked from liver failure. And if I hadn't spent those five years in court fighting over his bodily remains with the *other* wife he'd been hiding up in Buffalo, my memories of him would be nothing but sweet.'

Yes, Bunny. Love *is* a battlefield.

ROBERT AND THERESA THOMAS
AND
MS ABIGAIL BROCKTON STEWART
AND
MR JAMES W. STEWART

Joyfully Invite You to Share
in the Celebration as Their Children

Amy Sarah Thomas
&

Stephen Richard Stewart

Tie the Knot of Matrimonial Delight
on June 22nd
2 in the Afternoon
at the United Presbyterian Church

In Hopbrook, NY
Dinner Reception To Follow, Chez Thomas
RSVP
Festive Attire

7 May

My parents are refusing to discuss Nicole's divorce. Something along the lines of if they ignore it it will go away. Fat chance. I've been trying that with Gram since Christmas.

On another unfortunate note, Human Resources still hasn't found a replacement for Kate, and Barry won't stop grousing about it. Loudly. Especially when Mr Spaulding's within earshot. Our temps have ranged from English-as-a-second-language students to unemployed street performers. How a street performer can be out of work is beyond me. But suffice to say that not one of them has known Microsoft Office or where to buy a decent pair of wedding shoes.

That's right – I asked.

8 May

While Stephen and Mitch went to hear potential wedding bands at a Long Island club, Paula and Kathy came to my apartment to help prepare the invitations. I'd already had my temp address the envelopes on the laser printer at work but we still had to stuff the envelopes (invites, protective tissue paper, response cards) and stamp them. We were doing fine until I noticed that Kathy had started to slip. Her once neatly aligned stamps were suddenly slapped haphazardly on envelopes. Some listed to the left, others sloped to the right. How much skill is required to stamp an envelope? I immediately reassigned tasks.

We were done by midnight. After a crazed scramble back in March, the invitations were now under control: 120 beautiful invitations would be mailed out six weeks prior to my wedding. Eat your heart out, *BB*.

9 May

Having completed her five designated wedding tasks my mother decided to take the bull by the horns. Shooting straight from the hip it was Tough Love all over the place.

My menu is too outlandish. My floor plan has no 'flow'. My floral design is poorly conceived. And my caterer is a *pothead*?

'Come on, Amy. You honestly didn't know? Why do you think his eyes are always bloodshot?'

'I don't know. Onions, hayfever, a high pollen count?'

'Try a quarter ounce of reefer a day. Trust me. I teach public school. I know these things.'

Reefer, food, flowers, flow. Whatever. Just handle it. I hereby abdicate my throne.

10 May

Things are starting to come together. The July issue of *Round-Up* is falling into place with an extensive six-page article on hot trends in municipal playgrounds. My 'Faces In The City' issue is on schedule with four of the ten profiles already completed. And my wedding is now officially a Terry Thomas Production.

Welcome back, life.

11 May

Stephen hired a band for our wedding. Diggie's Delight will be headlining at the Thomas–Stewart reception. Though they favor classic rock songs, their repertoire ranges from classical to jazz instrumentals, they own their own sound system, and for an extra fifty bucks they'll provide the ceremony music.

Sold.

12 May

Mrs Stewart and Chuffy joined us at United Presbyterian for our second meeting with Reverend MacKenzie. We reviewed the basic structure of the ceremony and the wording of the vows.

Afterwards, Mrs Stewart reminisced about United Presbyterian – the moving Christmas pageants, the invaluable Sunday-school lessons – then broke down in tears about her life ravaged by divorce, a world that no longer appreciates heavy brocades and her preliminary stages of menopause. As Stephen comforted his mother the only thing I could think of was Reverend MacKenzie *peeing* in broad daylight, and how *not* to shake his hand.

On the train ride home, as Stephen and I cuddled in our seat, he happened to mention that Louise has cancelled her wedding. Something about cold feet.

12 May – 9 p.m.

> MANDY
> Okay, Amy. It's time to worry.

13 May

Due to insufficient postage all 120 invitations have been returned. My elegant invitations are now covered in hefty black RETURN TO SENDER stamps.

Can this be anything but an ugly omen?

14 May

My newest temp is a musical-theater aficionado named Fabrizio. Although he's a fairly good secretary, he can't seem to work without singing Sondheim. As much as this annoys me, it drives Barry absolutely nuts. Barry hates Sondheim. He's more the Andrew Lloyd Webber type. Think *Evita*.

So it was with mixed feelings that I interrupted Fabrizio's snappy rendition of 'I Feel Pretty' to send him down to Bunny's to get 120 new envelopes. When he returned I had him print the addresses and restuff all the invitations. I was about to have him mail them when I reconsidered. I'm already one week behind *BB*'s schedule so there's no room for error. I personally went to the twenty-four-hour post office and mailed them myself.

Afterward Mandy came to my apartment to show me the bridesmaid dresses. Ankle-length, sleeveless, and a stunning shade of rosy-pink, the dresses are classy and sophisticated. Everything that my wedding gown should be but *isn't*.

What the hell's the point of having a wedding if the bridesmaids look better than the bride? This event is supposed to be about *me*. I'm the center of attention. I should be the best-looking, or at least the best-dressed, woman in the room.

But what can I do? It's certainly not like I can say that to anyone. They'd think I was the most egoistic person on the planet. And maybe I am. But that's okay.

I'm the damn bride!

Meanwhile I can't help but worry that the man I'm about to marry is having an affair with his genetically perfect female co-worker. On a rational level I know Stephen is good, honest, and faithful. But he's still *human*. And anyone who watches daytime television knows that every man with proper urological functions has been unfaithful at some point in his life. Hell, if it weren't for infidelity and evil twins, soap operas would cease to exist.

And while Anita says my Inner Bride is insane, Mandy is convinced that no one gets cold feet and cancels their wedding unless they've met someone else. I'm just praying that someone else isn't Stephen.

Is there a non-confrontational way to ask your fiancé if he's nailing his co-worker?

15 May

Turns out Nicole's paramour Pablo not only works for the cable company but he is the guy who comes to your house and hooks up your service. Stephen suggested that if you can't beat them, understand them, or condone their actions, the least you can do is get free cable. I think he's on to something.

NEW YORK ELECTRIC WORKS

'We keep the energy flowing'

Dear Valued Customer,
Please be informed that your check to
New York Electric Works in the amount
of $45.19 has been returned unpaid. If
you do not pay the entire amount due
by the end of this minth a 19% interest
rate will be assessed on your balance.
Additionally, as per our company policy,
a $15 returned check fee has been
assessed on your account.

Sincerely,
Narda Mingala
Account Representative

16 May

This is great. Here I am throwing a ten-thousand-dollar party but I can't pay my damn electric bill!

17 May

We're Jewish.

18 May

At first I thought it was some old show tune. The forgotten 'We're Jewish' medley from *Fiddler*. But no. As Mrs Stewart, Stephen and I sat around the living room merrily telling my folks about the beautiful United Presbyterian Church I could sense that all this joy was really making Gram mad.

So I wasn't too concerned when she suddenly stood up and clutched her heart. I figured this was just the most recent in her string of attention-stealing ploys. The old heart-attack routine: clutch your heart, hold your breath and get that faraway look in your eyes. Standard summer-stock fare.

I am so naïve.

Heart-attacks are for amateurs. Gram is a world-class pro. 'We're Jewish!'

Excuse me?

'No church. No minister. It's an insult. It's a *shandeh*!'

A *shandeh*? Since when did Gram start honing up on her Yiddish? From the corner of my eye I saw Mrs Stewart clutch Chuffy tightly to her bosom, no doubt wondering what the hell a *shandeh* was.

Mom struggled to reason with Gram. But Gram just shook her head. Her parents were conservative Jews. They had a Judaica store in New Jersey for which she used to make ceramic *draydls*. But my grandfather was Protestant so she didn't mention it. After they were married she moved to upstate New York and raised her family in a Christian home. She didn't want to inconvenience anyone. Until *now*.

It seems that thirty-five days prior to my wedding is the

most convenient time to mention that my family is intimately linked to thousands of years of religious history and turbulent social events. That my people are strewn from New York to Jerusalem. That we are the Chosen.

Well, that's just swell. Had it been any other point in time I would have been interested to hear all about it. But not *now*. Not when I'm getting ready to tie the knot in a Presbyterian church under the eyes of friends, family, and Reverend MacKenzie.

'What do you mean "no church"? It's a done deal. We've reserved the date. Mailed the invitations. Had pre-marital counseling with the minister!'

My mother tried to calm me, to contain the situation, to make sense of those years spent painting Easter eggs. 'Mother, please. Are you *certain* you're Jewish?'

'Of course I'm certain. What do you think? Jews are stupid? Don't forget this makes all of you Jewish too.'

With enough of her own domestic problems to last a lifetime Mrs Stewart slipped Chuffy into her handbag and politely said her goodbyes. Two minutes later she was gone. Like a rat from a sinking ship.

How dare Gram turn my wedding into a sinking ship! I was furious. My parents were speechless. And Gram was on her way to bingo – but not before declaring me an anti-Semite and shoving my college graduation photo to the floor.

The up-side? Stephen finally agrees that Gram's a lunatic.

19 May

Chapter Thirty-nine of *BB* suggests that couples alleviate stress by taking mini-vacations prior to their wedding.

Where can we go on $23.50?

20 May

My family is still stunned by Gram's outburst concerning our Jewish roots. Considering how much energy we're already expending to plan my wedding, and to deny Nicole's divorce, it's a miracle we're not running to some clinic, begging for sedatives.

Thankfully my mother, who for the first twenty-four hours was leaning toward official conversion for the entire family, has eased up on the issue. She's come to her senses and agreed that my wedding should go ahead as planned – whether or not Gram chooses to attend. I suspect this has something to do with her realization that, as an observant, kosher Jew, she'd need to wash two sets of dishes and forgo bacon.

Meanwhile Mandy insists I resolve the Stephen/Louise issue a.s.a.p. 'How can you, in good faith, enter into a lifelong union with someone who may be cheating on you? A happy marriage is based on trust.'

She's right.

So we've decided to go behind Stephen's back and spend next Wednesday spying on him.

21 May

We got our first RSVP for the wedding today. It was so

exciting to see that familiar cream-colored envelope sitting in the mailbox.

And I can't tell you how pleased I was to learn that Hans Lindstrom will be attending my wedding.

23 May

More RSVPs. People are actually coming to my parents' house festively attired on 22 June.

Now I *have* to get married!

24 May

I've been trying to reach Anita for the past week. I know she's been busy – certainly every time I call her office she's either in a meeting or on an important call. But for Christ's sake, it's *Teen Flair*. How important can it be? Have the Hanson boys cut their hair? Has cherry-flavored lipgloss been linked to weight gain?

Doesn't she realize that my wedding is twenty-nine days away and I still don't have my beautiful rhinestone hair comb? Had she even remembered her promise to take her niece Molly to the Bridal Building and buy it for me? Sure Lucy's blue enamel barrette is beautiful but that hair comb is the finishing touch!

I kept trying.

> ME
> Hi, it's Amy Thomas calling again. Is Ms
> Jensen available?

ANITA'S SECRETARY

No, I'm afraid Ms Jensen is in the ladies'
room.

ME

Again? That's the fifth time today.

ANITA'S SECRETARY

Yes, well, I'm afraid Ms Jensen is
suffering from a urinary-tract infection.

Wait a minute . . . A *urinary tract infection*? Anita was
avoiding me just like I'd avoided Mandy![42]
And who could blame her? I've called her ten times a
day, panicked about Stephen and Louise, complained
incessantly about my dress, and even cried once or twice or
seventeen times over my non-existent shoes.

HAVE I BECOME A MANDY![43]

Anita's secretary must have sensed my sudden horror
because she put me on hold. Moments later Anita
answered the phone.

ANITA

Hi, Amy. What's going on?

ME

Look, I know you've been avoiding me

---

[42] Except her secretary was obviously more of a 'team player' than Kate
ever was. Kate absolutely refused to use the UTI excuse.

[43] So much for New Year's resolutions Nos 4 and 5.

and I'm sorry that I've called you ten
times today—

ANITA
Sixteen.

ME
Whatever. Just tell me if you and Molly
went and got my hair comb.

ANITA
Yes, we went. No, we didn't get the
comb.

ME
Why not?

ANITA
Because it's not a hair comb, Amy. It's a
tiara.

ME
Come on, Anita. You know how
important that comb is to me, and you
didn't buy it because Mrs Cho thinks it's
for kids?

ANITA
It *is* for kids. It's what prepubescent girls
wear in those pervy child beauty
pageants.

ME
But it's an integral part of my hairstyle!

ANITA
And you're a thirty-year-old woman
obsessing on some toddler's Taiwanese
tiara. Now calm down. I'll call you later.

First of all, it's Korean, not Taiwanese. Second, how the hell am I supposed to 'calm down'?

Single people just don't get it.

25 May

I no longer need to go undercover with Mandy in an effort to assess my fiancé's fidelity.

The truth is out.

I dropped by Stephen's office. Unannounced. Just a friendly 'in the neighborhood, thought I'd say hello' visit. But no sooner did I push the elevator button than the doors opened wide, and off stepped Louise – with her tongue jammed down the throat of a *hunky, six-foot-tall blond with the body of an Adonis!* Nothing at all like Stephen!

25 May – 11.30 p.m.

The fact that I so easily lost faith in Stephen's love is frightening. Nicole, the Stewarts, and Bianca Sheppard-Douglas-Izzard-Santos-Rabinowitz are all proof of the fragility of marriage.

But true love should be hard as a rock.

It's something I see between the Brocktons, my parents, and though Stephen would kill me if he heard me say this, I also see it with his father and Misty. Love is strong, binding, and brave. It rises to the top – even if it is unpopular.

I know our love is strong. I really do. But I've got to remember that nothing survives without faith.

26 May

We got our first official wedding gift today.

Stephen and I are now the proud joint owners of a shiny seven-speed blender with an adjustable base.

27 May

It's amazing how much progress has been made since my mother ascended to the wedding-planner throne.

Chairs, tables, table linens, a tent and the dance floor have all been rented. Bartenders have been hired. The floral design has been reconceived and orders have been placed. The menu has been revised.[44] And the wine has been purchased. All in just two weeks. Asking my mother to help was the smartest decision I've made since deciding to marry Stephen.

And work's back on track too. Since I'll be honeymooning until mid-July, D-day on the proofs for my 'Faces' issue

---

[44] After weeks of negotiation, Jeb finally agreed to serve chicken breast if my mother promised to stop pressuring him about entering drug rehab.

is set at the second week of June. To make sure I meet that deadline I've instituted a new rule – no wedding-related phone calls at the office. And this time I'm sticking to it. Be it the florist or the band-leader, leave a message on my machine at home. And if it's an emergency call my mother. I've purchased a pager for her, which has convinced her fourth-grade students that she's dealing drugs on the side. They are thoroughly delighted.

But that's not to say that things at work are calm. On the contrary, tensions are running high. Barry spent the morning short-tempered and muttering as Fabrizio serenaded us with a medley from *Gypsy*. Somewhere around the chorus of 'Everything's Coming Up Roses', Barry snapped. 'Dammit, Fabrizio, Sondheim's a wordy light-weight with no passion!'

Fabrizio gasped. Then shrieked, 'Andrew Lloyd Webber's a hack and a plagiarist!'

I was expecting fisticuffs.

But as much as Barry despises Sondheim, he knows Fabrizio's the best temp we've had since Kate's departure. So he directed the remainder of his frustration at me. 'You! This is all your fault. Kate didn't sing Sondheim! Kate didn't even know who Sondheim is! Now, for Christ's sake, would you hurry up and get married? *You're killing me here!*'

My pleasure, Barry, except I still don't have shoes!

LY EVIL AND ENDLESS
Official ∧ THINGS TO DO List
1. ~~Choose wedding date~~
2. ~~Tell boss wedding date~~

3. Vacation time for honeymoon
4. Decide on honeymoon
5. Get minister/church
6. Choose reception venue
7. Make guest list
8. Choose maid of honor
9. Choose best man
10. Register for gifts
11. Arrange for engagement party
12. Buy engagement ring
13. Buy wedding rings
14. Buy wedding dress
15. Choose maid-of-honor dress
16. Order wedding cake
17. Hire caterer
18. Hire band for reception
19. Order flowers for ceremony
20. Buy shoes
21. Plan rehearsal dinner
22. Invites to rehearsal dinner
23. Hire musicians for ceremony
24. Decide on dress code
25. Get marriage license
26. Hire videographer
27. Hire photographer
28. Order table flowers
29. Order bouquets
30. Order boutonnières for men
31. Order nosegays for women
32. Order invitations
33. Decide on wine selection

34. ~~Postage for invitations~~
35. Choose hairstyle and makeup
36. ~~Buy gifts for attendants~~
37. Buy thank-you notes
38. Announce wedding in newspaper
39. Buy headpiece
40. ~~Buy travelers' checks for honeymoon~~
41. ~~Apply for visas~~
42. ~~Get shots and vaccinations~~
43. ~~Order tent if necessary~~
44. ~~Order chairs/tables if necessary~~
45. ~~Make budget~~
46. ~~Divide expenses~~
47. ~~Make table-seating charts~~
48. ~~Choose bridesmaid dress~~
49. ~~Decide on menu~~
50. ~~Decide on *hors d'oeuvres*~~
51. Decide on dinner service style
52. Decide on staff–guest ratio
53. Decide seated or buffet
54. Reserve vegetarian meals
55. ~~Reserve band/photographer meals~~
56. Make photo list
57. Choose hotel for wedding night
58. Hire limo for church–reception transport
59. Buy guest book for reception
60. Find hotel for out-of-towners
61. Decide on liquor selection
62. ~~Hire bartenders~~
63. Verify wheelchair accessibility

64. Choose processional music
65. Choose recessional music
66. Choose cocktail music
67. Choose reception music
68. Choose ceremony readings
69. Prepare birdseed instead of rice
70. Schedule manicure/pedicure/wax

28 May

It was an act of desperation but I have less than *four weeks*. Can you really blame me for going to Manfield Blossom – one of the most expensive shoe stores in the entire world? Let ye not be the first to cast a stone lest ye be in possession of a fabulous pair of wedding shoes!

The store, located just off Fifth Avenue's rarified shopping district, looks like a fancy gift box. It's tiny and immaculate and filled with wildly expensive merchandise. Shoes for thousands of dollars. Handbags for the annual cost of an entire family of migrant laborers. You know you can't afford to shop there just by looking at it. So I dressed up for the occasion. Not to celebrate my folly but to avoid detection. The last thing I wanted was to set off some snotty salesperson's riff-raff meter. Just let me shop in peace, and quietly check out the price tags, without any hassle or humiliation.

And there they were. My wedding shoes. A pair of lovely cream-colored Mary Janes with a Holly Golightly twist – rich satin, a sturdy heel, and an understated square buckle.

One problem. They were *four hundred dollars*.

Quick! If I cancel the bridesmaids' bouquets and the band plays for three hours instead of four can I afford it? Yes! Minutes later a saleswoman dressed in skin-tight designer clothing was slipping the shoe of my dreams on to my foot—

Or was she?

My toes were in but the top of my foot wasn't. The saleswoman was pushing the heel. I was pulling the strap. But the shoe refused to surrender. It wanted nothing to do with my foot. Then, adding insult to insult, the saleswoman looked up and said, 'Your feet are too fleshy for our shoes.'

Too fleshy? What? Like they should go on a diet? Be shipped to fat camp for the summer? Walk off a couple pounds? Is it my fault Manfield Blossom's shoes are designed for anorexics with bony feet who can afford to pay exorbitant prices because they don't spend money on food?

So much for avoiding detection.

29 May

It's official. I'm having an afternoon reception with a chicken buffet, New York State wine and tap water. When I reminded my mother that some people don't eat chicken she just scoffed, 'It's a wedding reception, not an airplane ride. We don't need a *selection*.' She's right. Screw 'em. No lobster risotto, French wines or lamb. Value and size. Thanks, Mom. It'll go great with my dress.

At least my bridesmaids will look good.

30 May

Houston, we have a problem! Chapter Nineteen of *BB* clearly states that 25 per cent of invitees will decline. We already have eighty-five acceptances and only two declines with thirty-three still outstanding! What's wrong with these people? Don't they have anything else to do with their lives? Don't they know we've only budgeted for ninety?

To make matters worse, Stephen's brother Tom is suddenly refusing to wear a tuxedo. He needs to be 'special'. Oh, he's special all right. How about a strait-jacket and a muzzle?

Meanwhile we've got to go to Bianca's wedding this weekend. I would have completely forgotten about it if Mandy hadn't asked if we wanted to split a gift with her and Jon. She says that etiquette declares it unnecessary to send gifts for a fifth wedding but she felt badly sending nothing. Since I can barely afford to keep my utilities on, I think I'll just wait for wedding number six.

1 June

Barry has managed to convince Mr Spaulding to reschedule the 'Faces In The City' advertisers' meeting from 18 June to Friday, 21 June. Something about 'better timing'. For everyone but me.

Creep.

Barry knows that my rehearsal dinner is upstate that Friday night. He knows that I was intending to take the day off, to spend it with my parents, preparing for one of the biggest days of my life. But the advertisers' meeting is crucial to the 'Faces' issue. To *my* 'Faces' issue. It would be totally irresponsible of me not to be there. And there's no way in hell I'm letting Barry take my place.

Weasel.

So there's only one thing to do. When Stephen goes upstate on Friday morning to help his parents with the rehearsal dinner I'll have him bring all my wedding things. This way I can take the train straight from the advertisers' meeting to the dinner.

Work, dinner, wedding, clothes . . . I can do it. I can do it.

2 June

With Louise's help, Stephen has successfully delivered his computer program. Yip-pee![45]

The whole office finished the day with a case of champagne and a sigh of relief. They have a new product to release in September, the business will stay afloat, and Stephen still has a job. He's so happy!

And totally relaxed. He actually asked if there was anything he could do to help with the wedding.

There are barely three weeks left – is he kidding me?!

---

[45] And *Yip-pee!* for the lovely and talented Louise who has moved in with Sten, the sexy Swedish mechanic she was groping in the elevator.

3 June

Capitalizing on Stephen's free time we went to City Hall to get our marriage license. Luckily in New York State you don't need a blood test. Just a ballpoint pen, valid identification, and some cash will send you on your way to legal matrimony.

Welcome to the practical side of marriage.

Although the marriage office was dingy and cramped, anticipation filled the air. Stephen and I were among fifty couples all waiting to profess their undying love for each other – to the government. That's right. Tell the Census Bureau, the taxman and my congresswoman that we're in love, dammit!

You could almost hear the office clerks thinking, 'Fools. You'll be back. And next time, bring correct change.' But even the bureaucratic indifference to affairs of the heart couldn't dampen our spirits. Every couple was holding hands and grinning.

And when the clerk asked what my name would be after marriage, I proudly became Amy Thomas-Stewart. Legally able to call myself Amy Thomas or Amy Stewart I was still, most importantly, me.

4 June

The floodgates have opened and the presents are pouring in. According to Chapter Forty-two of *BB* guests have a year after the wedding to send a gift but already my apartment's teeming with cardboard boxes and Styrofoam pellets. It's almost enough to make me forget how much this event's costing us.

Almost.

Dear Mr and Mrs Kendilinski,

We greatly apreciate the blender you sent us for our wedding. It will undoubtedly aid in our culinary adventures.

Sincerely,
Amy and Stephen

Dear Cousin Jane,

We greatly apreciate the iron you sent us for our wedding. As neither Stephen nor I possess any skill in this area we are hopeful that your gift will assist us. I was, however, sorry to learn that you will be unable to attend our wedding. Perhaps we can get together some time after our honeymoon.

Warmest Regards,
Amy and Stephen

❀ ❀ ❀

Dear Mr Munson,

We greatly apreciate the Aboriginal
Death Mask you sent us for our
wedding. My future father-in-law informs
me that you spend much of your free
time in Papua New Guinea so we delight
in knowing the authenticity of such a
unique gift. Certainly I have never seen
anything like it. It will be a lovely
addition to our new home.

Sincerely,
Amy and Stephen

---

5 June

Our cake tasting is tomorrow at Piece-A-Cake but Mr
Spaulding has scheduled a 5.30 p.m. staff meeting and
Stephen's got a court appearance for his pothole débâcle.
   Surprise, surprise. It looks like my mother will have to
decide.

6 June

My mother has informed me that our wedding cake is
going to be mocha with a hazelnut filling covered in yellow
frosting and white sugar flowers. Hazelnuts and mocha.

I hope our guests enjoy eating our wedding cake since we can't without me swelling like a blow-fish and Stephen passing out from excruciating cranial pain.

7 June

While I'm thrilled to be on first-name terms with my UPS delivery person, receiving these wedding gifts is beginning to raise all sorts of unexpected feelings in me. Guilt, annoyance, resentment, shame . . .

After all, a lot of people made big sacrifices to send us such nice things. Not everyone's rolling in it like Mandy and Jon. And I don't want our marriage to nickel-and-dime those I love. Lucy actually sent us the serving platter from our dish set. That cost fifty dollars and she's on a fixed income!

Then there are our parents' friends, people we've never met. Complete strangers at our wedding for forty bucks a head. So is it any surprise that I get annoyed when they send cheap gifts like a set of dishtowels? Of course not. But after getting annoyed I begin to feel ashamed. Ashamed for judging the worthiness of complete strangers solely on the monetary value of their gifts. That's *really* gross.

But not as bad as the fools who send us gifts that weren't on our registry. How smug are people who decide they know what you want better than you do? Especially if they've never met you. It's one thing if someone happens to know your taste. But the complete stranger who sends you a hand-carved clock shaped like a cow that moos on the hour? These things aren't cheap. Nor are they returnable. I hate that.

Then you're faced with the decision of whether to keep a gift you hate just in case the person who gave it to you happens to come to your house. Who's got that kind of storage space? Forget it. Stephen and I have already decided that if we don't like it, we're exchanging it for something we need. And if we can't exchange it we're giving it to charity. Let the less fortunate listen to that damn mooing cow.

But of course I'll be sending everyone a thank-you note, regardless of what they give us. And I do mean 'I' because Stephen's chicken scrawl is so illegible people often mistake it for Arabic. It's long and laborious this process of writing thank-you notes. I've already written thirty-eight, which means I've had to devise thirty-eight different ways to say thank you and still sound sincere. But that's all right because I really am thankful.

Dear Jerry and Mimi,

We greatly apreciate the bowl you sent us for our wedding. Seldom have I seen so many brilliant colors on a single object. What an original selection. It will be beautiful on our coffee table.

Warmest Regards,
Amy and Stephen

❀ ❀ ❀

Dear Nancy,

We greatly apreciate the mosaic bowl
you sent us for our wedding. It reminds
me so much of the Roman antiquities I
adore. What an original selection. It will
be beautiful on our coffee table.

Warmest Regards,
Amy and Stephen

❀ ❀ ❀

Dear Katrina,

How thoughtful you were to send us a
wedding present. We greatly apreciate the
copper bowl. While both modern and
colonial, it will make a lovely centerpiece
for our coffee table. What an original
selection.

Sincerely,
Amy and Stephen

8 June

I'm going to kill Bianca Sheppard! It took me two months
to find 'Sweet Sugar Kisses', a song that's regal, moving
and romantic without being hackneyed like 'Here Comes
the Bride'. And Bianca stole it! I'm certain I mentioned it to

her when we spoke about wedding cakes in April. I mean, *please*. What are the chances of someone you know using an obscure B-side jazz instrumental as their processional music? Now all those people who come to my wedding who also went to Bianca's will think Stephen and I stole it from her. It was ours, dammit! It was ours!

9 June

Sure I've got seven decorative bowls, five saucers, two teacups, an iron, a blender, and an Aboriginal Death Mask but I still don't have wedding shoes!

10 June

I picked up my dress from Katrina today. She said she felt badly about taking my money since the dress is still just 'okay'. Nice. Real nice. That's my WEDDING DRESS you're talking about, lady!

But considering the speed with which she pocketed my check she couldn't have felt that bad. At least it fits well. And while it may not be perfect it certainly is unique.

That's got to count for something, right?

Nicole stopped by my apartment while I was trying it on. She was on her way to some dance club with Pablo and wanted to borrow the bustier that she mocked so mercilessly four years ago. It seems that Pablo's turned Mrs Suburbia into a city-loving club rat.

She took one look at my dress and shook her head. 'You're actually going to wear that?'

'Yes, I'm going to wear it. It was Mom's.'

Nicole lit a cigarette as she rifled through my closet. 'I know. She begged me to wear it when I got married but I refused. I can't believe you said yes.'

Excuse me – WHAT?

My mother offered this dress to Nicole *first*? What about sentimental gestures? And our big, emotional moment?

I am the world's biggest sucker, with the world's ugliest wedding dress.

Dear Suzy,

We greatly apreciate the framed reproduction of Poussin's 'Rape of the Sabine Women' which you gave us for our wedding. I am always amazed by how vividly the Baroque painters were able to capture the pain and misery of the human condition. Thank you so much for thinking of us.

Warmest Regards,
Amy and Stephen

Dear Mr Lindstrom,

We greatly apreciate the set of salad and

dessert plates you gave us for our
wedding. They will undoubtedly enhance
our dining experience for years to come.

We look forward to meeting you at
the reception as my mother-in-law speaks
very highly of you.

Warmest Regards,
Amy and Stephen

Dear Anita,

Stephen greatly apreciates the year's
supply of edible underwear which you
gave us for our wedding. He's always
been a fan of dessert.

Love,
Amy

11 June

I just got our wedding gift from Mandy and Jon. It's an
orange enamel stockpot and I just know it's a reject from
their wedding. It's not from our registry, it's not their taste,
and it's certainly not ours. Mandy knows we registered for
stainless steel. It's in a nondescript box without any store

name so I can't return it or check to see that they actually bought it.

The thing just screams RE-GIFT, RE-GIFT, RE-GIFT!

It'd be one thing if they couldn't afford to buy us a gift but they're the most affluent friends we have. And to think Stephen and I spent all that money on their damn fluted crystal vase. I feel like I should mail a thank-you note to the *original* sender.

12 June

After two hours of deliberation the jury has found in Stephen's favor. They are awarding him a hundred dollars for each of his thirty-six stitches. That's three thousand six hundred dollars! I almost wish he'd had forty!

Who knew Stephen cracking his head on the ground was a stroke of such luck!

This is a godsend. We need this money *so* badly. And to think we owe it all to Larry. And the best part is that since he agreed to represent Stephen for free – as a wedding present to us – we actually owe him nothing!

13 June

As soon as I'm back from my honeymoon, assuming I survive this wedding, I'm suing *Beautiful Bride* for everything they've got: 75 per cent acceptance rate my ass! We've got 115 people coming! That's 95.8333 per cent! There goes that 'extra' money from Stephen's lawsuit.

So much for solvency.

14 June

Having been actively involved in the wedding-planning process for a mere twelve days, Stephen has officially begun to worry – the rehearsal dinner, Misty's relatives, his tuxedo, his brother Tom's refusal to wear a tuxedo, Larry's prospective toast, the cake . . . Blah, blah, blah. Amateur.

Meanwhile a stray cat crossed the sidewalk in front of me today. I was fairly certain that it was dark brown but it *could* have been black. I'm not usually the finger-crossing, salt-tossing type of superstitious person but it's *eight* days before one of the biggest events of my life. Not to mention the fact that the proofs for my 'Faces' issue are due tomorrow. So who could blame me for chasing the cat down the block, across the street, through an alley and into a dumpster just to make absolutely positively certain that it was dark brown?

15 June

Lucy's doctors are concerned that travel will exacerbate her circulatory problems. She can't come to the wedding.

I've been crying all day. What's the point of having a wedding if Lucy can't be there to share it with me? It's been her unfaltering support that has gotten me through these past few months.

My 115-person wedding suddenly feels very lonely.

Anita called and invited me to dinner at Snap Dragon – a Chinese restaurant in SoHo. I assumed she wanted to apologize for callously refusing to buy my hair comb. But Snap Dragon's carnival atmosphere of music and booze hardly suited my mood. After all, hair combs, wedding dresses and obnoxious Tom were meaningless in the face of Lucy's absence. But Anita insisted and I reluctantly agreed.

Thank goodness because it turned out to be my wedding shower. Anita-style! Snap Dragon's back room was filled with my girlfriends – Mandy, Paula, Kathy, Jenny, Suzy . . . Even Nicole was there. And for the next four hours we ate, drank, laughed, reminisced, yelled at the top of our lungs, stood on tables, and made a total spectacle of ourselves.

It was one of the most incredible evenings of my entire life.

Here were all of my girlfriends joyfully celebrating not only my wedding but our years of friendship. Humorous stories were shared. Humiliating tales were told. And then there were the gifts: lingerie, sex toys, a *Dust-Buster*? Paula gave me a salon gift certificate for two. Nicole returned a doll she'd spent our entire childhood denying she'd stolen. And Anita, forever impressed with Gram's chutzpah gave me a book: *How To Make A Jewish Home*.

Later in the evening, as a man dressed like a firefighter strutted across tabletops stripping to a leather G-string, Mandy whispered quietly in my ear, 'By the way, have your sex dreams stopped?'

'Yeah, pretty much.'

Mandy smiled. 'That's good to hear.' Pouring herself another glass of wine she looked absently around the room. 'So what did you do? Use a book? A shrink?'

'No, the dreams just stopped on their own. Why?'

'No reason.'

Mandy never says anything for no reason. And I was acutely aware that she was changing the topic when she asked if I'd purchased wedding shoes. But I told her my humiliating fat feet/Manfield Blossom story anyway. She just shook her head. 'You really don't want to find wedding shoes.'

Is she kidding?! 'Of course I do. I'm getting married in *six* days.'

'Exactly. And if you find wedding shoes you'll have nothing left to worry about *except* the fact that you're getting married in six days. Those shoes are just a scapegoat for your wedding anxiety. Trust me. I did it too. Except my scapegoat was those damn Holland tulips.'

But before I could marvel at my own powers of deception Nicole sat down next to me and lit a cigarette. 'Hey, sorry to interrupt but I've got a favor to ask. Since Chet's obviously not coming to the wedding I'd like to bring Pablo.'

Great. 'First off, smoking's bad for your health. Second, don't you think it's a bit premature to be inviting Pablo to family events? Mom and Dad are going to be really upset.'

'True, but it's your wedding so they can't make a scene.'

That's what she thinks. But how could I say no? After all, if she's willing to celebrate my wedding as her own marriage falls apart the least I could do is allow her a date.

17 June

As a politically correct gesture Stephen came to my
apartment after his bachelor party last night. At three in
the morning he stumbled in, drunk out of his mind,
slurring his words, and stinking of cigars.

Oh, yeah. He was wearing a Viking helmet.

It was hysterical. After professing his love and slobber-
ing all over me he passed out partially clothed.

I took some Polaroids for posterity.

As soon as I got to work I called Mandy to compare
notes. Had Jon also returned home wearing a Viking
helmet? Mandy didn't know. She'd been in the shower
when Jon returned home at 7 *a.m.* 'What do you think
they did until seven in the morning?'

I don't even want to know. 'Played some pool. Ate
breakfast.' Yeah, right.

18 June – 1.35 a.m.

I've shredded my 'Things To Do' list. I now understand
that *Beautiful Bride* and Prudence, with her flawless skin
and million-dollar dress, are agents of the Devil. Who else
would promote the following?

No. 47. Table-seating charts
If my guests can find their cars in the mall parking
lot, then they'll have no trouble finding an empty
chair in my parents' backyard.

No. 52. Decide on staff–guest ratio

How's 1:115? Rest assured that my guests have all been to the salad bar at Wendy's. They'll be able to serve themselves just fine.

And my personal favorite:

No. 58. *Hire limo for church–reception transport*
Limousines and the Thomas family. It's like cooking truffles with margarine. How ridiculous.

Face it. My Things To Do list is simple: Find Shoes.

18 June

Anita called to confirm the plans for my rehearsal dinner.

> ANITA
> Oh, there's one more thing. It's not a big deal but I think I should mention it.

I thought she was going to harass me some more about the hair comb. But I was wrong.

> ANITA
> In the thank-you note you sent me, you misspelled the word 'appreciate'.

> ME
> What are you talking about?
> A-p-r-e-c-i-a-t-e.

ANITA
No, it's a double P.

ME
Are you certain? I mean, like you
absolutely verified it with a dictionary
and a secondary source?

ANITA
Yes, Merriam-Webster's and my higher
than average IQ. But don't sweat it. Just
spell it correctly in the rest of your
thank-you notes.

What 'rest' of my thank-you notes? I've already sent out
seventy-six with the line 'We greatly apreciate your gift
. . .' Every one of our wedding guests must think I'm a
complete moron!

ME
Are you certain that one P isn't some
alternative British spelling?

19 June

I used Paula's gift certificate and went to the salon after
work. I'm sure she assumed that I'd take Mandy with me
but I took my mother instead. After getting a haircut and a
massage we had our toenails painted matching shades of
red.

This was the first time since we started to plan this

wedding that my mother and I spent quiet time together. For the last nine months our meetings had been consumed with hysterical family members and the crazed minutiae of a Things To Do list.

But here we were, three days from the wedding, still breathing. It was a miracle. A miracle my mother had worked incredibly hard to bring to fruition. Without her, I might have had a decent wedding dress, but I probably wouldn't have had a wedding. Terry Thomas had delivered with flying colors for her firstborn. Sure, she did it without the fanfare and emotional fervor I had hoped for but, as I was finally beginning to realize, that didn't diminish her sincerity.

So, as our toenails dried a heartfelt shade of red, I told my mother how much I loved her, then thanked her for all her help.

Reclining in her pedicure chair, aglow with post-massage bliss, my mother put her hand over mine. 'I know you think Nicole is some sort of family favorite. But it's not true. My guarded enthusiasm for your wedding had everything to do with how much I love you. When your sister first decided to get married I was thrilled. I felt it was the natural conclusion to what had already been a long and happy relationship. And because of that I threw all my energy into her wedding, never once stopping to consider if it was a sound idea. Then, as time passed and I saw how her marriage was evolving, I began to reconsider. I began to wonder if it had been a mistake. It had nothing to do with Chet. I've always felt that Chet is an extremely decent human being. It's just that they were so young, and they'd really never dated anyone else. And since I never took the time to think about these issues before they wed, I've spent the last five years praying that they'd done the right thing. Except now that they're divorcing, I know they didn't. And I can't help but blame myself. Yes, it was Nicole's decision, but I'm the mother. I should have taken better care of my baby. Because that's what mothers do. And that's why I was cautious about your marriage. It wasn't because I'm indifferent to you. It's because I love you.'

Me too, Mom. I love you too.

20 June

After trying on every white shoe in the city of New York I returned to the Kenneth Cole store two blocks from my house and bought the same white satin slingbacks I tried on ten months ago. They're simple, they're classic, and they're affordable. If only I'd bought them ten months ago I could have saved myself a ton of anxiety. But Mandy's probably right. If I hadn't agonized over my shoes I would have found something else to agonize about.

One thing's for sure – I'm *never* taking them off.

21 June

TO: Backstabbing Barry
FROM: Amy Thomas-Stewart
MESSAGE: Kiss my ass!

I was *magnificent* at the advertisers' meeting. Featuring statements peppered with salacious details – the performance artist who delights in nudity, the reclusive novelist with the mysterious past – I eloquently discussed our ten profiles and held everyone's attention from start to finish. That's right, fellas, throw your advertising dollars our way because this issue's gonna sell out!

And when the meeting was over Mr Spaulding personally presented me with a wedding present from the magazine: a crystal picture frame from Tiffany's. I was speechless and touched.[46] I almost felt sorry that I'd decided not to invite any of my co-workers to the wedding.

Racing to catch my train upstate, my arms filled with a change of clothes, shoes, and makeup, I felt like I was floating. I'd impressed the advertisers, pleased my boss, received a picture frame, and in less than twenty-four hours would be marrying a wonderful guy.

But before leaving the office I called Human Resources and specifically requested that Fabrizio, the Sondheim fanatic and Barry's least favorite temp, be hired on a permanent basis. I considered it a wedding gift to myself.

Because I'd been unable to take the day off from work the church rehearsal for my wedding took place without me. It seems that Gram magnanimously stood in for the bride. Analysis, anyone? But, according to Nicole, the event took place without a hitch – except for Tom bickering with Mitch and Larry about which one of them was the best man. Tom's insistence that blood relations came before friends was countered with the announcement that Stephen didn't even like Tom. My mother finally solved the dilemma with a round of 'I'm Thinking of a Number'. Larry won. I'm certain it was rigged.

---

[46] Actually I was speechless and touched and mindful of the fact that it would require a trip to Tiffany's in order to exchange. It's really too fancy for us and, besides, we could *really* use the cash.

The rehearsal dinner was held at the Mayflower Grill. Only a thirty-minute drive from my parents' house, no one in my family had ever been there. Romantic and cozy, the restaurant was filled with heavy brocades. Mrs Stewart herself had been the design consultant. And while the menu featured traditional American food, I sincerely doubt that the Pilgrims ever paid $7.50 for an *à la carte* order of yams.

The entire wedding party and both our immediate families were at the dinner. That included April, Stephen's videographer cousin, who although still dressed exclusively in black had painted her fingernails blue for the occasion. And, to my surprise, Gram was also in attendance. Clearly unwilling to miss a good meal, she commanded court from a distant corner where it was reported she was nursing a sudden bronchial infection. Every toast mysteriously provoked a round of wheezing, followed by a meek apology for the interruption.

I know everyone raved about the meal but I can't remember what I ate. In fact, I was so consumed with excitement that I barely noticed the little things. Like the fact that someone had foolishly placed Mrs Stewart within smacking distance of Misty, and that Jon complained about the wine being too dry.[47] The entire evening just seemed magical. Even my mother's toast, which started with 'We never thought Amy was the marrying kind . . .' and ended with 'She was just waiting for the right man to come along.'

Amen.

Stephen and I stayed side by side for the entire evening. I

---

[47] Proving once again that Jon is undeniably a horse's ass.

think seeing our families assembled like this, with our wedding party present and the clock ticking down, really drove home the fact that by tomorrow afternoon we'd be married. That the months of preparation, anxiety, fights, and excitement were all coming together. Not next month. Not next week. But tomorrow afternoon – even though our photographer had never managed to see our site or check the lighting conditions. But it was too late to worry. We both knew that whatever was going to happen would happen. There was nothing we could do except hold each other's hand.

21 June – 11.30 p.m.

This is the last night I'll go to sleep a single woman. And before climbing into the bottom bunk of my childhood bed, I called Lucy and told her how much I love her.

5 July

South Carolina was fabulous. Beaches, sun, and absolutely nothing to worry about. We woke up when we wanted, ate where we wanted and wore what we wanted. Pure pleasure and love.

Which is the way it should be. Actually, it's the way the wedding should have been too. But it wasn't – exactly.

The night before the wedding a huge storm appeared from nowhere at 2 a.m. Despite our pricey tent, the twelve tables, 115 chairs, three serving stations and the dance floor all went flying. All the work that my family, my bridesmaids and Jeb had done that afternoon was lost. And to make matters worse, the wind was accompanied by rain so that everything that had been originally white became black and muddy. My parents and I dragged everything inside[48] then watched in disbelief as the beige living-room carpet, which had been shampooed the week before, turned a foul shade of gray.

Annoyed with the mess and her hysterical bride-to-be daughter, my mom chose that moment to scold my father for not getting a haircut for the wedding. She ranted about how he looked like a hillbilly who'd been raised in the woods.[49] And though my father protested that he'd been too busy retiling the downstairs bathroom to get to the barber, my mother would have none of it. At 3.26 a.m. she was cutting his hair with the kitchen shears as he sat on the closed toilet seat in his pajamas and a raincoat. By 3.30 a.m. he'd gone from a middle-aged hillbilly to a Cub Scout. An angry Cub Scout.

Unable to stand another moment I went to bed. This wedding had gone from my hands to my mother's, and now into Fate's. If the rain didn't stop there was no way to fit a band, the dance floor, a buffet dinner and 115 people inside my parents 1800-square-foot house. Needless to say, I cried myself to sleep.

I woke up the next morning comforted by the sight of my childhood bedroom. Sure it's been converted into a den with a La-Z-Boy chair and a color television, but my bunk bed remains, as does my Donny Osmond poster on the

---

[48] Gram conveniently slept through the entire ordeal.

[49] Which was an exaggeration. He looked more like a middle-aged hippie in search of a Byrds concert.

wall. For a moment I imagined putting on my clogs and overalls and running to catch the school bus outside Jamie Mitchell's house. Then it occurred to me that the light coming through the window was *sun.*

I jumped up and looked outside. The chairs, dance floor and serving stations had all been cleaned and restored. The tables were covered in linens and bud vases. Beautiful paper lanterns dangled gracefully from the trees. And some guys in low-riding jeans were bent over assembling a stage for the band. It was my wedding day. I looked in the mirror and smiled. Then noticed my first gray hair – a reminder of what a long, hard road it had been.[50]

Mandy arrived a few minutes later with a light breakfast in hand. I opted to skip the meal. For the first time in my life I was indifferent to food. Besides, Mandy's foot was tapping. We had less than ten minutes to get to the hairdresser's where we'd meet Anita and Nicole. Then the four of us would return to the house, change our clothes and head over to the church to meet my family, Reverend MacKenzie, the guests and, God willing, Stephen. Mandy had the whole thing planned out. She'd even borrowed her father's brand new Mercedes for the occasion – an 'S class'.

Since my town's not known for its upscale salons my bridesmaids and I had to settle for appointments at Glamorous Lady, a local beauty shop that's been coiffing my mother's locks for the last fifteen years. And since she still has hair, I figured how bad could they be? Besides, we're simple women. No high-voltage electrical appliances would be required for our appointments.

---

[50] Not one to dwell, I yanked it out immediately. From the root.

Unfortunately 'glamorous' is a subjective term.

An hour later I was seated under a thermal-nuclear dryer hood bearing a load of fifty-six rollers, struggling to comprehend how my beautician, Abigail, could possibly think a case full of curlers would in any way replicate the Gwyneth Paltrow hairstyle depicted in the magazine clipping I'd given her.

Meanwhile Nicole, who'd resigned herself to looking like Annette Funicello in *Beach Blanket Bingo*, was desperately shielding herself from the geriatric assistant who was bombing her with Aqua Net. To her credit Anita refused to allow anyone to touch her. After washing, towel-drying, and brushing her own hair, she used the remaining time to sniff my dryer hood for signs of singeing. And Mandy, who was supervising her beautician with an iron fist, finally lost her cool when the frustrated beautician resorted to subterfuge and tried to secretly slather Mandy's up-do with a floral-scented mousse. I'm not sure who slapped whom first.

Having officially destroyed my mother's long-standing relationship with the Glamorous Lady salon, my bridal party and I raced home. Nicole looked like she was wearing a helmet, Mandy smelt like cheap hand soap, and I, fifty-six curlers later, could have done dinner theater as Shirley Temple. Anita just shook her head and said, 'I told you so,' as she desperately pulled a wet comb through my curls.

According to Mandy's schedule we had exactly fifty-five minutes to make me look like a bride, then an hour to get to the church. After a frantic search for an AWOL shoe, Nicole steamed my wedding dress, Anita pinned yellow roses in my hair, and Mandy did my makeup: 'Daytime

Elegant, for the subtle, yet photogenic effect'. I then proceeded to rip three pairs of pantyhose without ever getting them above my knees.[51] With one eye on the clock and the other on our last pair of hose, a frustrated Mandy sat me on her lap and *put on my pantyhose for me*.

By one o'clock three stunning bridesmaids and one not-so-shabby rodeo bride were speeding toward the church in a borrowed Mercedes.

By 1.05 I was physically ill.

According to Anita, I looked washed out. According to Nicole I looked like death. Nice. As Mandy casually cited nerves and stepped on the gas, beads of perspiration clustered in my cleavage and I began to shake. It occurred to me that I hadn't eaten all day.

Mandy was hysterical. 'How could you not eat? I brought you breakfast! It was perfectly balanced for protein, carbohydrate and fat!'

Anita clutched her head. 'Would you just shut up and find some food?'

'She's getting married in less than an hour. Where am I supposed to go? Arby's?'

Just then Nicole's Girl Scout survival skills kicked in 'Look! There's a 7–11 on the next corner.' They don't give proficiency badges to just anyone.

Too panicked to argue Mandy floored her father's Mercedes into the 7–11 parking lot. As Anita bolted from the car Mandy yelled after her, 'Only white food! There's no way I'm letting her stain that horrible dress. Now hurry up!'

---

[51] God bless the veritable bridal emergency kit, which Mandy had loaded into the trunk of her father's car. Although I'm still not sure what that double-sided tape was for.

Without looking back Anita flipped Mandy the bird and raced into the store. Through the plate-glass window we watched customers stare with incredulity as the woman in stiletto heels and a sleeveless, ankle-length dress made of Asian nubby silk in an elegant cherub pink with a hint of silver sped past the porn aisle and rounded the Slurpee dispenser.

Minutes later Anita returned to the car with a bag of popcorn, vanilla ice cream, and a loaf of Wonderbread. The Wonderbread was on the house – a wedding gift from the day manager, Rajit. Ravenously stuffing popcorn into my mouth I began to feel my shakes disappear and my color return. Mandy flipped the key in the ignition. We had less than twenty minutes to make the thirty-minute trip to the church. There was only one problem. The car wouldn't start. Mr Alexander's ninety-thousand-dollar S-class engine was dead.

Mandy banged on the steering-wheel. 'I'm going to sue those bastards at Mercedes-Benz! Then I'm going to kill the guy who sold this piece of junk to my father. And I'm going to shoot his mechanic and . . .'

As Mandy planned her hit list Anita ran to the payphone to call a cab. Nicole looked at me, knowing full well that our town has three taxi cabs, only one of which worked on Sunday. 'Jeez, you'd think this wedding was cursed, or something.'

Nice. Real nice.

The clock was ticking. My wedding was starting in less than twenty minutes and I was stuck in a 7–11 parking lot with popcorn kernels wedged in my gums and vanilla ice cream melting on my dress. It was a disaster too large to comprehend. After an agonizing year spent planning my wedding, could it really end like this?

Was this what the wedding-shoe search, the venue hunt, the Barry fights, the Kate débâcle, the band crisis, the Louise scare, the dress disaster, the invitation rush, the pastor pursuit, and the near-collapse of my relationship with Stephen had all been for?

And just as I began to lose my mind, *he* appeared.

Like a knight in shining armor I turned to find Rajit, 7–11 day manager supreme, standing at my window with a look of genuine concern on his face. 'Are you having trouble with the car?'

It was all Mandy needed. 'Those bastards at Mercedes stuck us with a lemon and—'

Calmly Rajit raised his hand. 'I understand. If you want, I will leave the stock boy in charge and give you a ride to your church. My car is parked in back.'

We were never so happy to see a 1987 Mazda Miata in our lives. As my three stunning bridesmaids wedged themselves into the non-existent back seat, I sat alongside Rajit as he broke speed limits through four towns to arrive at the United Presbyterian Church in record time. We were eight minutes late for the ceremony.

While my mother frantically accosted me, and my bridesmaids dragged our bags into the church, I begged Rajit to come in for the ceremony. But he refused. Someone had to mind the frankfurter wheel. And before you could say, 'Big Gulp to go,' he was gone.

Seconds later I was hustled into the church foyer and bombarded with mood-altering substances – a Valium from Mandy and a shot of Jagermeiser from Anita. Already anesthetized by euphoria and fear, I refused both. So Nicole took them. Then off I went with something old (my mother's dress), something new (my shoes), something borrowed (Mandy's ruby earrings), and something blue (Lucy's barrette). I felt like I was dreaming. Even my horrible dress didn't seem so horrible anymore.[52] And the yellow roses which Anita pinned in my hair looked beautiful. Probably better than that comb would have since, truth be told, it really was a toddler's tiara. But I'll never admit that to Anita. Or Mrs Cho. How *embarrassing*.

As I moved down the aisle, flanked on either side by my parents,[53] the members of Diggie's Delight treated us to a moving interpretation of 'Greensleeves'.

And from there on it's a blur.

I remember that instead of a tuxedo Tom was wearing a blue sharkskin suit,[54] that my parents were crying,[55] that Gram had positioned herself at the center of the front pew, and that some skinny guy was running around taking photos of me. It was our infamous photographer whom we'd never met.

Before you knew it I was telling Reverend MacKenzie that 'I do' and Stephen was flashing his beautiful tilted smile while slipping a wedding ring on to my sticky vanilla ice-cream finger.

At the reception Diggie's Delight played everything from

---

[52] Although I suppose the final verdict won't be in until I see the wedding photos.

[53] It seemed right that we should take this walk together. For, while it may be a tradition for fathers to walk their daughters down the aisle, it's a reality that the majority of mothers spend every moment prior to that day worrying about report cards, doing laundry, and breaking their backs to ensure that their daughters grow up with common sense.

[54] Which actually made it easy for us to tell the photographer which guy *not* to take any photos of.

[55] Not just because Nicole invited Pablo.

classical music to funk. And upon the bride's request they played a kick-ass version of 'Brick House'.

While our guests enjoyed themselves Stephen and I spent most of the afternoon shaking hands and thanking people for coming. Yes, it was overwhelming, but it did give us a chance to meet Pablo, who was surprisingly nice – and nothing like Chet. He's witty, gregarious, and four years younger than Nicole. He's also generous. We're getting free cable as our wedding gift.

We also got to meet our photographer, finally. Thankfully he was festively attired, professional, and sober. Although he did take his photos with an abundance of urgency, as if he were dodging a sniper's bullets.

As for the food, our chicken buffet was delicious and the cake was divine. Or so I'm told. Stoned out of his mind, Jeb had three slices.

I think Mitch and Larry were also stoned, or maybe just drunk, because after striking out with all the single women in their twenties they hit on April who despite her Goth attitude and quasi-feminist beliefs found them fascinating. Ah, to be nineteen again. Maybe she was the one who was drunk. Needless to say Larry and Mitch are prominently featured throughout our wedding video. As is the classic moment of Anita shoving Stephen's sister Kimberly across the dance floor.

Apparently there were several classic moments I wasn't aware of: Gram discovering Reverend MacKenzie peeing behind my parents' garage, someone slipping a glass of New York Chardonnay into Chuffy's water-bowl, and my former boss Suzy Parks, the 'mad weeper', meeting Hans Lindstrom. According to Mrs Stewart, they've been dating ever since.

And Mrs Stewart didn't do too poorly herself. She danced for hours, exchanged family anecdotes with my parents, and by the end of the reception had agreed to go on a singles' cruise with my cousin Lydia. Love was in the air.

But when the time came for my bouquet toss it was the repeat offender herself, the current Mrs Bianca Carson, who caught it. You should have seen the look of horror on Mr Carson's face. That's when I knew it was time to call it a night.

Stephen and I piled into Pablo's car with Nicole and headed for our bridal room at a local bed and breakfast. Imagine our surprise when Pablo drove past the B-and-B and got on the highway. It turned out that Mr Stewart had booked us a suite at a luxury mountain resort located twenty miles away. It was an incredibly magnanimous gesture – and it had all been Misty's idea. Who knew?

The next afternoon we were on a plane to South Carolina for much-needed rest. Days on the beach. And nights under a cloudless sky that extended forever.

We also took a moment to write a few postcards. A Note of Thanks – to Rajit who abandoned his convenience-store duties to help a total stranger in her hour of need. A Note of Apology – to Kate who endured far more than she should have, and who, after witnessing countless scenes of wedding hysteria, has enough blackmail material to ruin me.[56]

And finally . . . a Note of Reconciliation – to Gram who, despite her recent antics, is still the only relative I have who reads *Round-Up*.

---

[56] A gift of two Backstreet Boys concert tickets, along with backstage passes (courtesy of a connection at *Teen Flair* magazine), to follow.

Before returning home Stephen and I took a few extra days and went to Wisconsin to surprise Lucy. She was so shocked that she started to cry. Then I started to cry. And when Stephen began to well up with tears, even though he'd never met her, we all started to laugh. Although there was no way to re-create our Grand America adventure from twenty years earlier, we did ride the Ferris wheel at the local state fair.

And now we're home. I can't wait to get back to work on my 'Faces' issue. I've got all sorts of ideas for the layout. But the *best* news is that Barry has quit his job at *Round-Up*. He's become the stage manager for a regional tour of SONDHEIM'S *A Little Night Music* – starring Fabrizio! Apparently in my absence the two got better acquainted and, during walks in the park and drinks at the bar around the corner, had a meeting of minds. And then some. Their tour leaves for Baltimore in August. Until then they're enjoying the summer at Fabrizio's house in Elizabeth, New Jersey.

Now *that*'s a wedding present.

Speaking of which I still have tons of thank-you notes to write. People to whom I need to express my a-p-p-r-e-c-i-a-t-i-o-n. I also need to recycle all the packing papers, boxes and Styrofoam pellets that came with every gift, start looking for our new apartment, check the photographer's proofs, choose our photos, buy photo albums, pay all the wedding bills, return Mandy's earrings, get my wedding-dress to the cleaners and have it hermetically sealed for posterity . . . You never know, maybe the frontier theme will be cool by the time my kids get married.

As for *Beautiful Bride*, I gave it to Anita along with a note warning her to take Prudence and all her rules in stride. I never got a chance to read the last twelve chapters but I figure maybe someday Anita will. I know she says she's not interested in getting married, and that's just fine. But you never know. After all, that's what I used to say.

Yet here I am. A wedding-day survivor.

There are so many emotional moments prior to a wedding. Some are euphoric, some are devastating. Peaks and valleys. Just like the rest of life. But without a doubt I'd say it was worth it. Sure I thought I could rise above the hysteria and have a hassle-free wedding. Instead I failed. Miserably. But in failing I didn't necessarily lose. In fact I won – I married someone I truly love.

The funny thing is that although we place so much energy and importance on our wedding day, it isn't the biggest day of our life. The biggest day of your life is every day thereafter. Because it's not the pledge to love someone that matters, but the act of fulfilling that pledge which is most important.

In other words, it's only just begun.